RESTLESS SEA LORD

LEGENDARY BASTARDS OF THE CROWN SERIES - BOOK 1

ELIZABETH ROSE

ROSESCRIBE MEDIA INC.

Cover created by Elizabeth Rose Krejcik
Edited by Scott Moreland

ISBN-13: 978-1537700670

ISBN-10: 1537700677

TO MY READERS

It is best to read the series in order so no surprises will be ruined. However, each book also stands alone.

The books in the Legendary Bastards of the Crown series are:

Destiny's Kiss – Series Prequel

Restless Sea Lord – Book 1

Ruthless Knight – Book 2

Reckless Highlander – Book 3

Legendary Bastards of the Crown Boxed Set

Highland Spring- Book 1

Summer's Reign – Book 2

Autumn's Touch – Book 3

Winter's Flame – Book 4

Enjoy,

Elizabeth Rose

From vengeance and strife, a legend is born.

PROLOGUE

SCOTLAND, WINTER 1356

Twelve-year-old Rowen Douglas looked up from his meal of eel and pottage as the door to the cottage burst open and his father limped in, being held up by their Uncle Malcolm. Rowen's brothers, Reed and Rook looked up from their game of chess – a game they'd been taught by their father that Rowen could never win.

"Ross!" Their mother, Annalyse, gasped when she saw her injured husband. She'd been tending to Autumn, the baby of the family, while Rowen's two other sisters, Winter and Summer, sat playing on the floor by her feet. "What happened?" Annalyse put the baby down and ran to help her husband. Ross Douglas was a big man with red hair and had a tremendous skill with the blade. But today, Rowen could see that his father had failed. Many times, Rowen's father returned from battle tired and dirty but never had he looked so broken, bloodied, and defeated as now.

"'Tis bad, lassie. Verra bad," said Ross shaking his head, his voice sounding low and gravelly. "Ye'd all better say a prayer." His mangled leg bled profusely and his green Douglas plaid was now black with soot. Malcolm looked no better.

Rowen's mother rushed around the room to collect water, herbs, and rags to use in aiding her husband.

"It's the English King Edward, isn't it?" she asked softly, looking over her shoulder at her triplet sons as if there was something she didn't want Rowen and his brothers to hear.

"Aye," Malcolm answered for them. "The English king has invaded with his troops and seized the castle at Berwick-upon-Tweed."

"Nay," said his mother, as she wrung out the water from a cloth and tended to her husband's wounds. "Tell me it isn't so."

"The Scots surrendered to him," said his father with despair in his voice.

"Not only that," added Malcolm, "but Edward Balliol surrendered to the English wretch and resigned his claim to the Scottish crown."

"Oh!" shrieked Rowen's mother with her hand covering her mouth.

"The coast is on fire and Edward's troops continue to sack our lands while his fleet of ships waits at the shore." Rowen's father gritted his teeth, holding his knee and then half-squinted his eyes as he looked up to the ceiling. "The Scots are burnin' anythin' that could be used by the English, includin' livestock as they flee for their lives! We have no choice. We need to head for the Highlands. We're doomed, Annalyse, doomed I tell ye, and it's all because of the faither of our triplet sons." He shot the boys an angered look, fire in his eyes. Rowen felt confused as to what he meant.

"Ross, quiet!" warned Annalyse, putting down the cloth and hurrying to pick up one of the crying siblings. "We promised to keep my sister's secret, now hush."

Rowen looked over to his brothers. They didn't need to speak to know they were all wondering the same thing. Rising from the table, they headed over to their father.

"Father, what do you mean?" asked Rowen. He and Rook used the speech and mannerisms of their English mother. But Reed, who was closest to their Scottish father, mimicked the man. He talked with the Scottish burr and even wore a plaid, though Rowen and Rook wore tunics and breeches.

"We'll get that bastard," said Reed, pulling his dagger from his waistband. "Let me fight the English king."

"Nay, let me cut off his head, instead," said Rook, pulling his dagger from his waistband as well.

"You fools! We can't fight with only daggers," said Rowen. "Father, give us our swords. You've trained us as warriors and we'll make the English king pay for what they've done to you and our land."

"Nay!" shouted his mother, trying to calm the squalling baby. "You boys will do no such thing."

"Why not?" asked Reed. "We hate the English."

"Reed, stop it," warned Rowen. "Mother is English, or did you forget?"

"Don't ever talk that way about King Edward," his mother warned them.

"Why shouldna we hate him? We're Scots," said Reed.

"Half-Scots," Rook reminded him.

"Stop the squabblin'," shouted their father, reaching for a bottle of whisky on the table. He pulled out the cork with his teeth and spit it across the room. "Yer mathair doesna want ye to hate King Edward, but I feel as if ye should. I dinna care if he's yer real faither."

"Ross!" shouted their mother and Rowen saw the tears in her eyes.

"Our real father?" asked Rowen. "What does that mean?"

"Ye're our faither," said Reed, going to his side.

Their uncle worked at wrapping up their father's leg, shaking his head and keeping silent. Ross picked up the bottle and took a swig of whisky, his eyes never leaving his wife.

"How could you break our promise to my dead sister?" asked their mother angrily.

"I dinna care any longer and neither will I pretend the boys are mine when they are that bastard's!" Ross finished off the whisky and threw the bottle across the room. It hit the wall of the cottage and shattered upon the dirt floor.

"King Edward of England is our father?" asked Rook. Rook's hair was as black as a raven, but his eyes were clear blue just like his brothers.

"You're saying we're bastards?" asked Rowen.

"Ye're no' really our faither?" asked Reed, sounding the most disappointed of the three of them.

"It's time they ken," said Ross, shaking his head and looking down at his mangled leg. "I'll ne'er be able to stand and fight again. And because of their faither, I've lost most of my family. Now our lands are being burned to the ground."

Shouting came from outside. Their uncle ran over to the door to talk to the passersby.

"What's happenin'?" asked Malcolm.

"Berwickshire is wasted and now the English king is headin' north to Haddingtonshire," said the man outside the door. "Ye need to get yer family to safety."

"Annalyse, take the girls to the Highlands where ye'll be safe," ordered Ross.

"I'll not leave without you," she said, sounding frightened and angry at the same time. Little Autumn started to cry again. Annalyse picked her up and went over to comfort the other two girls.

"I will just slow ye down," Ross told her. "I am too wounded to walk or even ride a horse."

"We'll take the cart," said Malcolm. "I'll go hitch up the horse." He hurried out the door. Reed looked at his brothers, able to feel their emotions and know they were just as upset as him.

"Mother, tell us the truth," said Rowen. "Are we really the English king's bastards?"

His mother's eyes interlocked with their father's. The glance they exchanged told him it was true. Finally, she answered in a soft voice.

"Yes, boys, you are. I'm sorry to have never told you, but your mother – my sister, begged me on her deathbed to not only keep it a secret but to raise you as my own."

"Nay! It's no' true!" Reed looked over to the only father they'd ever known and the man they most admired.

"It is true, boys," said Ross, his shoulders slumping as he leaned forward on the chair. "Yer true mathair was a mistress to the English king. She died birthin' ye and the king feared ye."

"Why would a king fear babies?" spat Rook.

"Because ye were born on the cursed day of the Holy Innocents and ye all looked verra much alike. Ye ken the superstitions surroundin' twins." He moaned in pain and tried to wrap his leg on his own. Rowen could see the shards of broken bone sticking out from his knee.

"But we're not twins," said Rook.

"Nay, but I was," answered their mother, putting down the baby and coming to gather the boys into her arms. "I was a twin. I will tell you that you're lucky no one in Scotland has considered you evil and spawns of the devil for not being the first born. We did what was necessary to protect you boys. We love you and don't you ever forget that."

"Nay," said Rook, pushing away from her. "If you loved us, you would have told us the truth years ago."

"Would ye have wanted to ken that ye were bastards of an enemy who ordered ye all killed at birth because he was afeared of bein' cursed by ye?" shouted Ross, having no more patience for this conversation.

"Ross! That's enough." Annalyse pulled all three boys to her in a protective hug. "We've got to get to safety before it's too late."

"I don't want to hide. I want to fight the man who wanted me dead!" said Rook, always the angriest of the three. They'd been called Rowen the Restless, Rook the Ruthless, and Reed the Reckless, their entire lives. Tonight was no different because they were about to live up to their names.

"I can't just hide. I want to fight, too," said Rowen, always feeling unsettled.

"Look at your father and what the king and his army did to him," said their mother in a stern voice. "You boys are young and can't yet fight like a man. What do you think will happen to you? It's too dangerous out there."

"He's no' our faither," spat Reed, eying the broken and bloodied man on the chair. "And we ken how to handle a sword. I'm goin' to get our swords from the barn and fight!"

"Me, too," said Rook. The two boys ran from the house.

"Nay! Stop!" shouted their mother. Rowen just watched what transpired, not knowing what to do. "Rowen, go stop your brothers," begged Annalyse. "Make them come with us to the Highlands."

Rowen understood his brothers' anguish because the same vengeance now flowed through his blood. He didn't want to cower in fear from the man who'd ordered his death when he was naught but an innocent and helpless infant. He wanted to fight as well.

"Tell me about our mother," said Rowen. "Did she love King Edward?" he asked, needing to know if his mother had been used as naught but a whore.

"Aye, she did love him," said Annalyse. "And she loved you boys, too. She was the one to name you. She said someday you'd all be legends."

"How did we survive death?" he asked, his eyes going back to the man he'd thought for the last twelve years was his father.

"Rowen, you don't need to know that right now," Annalyse spoke out.

"You spoke about the first born child of twins being favored," he said. "At least tell me which of us was born first?"

"You were the first born," she answered. "The king wanted only the first born baby and was going to kill your brothers. We couldn't let any of you die. So we didn't tell him which of you was born first. That's when he gave the order to kill you all. You have to understand, we love you and your brothers and didn't want to lose any of you. Now gather your things, we have to go."

"You should have told us years ago," said Rowen, knowing the time to leave had come. However, he and his brothers would not be going with this family. He headed toward the door.

"Where are you going?" asked his mother.

"I'm going with my brothers so we can claim vengeance on the man who wanted us dead."

"He's the man who sired you. You can't do that," said his mother.

"Just watch us," said Rowen, feeling a restlessness stirring in his gut.

"Ross, stop them," he heard his mother say from behind him as he headed out the door.

"Let them go, lassie," said Ross. "There's nothin' ye can do to stop a man with vengeance in his heart. I should be proof of that to ye."

"But they're not men; they're boys. They'll be killed!" she shouted frantically.

"I've raised them as my sons and I've taught them how to fight. They've also got Edward's hunger for war in their blood. There is nothin' we can do to stop them now."

"If you don't stop them and do something to protect our sons, I want nothing to do with you ever again," said Annalyse. It broke Rowen's heart to hear his mother crying as he headed to the stables. He got to the barn to find his brothers on horses with three swords strapped to the sides. The hawks and birds they'd helped their father raise and train squawked and fluttered in their cages knowing something was wrong. Rowen and his brothers loved these birds. But if they left them, they would die or be taken by the English. He knew what he had to do. Hurrying over to the cages, Rowen opened the doors, setting the birds free. He watched them fly up into the dark sky, disappearing into the thick, smoky air.

"Come on, Rowen," said Rook, reaching down his hand to help Rowen mount behind him. Their family only had three horses and one was being used to pull the cart for the rest of them. So two of the boys would have to share. Their uncle had a horse of his own and held the reins as he watched the boys.

"Ye'll ne'er beat Edward and ye'll lose yer lives tryin' to do it," he warned them.

"Nay, that's not true," said Rowen. "Our real mother said we'd be legends and that is exactly what we'll be."

"If ye get into trouble, hide in the church. Ye'll have sanctuary there."

"We're no' afeard," said Reed. "We'll bring vengeance upon the man who did us wrong."

"I hope ye're right, laddie," said Malcolm with a shake of his head. "I hope ye're right."

The boys rode toward Haddington, watching the sky turn an evil shade of red and orange from the fire that consumed the land in the wake of King Edward III. With swords in their possession, they were ready to fight. But not one of them realized how terrible the devastation really was or how much power the man who'd sired them held.

"Look," said Reed, stopping his horse and pointing toward the coast. The sky darkened over the sea, looking as threatening as the army of soldiers that appeared on the hillside. The English soldiers stretched out over the land for as far as the eye could see.

Shouting and screaming was heard in the distance as well as

the clashing of swords and the sound of thrashing about as Edward drove his men forward to pillage the land. Scots ran in all directions and Rowen realized the information they'd received was true. The Scots were setting fire to their land and homes to keep the English from getting any of their belongings.

"That's him," said Rook, pointing forward. He nodded toward a man mounted atop a horse in the distance. Another man rode at his side carrying his flag on a long pole. In the light of the fire, the English king's helm glowed red like the devil.

Rowen couldn't erase the fact from his mind that this was the man who ordered innocent babies to be killed. Whether their mother loved the man or not, it no longer mattered. King Edward had done them wrong. Now, Rowen understood the vengeance in the blood of their surrogate father because he felt it, too.

"I want him dead, just like he wanted to do to us," said Rook, urging his horse forward. Rowen, who sat behind him, reached around and grabbed the reins to stop him.

"Don't be a fool," he warned his brother. "We are three boys and can't go up against a blood-thirsty king and an entire army of men."

"Da was right," said Reed speaking of Ross – their surrogate father. "There is no stoppin' the bluidy bastard. We dinna stand a chance against him."

The army continued toward them and fear hung in the air. No vengeance was strong enough to risk their lives for a battle that was sure to claim them in the end. Even the Scots had retreated and surrendered. There was nothing at all that the three of them could do against the man now.

"What are we going to do?" asked Rook.

"We wait," said Rowen, acting opposite his character of never wanting to sit still.

"Wait?" asked Rook. "You are the one who is restless. Now you're telling us just to sit and wait for our imminent death?"

"Mayhap we should go back and head to the Highlands with the rest of our family," suggested Reed.

"They're not our family," Rowen reminded them. "And we can't let the king get away with what he did. We will wait until the time is right. No matter if it takes years. And then we will work together to hunt him down like a dog. We will take away everything from him, little by little, until he feels the same pain the Scots have felt here today."

"You think we can do that?" asked Rook. "We're not knights, lords, or even warriors."

"Not yet we're not. But in time, we will be," Rowen assured him. "Even if we are separated, we'll be sure to find each other again. The three of us once shared the same womb – we will share everything from now on, including our hatred for the king."

The army moved forward. The boys directed their horses to the side in order not to be trampled by the running Scots and their livestock.

"Get into hidin' boys if ye value yer lives," shouted a Scotsman taking his family to safety.

"We will hide," said Rowen, remembering the advice his uncle had given him before they left. "I see the church and monastery atop the hill. We'll go there for sanctuary and the king cannot touch us."

"Let's go," said Reed, leading the way with Rowen and Rook right behind him. They traveled up the hill and dismounted at the front of the monastery. There was no one in sight and the gates were closed and bolted shut.

"We can enter o'er that wall," said Reed. "Let the horses go or the king will take them." He slapped the horse on the rear and started to climb the stone wall next to the locked gate. Rook and Rowen gathered up their swords and did the same.

They'd just made their way into the courtyard when a shout

came from behind them. To their horror, a band of men on horseback with torches in their hands came toward the church.

"You fool, making us send the horses away," Rook said to his brother. "Now we're going to burn to death."

"Nay, we'll be all right," said Rowen, leading the way into the church. Inside, many torches burned brightly along with beeswax candles. He suddenly remembered this was Candlemas. It was the day when torches were lit to light the way and celebrate the day the Christ child came to the temple. In front of them was a shrine to the Virgin Mary. Candles burning brightly surrounded her. Jeweled necklaces and rosaries hung around her neck and were also tacked to the wall of homage behind her.

Loud thumping was heard as the soldiers outside tried to break down the gate.

"They're coming," said Rook. "We won't find sanctuary here – only death."

"Let's hide here in the temple and pray to the Virgin Mary to protect us from the hands of evil," Rowen suggested, knowing they had no other option.

"I'd rather use my sword than pray," said Rook, running his hand over the hilt of the sword at his side.

"Get down. Here they come," warned Rowen, ducking under a pew. The door opened and, with it, came a gust of wind that blew out most of the torches and candles in the church, leaving them in near darkness. Thunder rumbled outside. When lightning flashed through the windows, Rowen could see the statue's face and swore the Virgin Mary held sadness in her eyes.

"Get everything you can," came a man's rough voice. "We need to pillage quickly and get outta here before King Edward shows up with his men."

So the thieves were not part of King Edward's army. Rowen couldn't help wondering who they were and bravely stuck his head out to try to get a glimpse of the men. By what he saw, there was no doubt in his mind that this was a band of pirates. Dressed not in chain mail or crest-covered tunics, these men wore clothes of all colors that were dirty and ripped. Most of them wore colored strips of cloth that were used to tie back their hair and some even wore hats. With boots on their feet and rings on their fingers, they looked as if they'd collected a lot of booty in their time. The big man leading them had an eyepatch covering one of his eyes.

There was another crash and Rowen dropped back down as more men entered the church.

"Soldiers," he heard one of the pirates say, followed by lots of scuffling. In the dim light of a lone burning candle, he saw his foolish brother, Reed, stand up. As soon as he did, an English soldier grabbed him and started to beat him. Rook and Rowen jumped to their feet intending to help their brother, but a hand on Rook's shoulder stopped them.

"Boys, come to safety with me," a voice whispered. It was a monk from the monastery wearing a long robe. "We can hide in the catacombs."

"Nay, I'm going to help my brother," said Rook, pulling out of the man's hold.

"What's that I hear?" asked a soldier. When he turned to look, Reed managed to escape and head for the door.

"Run!" shouted Rowen to his brother. "Go get help."

"Get them," came the commanding voice of the soldier. That was followed by more crashing of items as they continued to loot the church.

"Come with me," whispered the monk, pulling Rook into the shadows with him. Rowen was about to follow when someone grabbed him from behind and a hand covered his mouth. He fought, but was no match for the strong man. When he managed to look up, he saw the blackened teeth and the eyepatch of a pirate. A weathered face that looked like leather came closer to peruse him in the dark.

"Come without a fight and I'll spare your life," said the man in a low voice. "But if you so much as call out for help, I'll slit your throat right here in the chapel. Savvy?"

Rowen's heart beat furiously. Looking down to his sword, he wondered if he could draw it before the man slit his throat.

"You won't be needing that," said the pirate, taking it from him and calling his friends over to help him. As they sneaked out of the church, lightning lit up the sky again. Rowen glanced back over his shoulder and saw the face of the Virgin Mary just before one of the soldiers knocked the statue over. He remembered Ross telling them to pray and decided he would do that now. His prayers to the Virgin Mary were for retribution against these men who not only ravaged and burnt the lands, but also killed many Scots and now devastated a place of sanctuary, too.

The pirate dragged him outside and led him to a waiting horse. Rowen heard another pirate shout from behind them.

"Bid the devil; there goes my horse with that boy who escaped. Shall I go after him?"

Rowen looked up and silently thanked the Virgin Mary when he saw his brother, Reed, getting away and heading toward the Highlands. His prayers had been answered so far.

"Nay, you fool," said the man with the eyepatch. "These horses aren't even ours. We need to get back to the ship quickly. Just steal one of the soldiers' horses and let's be on our way."

"What do you want with me?" Rowen asked bravely, hoping to be able to escape as well.

"I need a lackey aboard the ship and you look to be good and strong." The pirate grinned, showing his blackened teeth.

"Let me go," cried Rowen, struggling against his captor. The man grabbed him by the neck and squeezed.

"You do that again and I'll leave you here to be killed by Edward and his bloodthirsty soldiers. Now stop your fighting, boy, because I don't plan on hurting you unless you force me to do it. What's your choice? Will you be going with me on my ship or did you want to be killed by Edward and his men? Look around you. They wouldn't think twice about taking the life of even a boy."

Rowen's future looked dim. If the man left him there without a horse, there was little chance he'd escape Edward's soldiers. They were already aware of his presence and would be looking for him. Any men who would be low enough to ransack and steal from a church would think nothing of taking the life of a child. After all, the man who sired him wanted him dead and that thought infuriated Rowen, making him want nothing to do with the English. Mayhap his life wouldn't be much better with the pirates, but at least the man had said he wouldn't kill him if he didn't put up a struggle.

The soldiers emerged from the church with their hands loaded down with burlap bags containing golden crucifixes and chalices. Around his neck, one man even wore the rosaries and jeweled necklaces stolen from the statue of the Virgin Mary.

"Look, there's the boy," shouted one of the soldiers, pointing in Rowen's direction. Rowen knew it was now or never. He had to make a choice. Silently praying once more to the Virgin Mary, he looked up and nodded to the pirate.

"Aye. I'll go with you," he said, already regretting his choice.

"Smart boy," said the man, adjusting his eyepatch. He mounted a horse and pulled Rowen up with him. Racing across the land, the pirates directed their horses toward the ships docked at the coast.

Rowen looked over his shoulder as they rode, seeing the flames flare up from inside the church. He hoped Reed would make it to the Highlands alive and that Rook would be safely hidden in the catacombs by now. They would be together again someday; he was sure. He felt it in his bones. This wasn't the last of the legend that he and his brothers would create.

The storm raged out of control by the time they got to the docks and all hell broke loose. Winds whipped the pirate's long hair into Rowen's eyes, stinging like the bite of an adder. Rain relentlessly pelted down around them and the black smoke created from the fires billowed up to fill the sky. Ships churned in the water, being knocked around by the waves. Several of King Edward's ships hit the cliffs and broke apart. Screams filled the air and men ran to and fro on the wharf trying to secure their lines, but to no avail.

"Hurry," said the pirate, poking Rowen in the back with the tip of Rowen's own sword as he directed him down the dock and to their ship, waiting to set sail. They boarded along with the rest of the men and the plank was pulled up into place behind them.

"Raise the sails," shouted the man, but some of his crewmembers fought his decision.

"We'll be torn apart in this wind," yelled one of his crew, desperately trying to hold on to the side of the ship and not be blown off into the sea. Rowen did the same, his small body being thrown about like one of his sisters' rag dolls.

"We can't raise the sails now," complained another of the crew.

"We have no choice. If we stay here, we'll be finished," said the pirate with the eyepatch who was most likely the captain. "Edward's soldiers know we're here and this is the only chance for our escape. Try it at half sail, instead."

"We need to know what's on the horizon," called out a crewmember. "Will the storm let up or get worse?" He shouted to be heard over the wind.

"Get up to the lookout basket and find out," the captain growled.

"We don't have enough men," said the pirate. "We've lost nearly a dozen between the storm and Edward's blades."

"Boy!" shouted the captain. "Up to the lookout basket and tell us which way to go in the storm."

"Me?" asked Rowen sizing up the rigging that led to the small basket dangerously swaying back and forth atop the tall center mast. Lightning flashed a jagged stream across the sky and deafening thunder rumbled in his ears. The rain pelted down like metal-tipped arrows. All Rowen could think about was that his prayers had been answered. These men were getting what they deserved. But why did he have to be a part of it?

Having no choice, he gripped on to the lines and held tight as he climbed toward the lookout basket, silently praying that he wouldn't be tossed into the raging sea. Luck was on his side and he made it to the top without falling off into the water. He threw his body over the edge, landing safely inside the lookout post. From his position up so high, he was able to see far. Clouds started to part and the storm was breaking in the distance. He shouted down and told the others which way to go to get out of the storm.

Rowen's fingers dug into the edge of the basket as it swayed back and forth, threatening to dump him into the sea. His stomach twisted into a knot, and he retched over the side. As they sailed away, he saw the coast lit up in an orange glow with billowing black smoke rising in eerie tendrils. There was no missing the long, dark line of soldiers fighting their way inland. On the coast, dozens of King Edward's ships were being smashed against the rocky cliffs. Many of them broke apart and quickly sank to the bottom of the sea.

"I'll be back to get you," Rowen whispered, thinking of his brothers and the family he left behind. Then he saw in the distance the bannered pole held high by King Edward's squire as the man guided the English king to the sea to survey the incurring damages. Rowen smiled since the man had gotten what he deserved.

"And I'll be back to get you . . . Father," he said, hearing the hatred in his voice as a shiver ran up his spine. This wasn't the end of things tonight, but just the beginning. The consequences King Edward would have to endure from ordering the death of three babies of his own blood was far from over.

CHAPTER 1

CUMBRIA, 1366

Rowen the Restless downed another tankard of ale as he waited for his brothers in the Owl's Head Tavern on the coasts of Whitehaven. With his ship anchored just beyond the cliffs in a cove, he'd managed to stay hidden from the major dock. Rowen's first mate, Brody, sat at the other side of the tavern as his lookout, ready to give him the signal as soon as both his brothers and their men arrived.

Rowen's reputation preceded him and he was a legend in his own time, just as his birth mother had predicted. Only it was more of an infamous legend since he'd been labeled the Demon Thief. He and his brothers were careful never to be caught while stealing from King Edward III and, for the past three years, they always managed to escape. With three of them having the same face, people thought them to be everywhere at once and they also thought they were only one man. Rowen prided himself on his ability to disappear into the shadows and sail away on the fastest ship on the sea. He'd inherited the Sea Mirage when One-Eyed

Ron died three years ago and he'd been using the ship as a getaway to bring booty to Scotland ever since.

It had taken ten years but, finally, the triplets were able to get their revenge on King Edward. Three years ago, Rowen found his brothers after being separated on the night of the Burnt Candlemas when Edward burned and pillaged the coasts of Scotland and his soldiers even ransacked a church. Rowen and his brothers managed to escape alive, each going their different ways because of circumstances beyond their control. And each one of them still held vengeance for the King of England – their birth father.

Triplets were feared even more than twins that were thought to be spawns of the devil. Triplets born on the Feast Day of the Holy Innocents, like Rowen and his brothers, were considered the worst of luck and to be demons themselves.

It all stemmed from superstition, but Rowen and his brothers never believed in such foolishness. For three years now, they'd been teaming together to best the king in any way possible. Today would be no different. They'd received word from their informant that a shipment was arriving today from Ireland and would be delivered to the king by horse-drawn cart. Rowen spotted the king's guards outside the tavern waiting with the empty cart and the ship had already docked.

Killing the king, they'd decided, was too good for the man who didn't think twice about wanting them dead. Nay, to kill him would only bring war between the nations and they didn't need to risk more innocent lives. Instead, they decided to make the man miserable, by taking from him everything and anything that made him happy. Today, they would secure the king's shipment and deliver it to Scotland, instead.

The Scots needed to be paid back for all they'd lost that horrible night so long ago.

His eyes scanned the room. There were two English guards at a table in the dark corner and a small person covered in a black cloak with them. Still, there was no cause to worry. The king's soldiers were all outside the tavern and, as far as he could see, there were only a dozen at most. It was nothing that he and his brothers couldn't handle. They had to take the shipment before it got too far from the docks or it would need to be stored in the catacombs with Rook until they were able to get it to Rowen's ship. This looked to be an easy feat, the most aggravating part of the mission being that his brothers could never seem to show up until the final minute.

"Give me another ale." He stopped a wench passing by with two tankards of ale in her hands. He took one from her and pressed a shilling into her palm in its place.

"You really shouldn't have done that," said the blond girl who looked to be about four and ten years of age.

"It's all yours," he said, flashing her a smile. "There is plenty more where that came from." The girl was much too young for his liking, but he was hoping, perhaps, she had an older sister. If his brothers took any longer, he might have time to take a wench behind the tavern for a quick tryst before he accomplished his mission and headed back to the ship.

As captain of the Sea Mirage, he spent most his time on his ship – with no ladies present. And he did like the ladies. So he had to make the most of it whenever he set foot on shore.

"Do I know you?" asked the girl, surveying him from head to toe. He looked down into his ale instead of meeting her perusal. Perhaps she'd recognized him as the Demon Thief, although he'd tried to hide his identity. He had to be careful. If she said one word about him to the king's men, the mission would need to be aborted.

"Nay, I'm just passing through and haven't been here before." He reached back and pulled the hood of his cape up over his head to hide his bright blond hair. He'd been a little too carefree drinking the ale and it was all his brothers' fault. If they could show up ahead of schedule just once, he wouldn't have to wait in a tavern in the first place biding his time.

He glanced out the window at the far side of the room and up to the sky for the signal, but there was still no sign of his brothers. Damn it, where were they? He saw the dockmen hauling the king's shipment down the pier and towards the king's guards who waited at the wagon with their hands on the hilts of their swords, watching their surroundings intently.

"Lady Summer, you shouldn't be conversing with wharf rats," came a female voice from behind him. "It's bad enough we're in here in the first place."

"Wharf rat?" he grumbled, turning on the stool to see a lady in a black gown and cloak glaring at him. Covering her head was a black wimple. A stray, loose russet curl poked out from under her headpiece. Her skin looked smooth and pale – a clear sign that she was a noblewoman and not a mere peasant, even if her clothes were drab and dark. Curious but cautious green eyes studied him as she boldly – or stupidly, approached him by herself with her guards still seated at the table.

"Lady Summer, get back to the table with our escorts, and stop carrying drinks or every man in here is going to think you're a serving wench."

"Aye, my lady," said the girl, starting away, but the mysterious woman in black stopped her.

"Wait," she said, reaching out and taking the last tankard of ale from her. "All right, now go on, before I am forced to tell your mother you've been lacking in your training again."

Rowen chuckled heartily, seeing the lady standing there with the tankard of ale in her hand.

"Mayhap she's not the only one lacking in her training. Or is it customary for a lady to drink with the wharf rats?" he asked.

"My, how you assume you know of things you really know nothing of," she said with a sniff.

His mind went back to the young girl saying she recognized

him. He'd thought the same thing and, deep inside, he'd felt as if he knew her from somewhere. But that wasn't possible. He lived at sea on his ship and spent some of his time in the Highlands with his brother, Reed. He only docked on English shores when he needed to talk to his brother, Rook, who lived in the catacombs of Lanercost Priory in Northumberland on the Scottish border.

"You called the girl Lady Summer," he said, picking up his tankard, swishing the liquid around, and taking a swig. "That's an odd name." Not able to dismiss the thought that he'd once had a sister named Summer, he started wondering if the girl he'd just met was she. He needed to know more without sounding too inquisitive or he'd raise suspicion with this one since she seemed bolder and sharper than most Englishwomen. "I suppose next you're going to tell me she's got sisters named Autumn and Winter as well." He chuckled again, finishing his ale, waiting with baited breath for her answer.

"I don't see that it's any of your concern. But if you know the names of Lady Summer's sisters, then my guess is that she's recognized you from somewhere after all and you are denying it for some reason."

His eyes snapped upward at that and he slowly slid his empty tankard onto the worn, wooden table. This one was clever and he didn't like that. Feeling vulnerable at the moment, he didn't want to be speaking to anyone who might jeopardize his mission. He was sure, now, that he'd just met one of his sisters after all these years and it tugged at his heart. Cousins, not sisters, he reminded himself, although he would always consider the girls his sisters.

He didn't think he missed his family, but it was hard not to when he'd lived with them the first twelve years of his life. Aye, he did miss them and wondered about his two youngest sisters and his mother as well. His aunt, he mentally corrected himself. But still, Lady Annalyse had been the only mother he'd ever known.

Reed, who lived in the Highlands with their surrogate father, told him that their mother had taken the girls and left for England with the nursemaid the night of Burnt Candlemas. It happened after she argued with Ross. She'd left and never returned.

A sharp whistle from the other side of the tavern caught his attention. Rowen looked up to see Brody motioning with his head toward the window.

A raven and a red kite could be seen circling the sky. Rowen's bird, an osprey, sat perched atop the roof of the cordwainer's shop next door. It was time. His brothers had arrived and he had a job to do, as much as he wanted to stay to find out more about his sisters. He slid off the stool and looked over to the table across the room where Summer now sat with the guards. One of the guards looked up at him, touched the hilt of his sword, and got off his chair. Rowen longed to talk to Summer and find out more but now was not the time. He dug a half-crown out of his pocket and handed it to the woman in black.

"Here, give this to Lady Summer," he said and watched the woman's eyes open wide in surprise at the amount he offered. Still, she did nothing to take it. Instead, her eyes narrowed to slits and her mouth stiffened into a straight line. She wasn't happy. Then to his surprise, she doused him with the ale from the tankard in her hand and threw the metal cup at him as well. It thunked against his chest and hit the soiled rushes on the floor, just missing his foot. Both guards stood up now, but the woman stopped them from coming forward just by lifting her hand in the air.

"What the hell was that for?" he growled, backing up with his arms widespread. His clothes were soaked and he now smelled like the rest of the tavern.

"I told you, Lady Summer is a lady!" she retorted "So don't insult us again by trying to buy her services because she is not a whore."

"I didn't think she was," he spat, shaking the ale from his hands and putting the half-crown down on the table. "I can see now that witches don't drink ale, they throw it."

"I'm not a witch and you have no right to speak to me that way." She stuck her chin in the air. "My name is Lady Cordelia de Clare of Whitehaven."

"You're never going to get anyone to believe you're a lady dressed like that."

"I am the widow of Lord Walter de Clare and in mourning. And you are not acting like a chivalrous knight."

"That, my lady, was your first mistake to think I was a knight." He looked over her shoulder and saw the guards watching his every move. She had to be powerful to command them to stay there and have them do so.

"You're not a lord?" she asked, sounding as if she thought he actually was.

"Oh, I'm a lord all right, but not the kind you think I am."

"Then what kind are you?"

"Sea lord," was all he said and quickly made his way across the room with Brody following him out the door.

"MY LADY, is that man giving you trouble?" asked one of Cordelia's guards coming to her side.

"We can go after him and have him arrested," said the other.

Cordelia watched the sea lord from the corner of her eyes, wondering about him. She could read people easily and this man was hiding something, she was sure of it. He intrigued her and it had been a long time since any man had taken her interest. She needed to know more.

"Nay, he's harmless," she said, picking up the half-crown from the table and staring at it in her palm in thought. It was still warm from his touch. She wondered where he'd gotten it. If he wasn't a lord, then why did he even have the coin in the first place? Half-crowns weren't seen much and especially not in a tavern on the docks. Her instincts told her something was about to happen. By the look of the three birds in the sky outside the tavern, she had a feeling she knew what that was.

A raven, an osprey, and a red kite were not a common combination. Hadn't she heard these were the birds of the legendary Demon Thief? The birds always seemed to appear just before there was a raid on the king's shipments. Rumors through the years were that the Demon Thief could disappear and appear suddenly, being in three places at once. He'd been reported as having red hair, blond hair, and even hair of midnight black. Most people thought it was magic since his face was always the same. But lately, she'd heard rumors the Demon Thief might be three separate men. The demons' names were whispered through the rushes and she remembered them all.

"Rowen the Restless," she mumbled under her breath, remembering the name of the thief with the blond hair. Fascinated to see the dangerous man up close, a shiver ran down her spine thinking she'd not only been talking to him but had dumped ale on him as well. She was surprised he hadn't raised a blade to her throat or buried his sword in her heart for soiling his clothes.

The legend of the infamous Demon Thief made him out to be a hideous, horrible monster feared by all. However, this man was handsome and seemed ever so calm. He looked to be only a little older than her age of twenty years. He appeared cunning and dangerous. She should fear him, but his presence only excited her. After being married to an old man for the last five years who never excited her in the least, she wondered how her life might have been different if she had married someone like Rowen, instead.

"We should be getting back to the castle, my lady," said her guard.

"Aye," said Lady Summer coming to her side. "My Latin lesson will be starting soon."

"Yes, we'll go," she said, following the two guards with Lady Summer at her side. As soon as they exited the building, she saw the sea lord and two other men ducking into the shadows behind the tavern. "Just a moment," she whispered to Lady Summer, pulling her to the side while the guards talked and headed toward their horses.

"What is it Lady Cordelia?" the girl asked.

"You said you thought you knew that man in the tavern. How do you know him?"

"Oh, I suppose I don't know him," she said with a smile and shake of her head. "I guess he just reminded me of a brother I used to have."

"Did your brother die?" she asked.

"I had three older brothers, though I don't remember them well. They were triplets."

"What were their names?"

The girl thought about it, but a shadow clouded her face and she shook her head again. "I'm not sure, my lady. I was only four at the time when my brothers left home. My mother says they're dead, but somehow I don't believe her. She won't talk about them or my father that we left behind in Scotland. Neither will she even tell us our brothers' names. The one thing I do remember is that my father used to have a lot of birds and my brothers loved them and helped him raise them. We lost them the night of Burnt Candlemas when we left Scotland forever. I don't remember anything else."

"Birds?" she asked, looking up at the sky where the osprey and red kite circled the air, flying together in harmony as if they were friends. A large raven squawked from atop the roof of the tavern. "Go mount your horse and wait for me," Cordelia told her, looking in the direction where she'd seen the sea lord and his friends disappear into the shadows. She had to know if she was right in her assumption of the man's identity.

"Where are you going?" asked Summer. "It isn't safe to be away from the guards, especially here on the wharf."

"Tell the guards I need a minute to relieve myself or make up something else. Just don't let them come looking for me yet."

"Nay, my lady. Please don't ask me to do that for you. You've already bribed the guards to bring us here and I feel as if it were a mistake."

"Nonsense," Cordelia told her. "I'm here to make sure the shipment my father sent from Ireland gets back to the castle. The king will be arriving for it soon."

"That's what the king's guards are for, my lady."

"Yes," she said, suspicious that the king would send his own men to watch over her small fortune or that he would choose to travel to Whitehaven to collect it. But then again, it would be his soon since it was the payoff he'd receive in exchange for allowing her to choose her next husband. After what she'd been through, she was willing to give even more than a small fortune to ensure she wouldn't end up miserable once again. "No one is going to bother me dressed like a witch, so you needn't worry." She had ordered her guards to give her breathing room in the tavern or they would have been at her elbow the minute she'd started talking to the sea lord. Pulling her black cape around her tightly and tucking a stray red ringlet of hair under her wimple, she slipped into the shadows behind the tavern looking for the sea lord.

"It's about time you two showed," mumbled Rowen, keeping his head down as he ducked behind the tavern to meet up with his brothers, Rook and Reed. Rook had hair black as a midnight sky and wore chain mail and leather under his cloak for protection. He'd been living hidden away beneath the ground in the catacombs but still managed to find mercenaries to train and spar with. The fool had some absurd idea that he was a knight.

Reed, on the other hand, prided himself on his Scottish heritage even though there wasn't a drop of Scottish blood in his body. He had a shield hidden under his cloak along with his sword and wore the dark green Douglas plaid. He did his best to hide his flaming red hair and keep from being noticed, but it wasn't easy to conceal a giant dressed like a Scot on English soil. The brothers were much taller than the average man and that only added to the rumors that they were a demon spawned by the devil. If the Scots hadn't been so happy with all the bounty the brothers had given them over the last three years, they would have rejected the trio. Instead, the Scots welcomed the triplets' devious antics with open arms, knowing anyone who worked against King Edward to help them was a blessing sent from God.

"We're not late - you're always early," said Rook. His large raven shrieked and flew to him, settling on his outstretched leather-clad arm.

"Dinna do that here," Reed warned him. "Ye're goin' to alert the soldiers of our whereabouts."

"You worry too much," said Rook, running a finger over the raven's feathers. The raven cocked its head and opened its beak as if it enjoyed the attention from its master. Then with a shake of Rook's arm, the bird flew back up to the roof of the tavern.

"Ye dinna see me callin' my bird over. I'm more discreet than ye are." Reed glanced up to the sky where his red kite kept circling right above him. The hawk-like bird finally landed in a tree near the tavern.

"You both need to train your birds not to follow so closely," snapped Rowen, seeing his osprey out over the water, heading back to his ship. "It amazes me that the king's men haven't caught on by now."

"They're too busy watchin' that shipment for the king," said Reed. "Do we ken what's in it?"

"Nay," answered Rook. "Brother Everad said he'd heard from

our informant that it has something to do with a woman, but that's all he knew."

"If there are gowns and shoes in that shipment instead of gold, I'm goin' to strangle ye," said Reed. "I dinna want to risk my life for a lady's clothes."

"If that's all that's in there, I don't think the king would send his men to guard it," Rowen pointed out. "But still, Rook, you might want to find a new informant who can give us a little more information." None of them knew the informant personally. The monk said he was sworn to secrecy of their informer's identity, so they went on blind faith alone.

A breeze blew past them and Reed sniffed the air, made a face, and glanced over to Rowen. "Brathair, why do ye smell like a soused Scot after a night of celebratin'?"

"Don't ask," answered Rowen, not wanting to have to tell them of his episode from inside the tavern. "Are your men ready? Last time, they were a little slow, so I hope you told them to be on their toes. I have a feeling this won't go as smoothly this time."

"My Highlanders are waitin' in the trees," said Reed. "Whose ship is meetin' us to take us back to the Highlands after the raid?"

"Fletcher will meet you at the inlet of Maryport in three days' time at daybreak. If you're late, he'll leave you and your men behind, so be sure to be there."

"Maryport? Why so far?" complained Reed. "Couldna ye just have had him meet us on the docks of Whitehaven?"

"Nay, it's too risky," said Rowen. "You'll be out of the general eye over there, now don't complain. It's better than walking all the way back to Scotland."

"I still think ye should take us aboard the Sea Mirage since ye're headed there with the bounty anyway," said Reed.

"There won't be time to get your men aboard before we set sail. I'd rather have you work with Rook to make a distraction so I can get away with the shipment before they even notice."

"Aye, but three days, brathair, och! That's a long time to hide two dozen burly Highlanders."

"It's all I could do on such short notice. I had to pay Fletcher twice the fee since he rearranged his schedule for us. I have a bad feeling about this mission," said Rowen, looking around. "Something's not right. So make sure the king's guards are convinced we've all gone before you show your faces anywhere near the docks of Maryport."

"I'll keep them hidden in the catacombs again," said Rook. "Brother Everad helped me stock the larder from the last shipment we pilfered from our dear old dad. Reed, your men will be dining on salted herring and dried pork this time instead of root vegetables and stale bread."

"You weren't supposed to keep that," said Rowen with a shake of his head. "This time, I'm taking the entire shipment. I'll be sure everything is delivered to the Highlands by my hand alone."

"We're supposed to split everything three ways," said Rook, always wanting more.

"We will split what's left over after I make sure the Scots are taken care of first," announced Rowen. He noticed the men were just about done loading the shipment into the cart. "It's time," he told his brothers with a nod of his head. "Allow me a minute to get into position. I'll give you the signal as soon as I'm ready and we'll attack. I've got Brody waiting to drive the cart. You two keep your men busy creating a distraction and we'll get the goods out of here and to the Sea Mirage before they know what happened." Rowen started to go, but stopped and turned back around. "Oh, I forgot to tell you. I saw Summer in the tavern and she has grown into a beautiful young woman."

"Summer?" Reed looked up. "And our other sisters, too?"

"Nay. Just her," said Rowen. "She didn't know me but thought I looked familiar. I wish I knew more." Rowen and his brothers, being triplets, often shared each other's feelings and knew what the others were thinking without even saying a word. Rowen couldn't hide the fact he wanted to find their family again after all these years.

"Don't even think of it," warned Rook. "That was a long time ago and they're not our sisters."

"I know," said Rowen with a slight nod. "But I couldn't help wondering what happened to them or what happened to Mother."

"She's no' our mathair," spat Reed.

"And Ross isn't our father, either. Yet you choose to continue acting as his son." Rowen threw back the words in his brother's face.

"Enough of this," said Rook. "They've finished loading the wagon. It's now or never."

"I'm on my way." Rowen walked around the corner of the building and when he did, he thought he saw movement in the shadows. Someone had been eavesdropping on their conversation and was hiding behind the rain barrel.

He ripped his sword from his side, reaching around the barrel with his free hand, and yanked the eavesdropper out into the open. He planned on slitting the man's throat but stopped when he felt the small size of his arms. The sneak's hood fell back revealing his face. Rowen swore under his breath when he realized it wasn't a man at all but rather the witch lady from inside the tavern.

"Damn you!" he spat. "How long have you been hiding there?" He'd been so distracted by thoughts of his sister that he hadn't even noticed the wench had followed him. This wasn't good. If she'd heard their entire conversation, she could ruin everything.

"Let me go, Rowen the Restless," she said, struggling in his grip.

"You know who I am?"

"I didn't need to hear you and your brothers to figure it out. I saw your birds."

Damn. Rowen knew those birds were going to give them

trouble someday. His brothers had been way too careless. "You know too much," he growled.

"Lady Cordelia, are you back here?" Her guard came around the corner. Just when Rowen was sure she was going to shout out, he did the only thing he could to shut her up. He pulled her into his arms and covered her mouth with his and kissed her hard.

"Lady Cordelia?" asked the guard, stopping in his tracks. "Are you all right?"

Rowen heard the sound of shouting and the war cries of his brothers and their armies, realizing the fools must have thought his kissing the wench was the signal to attack. Well, now that the plan was in action, he had no choice but to join them in their ploy.

Spinning on his heel, he hit the guard in the head with the hilt of his sword, sending the man sprawling on the ground.

"Nay!" Cordelia cried out. Rowen pulled her out of the way as a dagger whizzed past her ear and embedded itself into the rain barrel. Water spouted out, hitting the guard in the face. The man's eyes opened and he sputtered, hurrying to get to his knees.

"God's eyes, I don't have time to protect you now," Rowen said, kicking the sword out of the guard's hand and then turning around to meet one of the king's soldiers head on. Swiping his sword forward, he sank it into the soldier's chest before the man could do the same to him. Cordelia screamed at seeing all the blood. She was going to ruin everything! "Keep your mouth shut unless you want to lose your head," he warned, this time blocking her with his body as his brother, Reed, tossed a guard through the air. The man landed at their feet, and Cordelia peeked out from behind him and screamed again.

"Sorry about that," called out Reed. "I didna see the lassie there."

"You've got a girl?" shouted Rook, taking down two guards

with ease. "This isn't the time for that, you fool. Do something with her."

"Just do your job and get the guards away from the cart and let me worry about the wench," he spat, seeing a soldier running toward him with his sword drawn. Dressed the way she was, looking like an old hag, no one was going to think a noblewoman was right in the midst of the battle. And they wouldn't care if a peasant was killed in the fight.

Brody climbed into the driver's seat of the cart and waved his arm through the air to get Rowen's attention, while his brothers kept the rest of the soldiers at bay. They had to leave now if they were to have any chance at all of getting the goods to the ship and away from the coast without being caught.

"Go," he shouted, signaling Brody who slapped the reins and started the horses moving forward. The battle was still in full swing and he couldn't just leave the wench there unprotected. Besides, she'd heard too much. With one word from her, their operation could be blown apart. He had no choice but to take her with him.

"Let me go," she cried out as he pulled her by the arm toward the approaching cart. When Brody passed by with the goods, Rowen tossed her into the back of the wagon. Managing to fight off another soldier, he then jumped up into the cart with her. They sped away toward the Sea Mirage, with Rowen wondering how he was going to explain this one to his brothers and his crew.

CHAPTER 2

Cordelia held on for her life as the cart jostled and sped over the hard ground so fast that the barrels inside started to roll. The sea lord reached out, stopping them from hitting her, righting them and putting his body in between the barrels and her. Pushed up against the hard wood, she dug her nails into the side to keep from being thrown off.

Behind them was the battle in full swing. When she looked over to the tavern, she saw her guards and Summer riding away on their horses – without her. Her guards were cowards and if she got out of this alive, she'd have to throw them in the dungeon for not trying to save her.

"Help!" she cried out, hoping they'd hear her and turn around. But the sea lord leaned his wide chest against her back, reaching around and clamping his hand over her mouth. His other hand came around her holding his sword and she realized the man fought left-handed. That was a sure sign of a demon because knights always fought with their right hand – their sword arm. Her hands went to her mouth and she dug her nails into his flesh.

"Stop that!" he ground out into her ear. "Do you hear me?"

She squinted her eyes in aggravation and used the heel of her riding boot to stomp down on the man's foot.

"Aaaah," he shouted, moving backward and removing his hands from her.

"How do you expect me to answer when your hand is over my mouth?" she retorted, turning around to meet him face to face. Angry blue eyes the color of the sea met her in challenge.

"Well, if you'd rather I use my lips again, I will." He covered her mouth with his and, this time, instead of feeling helpless, she bit him.

"Bid the devil," he spat, pulling away and touching his hand to his bleeding lip. The cart hit a bump in the road at the same time and he almost fell out. This made her laugh. "Why are you laughing?" he growled, as it only seemed to make him angrier.

"Excuse me, but I thought the legend I've heard of the Demon Thief was that you were invincible. Apparently not, since I've managed to wound you more in the last minute than any of the king's guards have done in the past few years."

His tongue shot out and licked the blood away from his lip, and she couldn't help thinking of his kiss. It was powerful, strong and exciting, even if it was forceful. It managed to stir something inside her that the past five years of being married to her late husband had never come close to doing. Sir Walter of Whitehaven had been a poor excuse for a lover and she'd despised every minute of being married to the man who was old enough to be her father. She'd been young and frightened at the time of their marriage and thought this was the way it should be. But over time, she realized that she didn't want someone like him. She'd often wondered what her marriage would have been like if she'd been betrothed to a younger man who was exciting or handsome. Aye, someone like Rowen the Restless.

"You have a mean bite, my lady," he said, touching his split lip again.

"What will you do with me?" she asked, feeling her heart

pounding all the way up to her throat. She had to ask him this question, though she wasn't sure she wanted to know the answer right now. Hopefully, he wouldn't kill her since he'd gone to extreme measures to protect her during the battle. But then again, he was a pirate and pirates were known to pillage, plunder, and use women for their personal pleasures.

"I haven't decided yet," he said as the horse-drawn cart made its way around the cliffs and a ship came into view. Hidden from sight, the ship was anchored in a small cove that wasn't used for docking. It was a large ship and she could see at least a dozen or more men aboard watching them. Two shuttle boats were being manned by eight pirates at the shore as the men prepared to carry them and the bounty back to the ship.

"That can't be your ship," she said, not seeing another one nearby. With the main sail furled, she couldn't see it well, but the small sail on the back was white.

"Why can't it?" he asked, getting ready to jump from the cart.

"Because I don't see black sails. After all, it's common knowledge that pirates have black sails on their ships."

"Not unless they want to announce their arrival," he told her, reaching his hand up into the air. An osprey swooped down from the sky, landing on his leather-clad forearm, causing her to jump in surprise.

"No need to be frightened, my lady." He brought the bird closer to his face. "This is my good friend, Mya." Just as he said that, the bird noticed the blood on his lip and reached over and pecked at it.

"Ow!" he said, shaking the bird from his arm, sending it back up into the sky.

Cordelia laughed. "It seems she's not as good of a friend as you think."

"She's temperamental around strangers," he told her. "Just like you, I guess."

That made her stop laughing. "I am not temperamental."

"Oh, really? Kissing me one moment and biting me the next – I beg to differ with you, my lady." He jumped from the cart even before it stopped and started shouting orders to the crew on the shore.

"Hurry!" he called out. "They'll be on our tails in a few minutes. Unload the cargo and get it into the hold quickly."

"Aye, Captain," she heard from several of the crew that looked to be pretty frightening. Rugged men with blackened teeth, scars, ripped and dirty clothes, and wandering eyes did their work at the same time they surveyed her as if they hadn't seen a woman in some time. She stepped away from their grubby hands and backed against the side of the cart, holding her cloak tightly around her.

"Who's the wench?" asked a crewmember with a gravelly voice. She saw a scar across his throat and realized it had been slit at one time.

"Never mind," Rowen told him, reaching out and grabbing her around the waist, lifting her from the cart. Her hands automatically shot out and rested on his shoulders so she wouldn't fall. Under her fingers, she could feel his hard, corded muscles. When he slid her downward, she felt every muscle in his chest against her body since he didn't wear chain mail like a knight. "Like that lassie?" he asked so only she could hear. She looked up to find herself staring into the bright blue bird-like eyes of a very handsome man with blond hair and a short blond beard and mustache. Her heart skipped a beat being so close to him and she wondered if he were going to try to kiss her again. Although he was one of the most dangerous men alive, she oddly felt safe when she was in his arms.

"I'm sure I don't know what you mean." It was hard to pull her gaze away from his mesmerizing eyes that looked inviting and honest and as if light shone out from behind his blue orbs. It was almost as if there were another side to him, hidden behind his tough and dangerous façade. She looked down and stepped out of the way of the men who were loading the ship. "Will you leave me here then?" she asked, peering over her shoulder, watching for her guards or, perhaps, some of the king's soldiers. To her dismay, there were none in sight.

"What do you suggest I do with you?" he asked her in return.

A few of the men unloading the last crates and barrels overheard him and spoke up.

"The wench has seen where we dock," said one.

"Kill her," said the other. "She's seen us all and could talk. We can't risk it."

"Kill me?" she asked, not liking the way this conversation was going. "Oh, no," she said shaking her head. "I don't know anything, I swear."

"Why did you follow me out of the tavern to begin with?" asked Rowen.

"I was curious as to how you knew Summer, that's all."

"So my lover told you about us then?" he asked, taking her by surprise.

"Lover? Summer is only four and ten years of age. And I thought she was your sister."

"Sister? What's she talkin' about Cap'n?" asked a big man with a scar down one side of his face.

"Nothing," he answered quickly. "Now get the cargo to the ship and someone bring me a lit torch." He looked up to his ship and waved his hand through the air. A man standing on the sterncastle did the same in return.

"Aye, Cap'n," said one of the men taking the rest of the cargo – her dowry, from the cart and bringing it to the shuttle boats. Then the last of them disappeared, leaving her and the sea lord alone.

He went about unhitching the horses, not even looking at her as he worked.

"You tricked me," she said, knowing now what he had done. "You're not Lady Summer's lover at all. You're somehow her brother, aren't you? You only said that to get me to tell you what I know."

"You are a bright woman and I had to find out how much you'd heard." He looked up slightly as he finished unbridling the horses. "But now I know that you've heard too much and leaving you behind is a risk that I'm not willing to take."

"Wait!" she said as he slapped the horses on the rear and sent them away. With them went her only means of escape. "Why did you set the horses free?"

"Did you want me to kill them?" he asked. "I'm not fond of killing an animal unless I plan on eating it. And there is no way to get them onto my ship to take them with us."

"Please," she begged. "You're not going to take me . . . on the ship, are you?" She looked up and swallowed deeply, watching the pirates aboard the ship climbing the rigging and tightening the lines as they prepared to set sail. Visions of being ravished by each and every one of the vile men filled her head. She cursed herself inwardly for ever getting herself into this situation in the first place.

"Soldiers approaching just beyond the ridge," shouted out a man from the lookout basket atop the main mast, waving his hat in the air to get their attention.

"Cap'n, here's your torch," said a man with a limp as he handed it to Rowen. Then the man's eyes roamed over to her again. "Did ya want me to load the wench into the shuttle as well?"

"Nay, I've got her," he said, using the torch to set fire to the hay scattered inside the wagon.

"You're burning it?" Her heart almost stopped. Every moment, her future looked dimmer and dimmer. She needed to do something to try to get away.

"It'll keep the soldiers busy long enough for us to make it out of here safely."

She waited until the other pirate left. When Rowen looked

over to throw the torch into the burning wagon, she clutched her skirts and made a run for it, hoping to get away.

"Stop!" she heard him call out. When she didn't, the sound of something whizzed past her ear. A dagger lodged itself into a nearby tree. She stopped immediately, not even daring to breathe for fear he'd fling a dagger into her back next. "The next one won't miss," he warned her. "And that was your only warning. Now stop playing games because I don't have time for this." He approached the tree and yanked his dagger free. Then, he grabbed her hand and started pulling her quickly toward the ship.

"Nay! I won't go with you," she said, stumbling over the ground, struggling not to fall since he was moving so quickly and dragging her behind him.

"If you do as I say, I promise you won't be hurt."

"You're taking me aboard a pirate ship full of cutthroats who probably haven't seen a woman in years. How can you promise me anything?"

"We prefer to be called Voyagers and I make sure my crew and I have the pleasures of a warm woman every time we come to port."

"When is the last time you did that?"

He stopped and turned and looked her in the eye, causing a shiver to go up her spine. "Today. But I assure you, one or two kisses isn't enough to sate me."

She'd been talking about the crew, but he answered the question as if she had referred to him.

"Cap'n, we need to hurry! They're coming," came a shout from the ship. Rowen looked over her shoulder and his jaw tightened as he shook his head.

"There is no way I'm letting you put an end to my legend when it's just begun." Before she knew what happened, he picked her up and threw her over his shoulder and took off at a run for the shuttle. There was no pier or dock and he splashed through the water. When he got to the small boat, he tossed her inside and flopped into the boat after her. Four of his men were inside holding on to the crates and barrels, and one was preparing to row. The second shuttle boat had already been unloaded and the men were hauling the small vessel up onto the ship. Grabbing the oars from his crewman, Rowen rowed the boat himself.

Her eyes fastened to his thick arms and bulging muscles peeking out from his open black tunic as the shuttle glided quickly over the water toward the ship. Men shouting from behind her took her attention and she looked back to the shore to see angry soldiers running into the water after the ship with their weapons drawn.

"I'm here, I'm here," she cried out, raising her hand above her head, but Rowen's stern voice stopped her in mid-motion.

"Did you already forget what I said?" he growled. "Now put your hands down and close your mouth or I'll have Spider here hold you to keep you quiet."

She looked over to the man named Spider. He was already reaching for her with a huge smile on his face. His forearms were hairy and he looked as if his fingers would be sticky.

"I'll be quiet," she promised, trying to get as far away from the disgusting man as she could. She closed her eyes and wished this was a dream.

They made it to the ship quickly with the strength of Rowen's rowing. In a matter of seconds, Rowen had hauled her up to the rope ladder and was climbing after her. Spider and the others moved the cargo onto the ship as fast as they could and then used ropes to lift the shuttle boat. A gust of wind filled the large, square sail with air and the ship headed across the water.

Looking up, she realized someone had not only raised the sail but also changed it. The sail was now black, the color used to denote pirates. It made it all even more real and horrifying since she was aboard. Her heart about stopped.

"Yes, Lady Cordelia. You see, I do have black sails after all, so you won't have to be disappointed," said Rowen with a smile. "Now try to relax and stay away from the edge so you don't get dumped into the sea. If you value anything at all, including your honor - although I know you are far from virtuous - I warn you to also stay away from my crew."

"What about you, Captain?" she asked, raising her chin, pretending not to be frightened, although her body was trembling beneath her cloak. "Do I need to fear you as well?"

"All you need to do is follow my every order and I will keep my word of making sure you are never hurt."

She held back the tears and her knuckles turned white from gripping her cloak tightly around her. Rowen headed up the stairs toward the helm, calling out orders to his men in the process. She watched in terror as the ship sailed further and further from the English shores. There in the distance was her homeland, her protection, and her life. The soldiers got smaller and smaller and eventually disappeared from sight as she sailed away with the most legendary, notorious pirate, feared by all and known as the Demon Thief. Rowen the Restless was her captor now. He was also the only man who could keep her safe, if she could at all believe the man's promise.

CHAPTER 3

Rowen watched from the forecastle of the ship as Lady Cordelia stood transfixed at the rail, staring at the shore as they sailed away. This day hadn't gone at all as planned. Now, he had a blasted English noblewoman aboard his ship, which was the last thing he needed.

"Captain, what will you do with her?" asked Brody, joining him on the raised deck. The Sea Mirage had a clinker built hull with wide wooden planks that overlapped. This was a method used by the Vikings on their longboats and was tried and true. At each end of the ship was a raised platform where they could fight if attacked. The front was the forecastle and the back where they steered the ship was the sterncastle. Having the tiller at the aft center of the vessel enabled the ship to be more maneuverable. And since the ship had a second mast toward the aft with a lateen-rigged sail, it made the Sea Mirage faster than most and too elusive to catch.

Rowen's personal cabin was situated under the sterncastle, while his crew slept on the deck. The main mast held a huge square sail supported by the yardarm. The ship carried seventy tons in the hold.

Rowen's crew had consisted of two dozen men at one time, but every time they stole from Edward, there was a chance some of them would not return alive. Over the years, he'd only lost five men. Now his crew consisted of seventeen men, a boy, and an old man, and all of them pulled their weight. Brody had been a boy, just as Rowen had been, when he'd first been captured by One-Eyed Ron. They'd grown up together being trained to sail the seas, pillage, lie, cheat, and steal to get what they wanted. It didn't seem that bad at the time since the alternative was death.

Rowen's rage after finding out he was a bastard of the king was what fueled him to learn all there was of this black-hearted trade. He wanted to find justice and bring vengeance upon his true father someday.

"When One-Eyed Ron brought me here, I never thought I'd be stooping so low as to be kidnapping noblewomen. What's happened to me, Brody?" he asked his first mate. Brody was not as tall as Rowen's height of well over six feet. The man's hair and eyes were dark.

"Hell, I don't think you're that bad, Captain. After all, you did it to save the crew from being exposed."

"Did I?" he asked, working the till and looking out to sea. The water and swaying of the ship had always calmed him like being rocked in a mother's arms, but today it only roiled his stomach and jittered his nerves. He wanted to believe that he did the deed only to protect his crew, but something inside told him he had done it for selfish purposes as well. He'd liked the girl's kiss, not to mention she knew his sister. Right there were two more reasons why he'd kidnapped her.

If he had left her back at the shore, he would never see her or Summer again. Lately, he'd felt a restlessness deep inside and it had nothing to do with his inability to stay in one place for more than a day or two at a time. Nay, this was different. He didn't quite understand it but, after meeting his sister today after all these years, he discovered there was an empty spot in his heart that needed filling. For the last ten years, he'd cared about no one but himself. Mayhap this feeling had something to do with not being close to anyone other than his brothers. He'd known how it felt to have a family at one time. But after he'd learned that everything in his world was naught but a lie, he'd decided he didn't need anyone at all.

"What's wrong, Captain?" asked Brody, always able to tell when something was troubling him. Rowen had confided in Brody and told him his secrets, but there were things he'd never told any of the crew. They all knew that Reed and Rook were his brothers and that they were triplets, but only Brody knew of the fire in Rowen's belly put there the day he found out the biggest secret of his life. Rowen never shared his personal life if he didn't have to, but felt as if somehow this woman aboard the ship was going to find out anyway. "You know it's bad luck to have a lady aboard the ship."

"Believe me, my bad luck stems from the day I was born. There is nothing that can happen from having a lady aboard the ship that is going to make a bloody bit of difference."

"Anything you say, Captain. But if you want her for yourself, you'd better keep a close eye on her. I noticed the rest of the crew's interest growing now that you've brought her aboard."

"I plan on it. Take the helm, Brody. I'm going to my quarters and I don't want to be disturbed."

"Aye, Captain."

Rowen made his way down the stairs, realizing he couldn't leave the girl out here or it would be like throwing her to the sharks. Mack, who everyone called Old Man Muck, was twenty years older than Rowen and the oldest man on the ship. He was also One-Eyed Ron's brother. It had never sat well with the man when his brother died a few years back and the crew elected to make Rowen their captain instead of him. Muck was loyal to a point, but Rowen honestly didn't think he could be trusted, especially around women - even if this one was dressed in drab, black clothing and reminded him of a witch.

"You're coming with me," he said, walking by and taking Cordelia's arm and continuing toward his cabin.

"Where are we going?" she asked, innocently.

"To my quarters," he said and she pulled against his hold.

"Nay! Don't touch me." She was back to clutching that damned cloak around her again even though the sun broke through the clouds and the day was getting hot and muggy.

"I promised to protect you, but I can't do it if you're out of my sight."

"It's not proper for a lady to be going into the quarters of a pirate." She adjusted the wimple atop her head.

"Nor is it proper having a lady aboard the ship to begin with, but I haven't thrown you overboard. Yet."

"I'll stay out here if you don't mind."

"Have it your way," he said. Rowen ducked down to enter into the room under the sterncastle where he bunked.

CORDELIA SAT down on the centerboard attached to the bulkhead as the crew continued to work all around her. The men took commands from the first mate and maintained their course. They tugged at the lines and, before she knew it, she had to duck to keep from being hit by the rigging. Some of the crewmen swabbed the deck while others scurried about maintaining their posts.

"So, what's your name?" asked one of the younger men near her. When she looked up from her sitting position, she realized he was naught more than a boy of about twelve years of age. Long and lanky, he didn't have a weathered face with leathered skin or the large muscles like some of the other men.

"I'm Lady Cordelia of Whitehaven," she told him. "Who are

you and what are you doing aboard a pirate ship? Do your parents know you're here?"

"Everyone calls me Link," he told her. "I'm an orphan. I don't have any parents. Captain Rowen caught me trying to steal food from his ship one day. Just when I thought he was going to make me walk the plank, he asked me to stay and be a part of his crew, instead."

"Why would you stay in such an awful place like this?" She glared at the other men who were slowly creeping toward her. The sun beat down upon her. Although there was a sea breeze and she longed to remove her cloak, she wouldn't do it with so many lustful-looking men aboard.

"This place is home, my lady," the boy told her. His big brown eyes lit up happily and he straightened his spine and stood taller as if he were genuinely proud. His blond hair was long and tied back in a queue that hung down the back of his neck. "The Sea Mirage is the fastest ship on the waters and can disappear at a moment's notice. It always escapes its pursuers."

"So . . . the king's ships have never been able to catch it?" she asked, not liking the sound of this.

"Not only can they not catch us," said another man limping over to join them, "but they can't find us either. We hide away and those fools don't know where to look."

"Lady Cordelia, this is Ash," Link introduced her. "He didn't always limp, but a few years ago he got a sword to the leg while trying to escape the king's men."

"I see," she answered, not sure how to respond to that. "Where do you hide?" she asked curiously.

"We are able to disappear and turn invisible amongst the many islands and cliffs at the Firth of Lorne," said Link excitedly.

"The Firth of Lorne?" she asked. "You mean – by Scotland?"

"Aye, that's where we bring the stolen goods," explained Link. "We take everything from the English and give it to the Scottish, just as it should be."

"You do, do you?" she asked, feeling like scolding the boy.

"Don' tell her another thing," came a stern voice. An old and weathered man with bowed legs pushed his way through the crowd that had started to gather around her. He made his way to the front of the group. The wind whipped past her head, almost managing to take her wimple with it, and she reached up and held it in place. The creak of the ship sounded louder and louder. The sail filled with air and the ends flapped in the breeze.

"Who are you?" she asked, clutching her cloak tighter and scooting back on her seat.

"That's Old Man Muck," Link told her. "Usually he doesn't even talk at all."

"Muck?" she asked, not sure how the man got his name and not wanting to find out.

"I talk plenty when there's somethin' to say." Old Man Muck leaned forward, so close that she could smell garlic and rum on his breath. His scarred and wrinkled face relayed that he'd spent years in the salt air and sun. Stiff gray hairs stuck out from his face in all directions. When he opened his mouth to speak, she saw lots of rotten teeth. Her stomach churned at the sight of him. "This girl is trouble and will bring bad luck upon us, mark my words."

"I think she could bring me good luck if you know what I mean," said one of the crewmembers and they all started laughing and moving closer, reaching out to try to touch her.

"Leave me alone!" She pushed away their dirty hands and jumped to her feet. If she stayed out here with these scallywags any longer, she was either going to get raped, retch, or jump overboard of her own free will. Frantically, she turned and ran for the door that she'd seen Rowen go through that led to his personal cabin.

Ripping open the door to the cabin, she rushed inside and slammed it closed behind her. The crew's raucous laughter became muffled on the other side of the wood. Leaning back against the door, she let out a deep breath and tried to still her racing heart. Dimly lit, the cabin only had one small open window with a shutter attached and it took a minute for her eyes to adjust from the bright sun out on the deck.

"Decided to join me after all, Lady Cordelia?" came Rowen's rich and sultry voice. "I guess I was the lesser of the two evils once you met my crew."

Finally, her eyes adjusted to the dim light. She saw Captain Rowen standing there bare-chested with bare feet, clad only in a pair of saffron-colored braies.

"Oh! I'm sorry," she said, holding her hand up to her face to hide her eyes. She'd left one dire situation and walked right into another.

"What's the matter? Never seen a half-naked man before?" he asked with a chuckle. She heard the splashing of water and peeked out from between her fingers to see him standing at a wash area. He used water from a pitcher and poured it over his head, the water being caught by a large wooden bowl.

She'd never seen a half-naked man with such a good-looking body before. With his back to her, he leaned over the bowl and splashed water up to his elbows and then over his face and against his chest. Then with a sharp intake of breath as if the water were cold, a slow stream of air released from his lips and he made a sound of pure satisfaction. Shaking his head, his shoulder-length, wet, blond hair sent water flying in every direction, reminding her of a dog after falling in the lake.

"Of course I've seen a naked man before," she answered. "After all, I'm a widow, not an inexperienced virgin if that's what you mean."

He turned and grabbed a drying cloth, running it over his face but stopped before he dried the rest of his body. Water rivulets ran down his chest. Her eyes followed the path as the drops continued down to his waistband and disappeared into the top of his braies.

"I said half-naked, not naked, Sweetheart. And I never questioned your virginity, but now I see what's on your mind." His eyes fastened to her and, by the way he perused her, she felt as if she were the unclothed one, instead. Obviously, it was the wrong thing to say to a pirate standing there half-naked, locked in a room with her with no one else around.

"I – I have nothing of the sort on my mind, but I'm sure you do or you wouldn't have brought me to your cabin in the first place when you'd planned on taking off your clothes." She broke the intense connection between them and looked away.

"I had to change my clothes and wash because someone decided to douse me with a tankard of ale – or have you forgotten? Besides, you were the one to burst in here while I was changing." He came toward her like an animal on the prowl, his stealthy steps making it seem as if his golden body were gliding across the floor. His gorgeous blue eyes scrutinized her, making her feel uncomfortable.

"I haven't forgotten," she answered, ignoring the part about her bursting into the cabin altogether. "Mayhap you've forgotten that you kissed me when you had no right to do so. So you deserved to have ale thrown in your face."

"Is that the way you remember it?" He made a full circle around her as he spoke and she refused to turn to look at him. Instead, she stood still with her spine straight as a rod. "Because the way I remember it is that you threw the ale at me long before I kissed you."

She suddenly felt like a fool. He was right. If she hadn't been so distracted by his naked chest and perfect body, mayhap she would have remembered this as well. "That's correct," she admitted with a slight nod. "You were trying to pay for Summer's services like she was a whore and that's why I did it."

"I never considered her a whore and wasn't trying to pay for a thing. That, my lady, was your interpretation of my kind act of generosity." He walked over to a trunk and pulled out a pair of breeches and donned them but remained naked on top. "Take off that cloak," he ordered. "Or do you plan on hiding under there for our entire trip?"

She did nothing to carry out his order, so he walked over to her and reached out and slid her cloak down her shoulders. Slowly, her fingers released her grip. She trembled being so close to this dangerously handsome man. Her covering fell to the floor and pooled around her feet. With her mouth so dry that she could barely swallow, her tongue shot out to wet her lips. Then the ship lurched to one side and she stumbled and fell against him. His arms closed around her protectively and he never once lost his footing.

"I'm sorry," she said, looking up into his eyes. He did nothing to release her and their faces were so close she could feel his breath on her wet lips. "I suppose I'm just not used to being on a ship. I'm feeling lightheaded and my stomach is turning."

"It's something you'll get used to in time. You'll be as sure-footed as the rest of us if you're here long enough."

ROWEN LIKED the feel of Lady Cordelia's curvy body in his arms. He knew nothing at all about the woman but planned on changing all that soon. Her actions intrigued him, as he'd never expected she'd be so strong as to keep from swooning or crying in this dire situation. She also knew his sister and that was what took most his curiosity.

Her emerald green eyes held determination and challenge, reminding him of a cat. Long, reddish-brown lashes flicked upward to look at him and then back down with a touch of shyness although he didn't think she had a shy bone in her body. Those big round orbs held strength, to be sure. But behind the façade, he could see more than a tinge of blatant fear. Her straight, regal nose and her oval face were delicate and quaint with her chin coming to a slight point that made her seem even more like a noble lady. And those lips, those tantalizing lips, were full and lush and just right for kissing. He could think of naught else and leaned his head down to taste them once more, drawn to her like a bee to a delicate flower. However, before he could kiss her, her hand went up to block her mouth. Her face turned a shade of green and her eyes opened wide. Then she bent over and retched.

His quick reflexes kept him from being in the direct line of fire, but she managed to soil her gown in the process.

"Well, I can see this is going to be a very long trip," he said, shaking his head. "You can't wear that any longer." He dug through a trunk and found what he was looking for and handed her a blue velvet gown.

"A – gown?" she asked, looking not quite so green anymore. "Whose is it? I won't wear clothes from one of the whores you've tumbled along the way."

"It's the gown of a lady so you need not worry. I absconded it from one of my latest runs and was wondering what to do with it. It's yours now. Do you need help undressing?" He pulled out a piece of red cloth and wrapped it around his wet hair, tying the cloth into a knot at the back of his head. He didn't bother with a tunic or even boots. He'd wait until she had her sea legs about her or he might be changing his clothes and washing several times a day. He didn't like a sweaty, stinky crew and often dumped his men into the sea just to cleanse them.

He was about to walk away from her when he realized she did need help disrobing after all. Her back was toward him and she'd laid the gown he'd given her on his bunk. She removed the wimple from her head, but he noticed her kirtle was laced up the back. This was a gown only worn by a lady who had a handmaid to help her dress and undress. There was no way she'd be able to unlace it herself.

"Allow me," he said, walking forward and gently moving her long, red hair over one of her shoulders. He caressed the long curls between his fingers, reveling in the feel of soft silk. The scent of rosewater and lavender wafted upward, bringing a freshness to the stale air in the room, about driving him out of his mind.

"I forgot this mourning gown had laces in the back," she told him. "I guess I am used to having Lady Summer help me dress after all."

His ears perked up and he figured this was the perfect time to ask her about his sister.

"So, is Lady Summer your lady-in-waiting?"

"Yes," she answered. "Actually, I'm teaching her how to be a lady so she can marry soon."

"Marry?" His large fingers fumbled with the intricate laces. The idea of Summer getting married disturbed him for some reason. "She's too young to be wed."

"Nay, she's not," said Cordelia, glancing over her shoulder. "She is four and ten years of age and it's not uncommon for a noblewoman to marry at the age of twelve," she reminded him. "I, myself, married at five and ten years of age."

Mayhap so, but in his mind, his sister was that smiling little four-year-old girl that he'd last seen on Burnt Candlemas. "Whom is she going to marry?"

"She's not betrothed yet, but I suppose the king will choose for her since she hasn't a father to make an alliance for her."

"The king?" He undid the rest of the ties and dropped his hands to his sides. Just hearing the king mentioned made his jaw tick. "What do you mean she doesn't have a father?" He'd almost shouted out that she did have a father who was a Scot named Ross Douglas, now living in the Highlands, but stopped himself at the last minute. She didn't need to know.

"Her mother left the man and never remarried. I don't know what happened, but I do know the girls and their mother traveled here from Scotland ten years ago without a male escort."

"Well, I don't think the king should choose a husband for Lady Summer."

She turned to look at him, holding the gown in front of her to hide her chemise. "This seems to bother you," she noticed, being much too observant. He'd made it his personal goal to never show his emotions and, because of it, he'd gained the respect of every man on his ship. Only Brody could tell when something troubled him. This woman seemed to see right through him and that unnerved him. "Why does the king choosing her husband disturb you?"

"I never said that." He clenched his jaw so firmly it ached as he turned and headed toward the door.

"You didn't have to because I can see the turmoil on your face and hear malice dripping from your words."

"You know nothing, so don't pretend that you do." He opened the door with his back still toward her but stopped when he heard her next words.

"Lady Summer told me she once had three brothers, but no longer remembered their names."

"That's ridiculous," he said looking over his shoulder. "I'm sure her mother would have told her their names."

"Nay. She said her mother never speaks of them and told her they are dead."

"Dead?" That surprised him and angered him at the same time that the woman who'd pretended to be his mother for the first twelve years of his life was now dismissing him and his brothers as if they never existed. Perhaps she was no different than everyone else who thought he and his brothers were naught but a curse. Even so, she had no right to tell the girls that they were dead when, in reality, he and his brothers were legends of the land.

"Her brothers are not dead, are they?" Cordelia studied him knowingly, as if she were waiting for him to admit the truth.

"How would I know?" he growled. "I don't even know the girl."

"I overheard you talking with those other men behind the tavern. They all looked just like you but with different colored hair. You're triplets, aren't you?"

He didn't answer. She just kept firing suspicious questions at him one after another, faster than an archer emptying his quiver. "There is no use denying it; I know that Reed the Reckless and Rook the Ruthless are your brothers and that you three are the feared and infamous Demon Thief. And while I don't quite understand it, I heard you say that Lady Summer, Lady Autumn, and Lady Winter, are your sisters."

His body stiffened and he turned back to the door, talking over his shoulder rather than looking her in the eye or she would see how upset he was right now. He didn't know what had happened to Annalyse once she left her husband and took her daughters back to England. He didn't think she would announce to everyone the fact her nephews were not only the most notorious legends of the land but also the king's bastards. He also hadn't considered she would lie to her daughters and tell them that he and his brothers were dead, but mayhap things were better this way. He needed to let it go and not allow it to upset him.

"You'd be best to keep your mouth closed and your suspicions to yourself while you're aboard my ship, my lady, because you have no idea what you're talking about or how angry you're going to make me if you keep it up. I warn you - when I'm angry, I'm not going to be in such a generous mood to protect you at the same time.

He exited the cabin and slammed the door behind him.

CHAPTER 4

As soon as Rowen exited the cabin, his crew gathered around him.

"Where's the girl?" asked Odo, the dark-haired man with the nervous eye twitch. "Are ya goin' ta be sharing her?"

Rowen spotted his sea hawk circling the ship. He took off the cloth from his head and wrapped it around his forearm and held out his arm. The bird landed with stealth upon it holding a fish in its beak.

"Thank you, Mya," said Rowen, taking the fish and tossing it to Big Garth, his cook. Big Garth was a jolly man, short and round and always smiling. He'd gotten the nickname of big, because of the gut hanging over his belt. Garth would never admit it, but Rowen knew he tasted good amounts of food while cooking. The man was usually calm and collected, but he turned into a madman when he picked up a cleaver. "Garth, add that fish to our supper."

"Aye, Cap'n," said the cook, catching the fish, but it wriggled out of his hands and hit the deck. "Get back here," he shouted as it flopped around and two other men chased after the fish, trying to pick it up, but it kept slipping through their fingers.

"Everyone, listen!" Rowen ordered. "We have a lady on board and no one – I repeat, no one, will touch her or you'll have to deal with me. And I warn you the consequences won't be mild."

Groans and complaints filled the air. Rowen just ignored them and ran a finger over his osprey's head. He and his brothers had always loved birds while growing up and each of them had a particular bird of his own now. "Ladies can get temperamental sometimes, can't they, girl?" he said to his bird.

Just then, the squeak of a door was heard and he looked up to see Lady Cordelia walk out of the cabin, straightening the long sleeve of her clean gown. When the men all became silent, she looked up with wide eyes, glancing from starboard to port.

"What?" she asked. "Is something wrong?" She looked down to her gown's front laces that squeezed her breasts together creating some very nice cleavage. The gown was bright blue velvet and constructed as one piece, so she was able to wear it without an undertunic. It was long and the hem, as well as the tippets of the sleeves, dragged on the ground. He could see it would be ruined on the ship from the salt water in no time.

One of the crew gave a whistle and Rowen silently agreed with the reaction because he couldn't take his eyes off her. Cordelia's auburn hair hung down long and loose to her shoulders in dainty curls that lifted in the breeze, making her look like a goddess of the sea. He wanted to feel the soft locks and caress them in his fingers again. Who would have guessed that under that witch's attire was such a beautiful woman? She certainly didn't belong on a ship full of lusty men who had no morals at all.

There were a couple of crude comments that he hoped she hadn't heard because he knew he had his hands full now. He'd have to sleep with one eye open or this girl was going to get rogered at the rail by his crew.

"Come here," he told her. As she slowly walked toward him, the fish flopped on the deck past her feet and she screamed, making all the men laugh. "Go get it, Mya, and just keep it for yourself," he told his bird, sending the osprey to collect the lost fish. It flew down, snagging it with its talons, and then headed up to eat the fish perched on the edge of the lookout basket atop the main mast.

"Oh!" she said, jerking backward in surprise just as the ship lurched. Not being used to the rocking of a ship, she stumbled and frantically tried to right herself, ending up heading for the sidewall. In two long steps, Rowen hurried forward and grabbed her before she took a dump in the sea.

"Careful, my lady, as I can see you don't have your sea legs about you yet."

"I'll help her," said the pirate they called Lucky Dog, who'd had his throat slit and lived to tell about it. He looked uglier than a weathered buzzard with his bald head and scarred neck. He also sounded frightening with his low, gravelly voice. When Cordelia noticed him coming toward her, she turned and vomited over the hull into the sea.

"Ooooooh," Rowen heard his crew remark. All of a sudden, they weren't so eager to help her anymore and that pleased him.

"Link, get a rag and bucket of water and go clean up my cabin," he told the boy.

"Captain, I cleaned it just this morning." Link seemed confused to be asked to clean it twice in one day.

"Lady Cordelia had a little accident in there. So leave the door open to air it out as well."

"Oh, I understand," said the boy making a face. "Aye, Captain."

"I'm sorry," said Cordelia meekly, wiping her mouth with the back of her hand. "I don't want the boy to have to clean up my mess."

"Would you rather do it?" he asked with a raised brow. She said nothing. "I thought not." He spied Old Man Muck lifting a bottle of rum to his mouth. "Muck," he called out. "Bring that over here for Lady Cordelia."

Muck hesitated, frowning at the suggestion, but did as

ordered. The ship shifted back and forth in the waves, but Muck's bowed legs were sturdy and he was used to the sea, just like the others. The only time he ever wavered was when he'd had too much rum. Rowen took the bottle from him and held it out to the girl. "Here. This might help."

"What is it?" she asked, making a face since Muck had just drank from the bottle.

"Rum."

"Rum?" Her eyebrows arched. "Oh, no, thank you."

"Have you ever had rum before?" he asked.

She looked up and saw everyone staring at her. Rowen noticed a look of sheer panic cross her face.

"Of course I have." She forced a smile that didn't reach her eyes.

"Then I guess you're not having any because you don't want to drink after Old Man Muck here, but I assure you he doesn't have the plague. However, I can't be so sure about lice," he added under his breath.

Cordelia made another face at the mere thought.

"She's a curse, Cap'n. Dump her overboard before she brings bad luck upon all of us," growled Muck.

"She's not a curse. Now still your tongue and everyone get back to your posts," Rowen ordered.

The crew grumbled as they returned to their duties. Rowen eyed the sky, feeling the salty breeze against his face. Sailing across the open waters made him feel so free. He'd learned to love the sea and it brought him to life. If he ever had to live on land again, he wasn't sure he could do it.

The sun would be setting soon. If he had to watch the girl, it was going to take a lot of his time. That is, time he didn't have. He lifted the bottle and drank from it, liking the feel of the rum burning a path down to his belly. Cordelia moistened her lips with her tongue and stared at the bottle.

"Well, mayhap just a little might help get this wretched taste out of my mouth," she finally agreed.

"Here you go," he said, handing her the bottle, still not believing she'd ever tasted rum before. She used the sleeve of her gown to wipe off the rim before she brought it to her mouth. It was clear his suspicions were correct when she tried mimicking him by taking a large swig and started to cough and gag. She almost dropped the bottle. He reached out and took it from her.

"Are you sure you've had rum before?"

She gasped and regained her breath and coughed again, covering her mouth with her hand and shaking her head. "Mayhap I was thinking of something else."

"Something like ale, perhaps?"

His crew had been watching and started laughing. So he threw them a daggered look, warning them to get back to work.

"Cap'n, when are we goin' te see the bounty?" asked Ash.

The girl's eyes snapped upward. "Those things you've stolen are mine," she boldly stated.

"I'll see to the bounty," he said, starting to go to the hold. Not wanting to leave the girl there alone, he stopped in his tracks. "Odo, you and Muck bring a few crates and barrels atop deck and we'll see what we've got."

"We always open the bounty in the hold," complained Muck. "I don't want to have to haul it back up here."

"Then don't," he said, having no tolerance for Muck challenging his command. He would teach them all a lesson. "Matter of fact, none of you will even know what's down there because I'm going to discover that by myself."

CORDELIA WAS ABOUT to object when Rowen reached out and took her hand and pulled her along with him. He gripped the bottle of rum in his other hand as he made his way to the hatch that she supposed opened to the undercroft of the ship. Her feet were bare since she'd removed her shoes when she'd changed. This caused her to slip on the deck as the ship tilted again. He pulled her against him while he opened the small door to the hold. Then he ducked his tall frame and entered, starting to descend some steps.

"You're takin' her with you?" asked Odo in disappointment.

"I am. And not a one of you will follow," he told them, heading down the stairs.

Cordelia's gown was long and the ship was rocking. Though he'd descended into the depths of hell like a sure-footed goat, she stopped and tried to grab for something to help her keep her balance. It was of no use since there wasn't a railing or rope of any sort.

"Come on, my lady," he said, looking upward and holding out his hand. It was dark and musty down there. If she wasn't mistaken, she thought she saw him standing ankle-deep in water.

"Nay. I can't." She shook her head, feeling like vomiting again.

"Then I'll help you."

Before she could object, he put his hands around her waist and lifted her into his arms.

"Please, don't put me down in the water," she begged, not knowing what sort of evil dwelled within it.

"I don't plan on letting you ruin the only dry gown we've got." He carried her in his arms toward a stack of crates and deposited her atop the largest one. She recognized the crate as one of her father's. His hands lingered on her waist and hers rested on his shoulders. Their eyes met. Through the light from the open door of the hold, she noticed a kindness and softness in his eyes that hadn't been there before. Then he looked at her lips and she thought, for a moment, he was going to kiss her again. She wouldn't have objected and this made her realize her mind was muddled from her harrowing experience today. What was the matter with her that instead of planning her escape, she was wondering if she'd experience another kiss from the infamous Rowen the Restless?

He cleared his throat and stepped away. With him went the warmth from his hands and also her silly daydreams.

"So tell me, Lady Cordelia, why aren't you swooning or crying like most women would in a situation such as this?" He dug around for something in the hold, his head dipping down between the crates and barrels. The ship creaked and moaned as it rocked on the waves. She heard the water on the floor of the bowels of the ship swishing back and forth. Looking upward, she could see the cause of the water. The deck above them had slight spaces in between the planks. Sunlight filtered through, splashing stripes of light over the cargo in the hold as water dripped down into the underbelly of the ship. The walls didn't seem to be watertight, either.

"Would it change matters any if I cried?" she asked, trying to stay strong. She wasn't one to break down easily, but it was warranted in such a situation. Still, if she cried, it would only make her look weak in his eyes and that would give him the advantage. She needed to stay in control of her actions if she planned on getting out of this alive and unscathed.

"It might." He found a crowbar and lifted up his head. "That is, if you cried, I might think you needed my protection from the crew more than you actually might believe you do right now."

"Oh, I do need your protection!" she exclaimed, not wanting to think about what would happen to her if he left her alone with the men. "Although I'm furious that you abducted me, I also want to thank you for protecting me from those lusty men."

He cocked a side grin and his blue eyes drank her in. "They aren't the only ones feeling lusty." He continued to use the crowbar to pry a lid from a barrel.

She felt her cheeks burning at his comment and wondered if her face were turning red right now. She had to say something before he started to have not-so-moral thoughts about her. "I'd also like to thank you for protecting my virtue."

He laughed at that and his deep chuckle filled the hold of the ship. "Listen, Lady, you seem to be forgetting where you are. You're on a pirate ship loaded down with men who would slit your throat in your sleep or roger you at the rail without thinking twice. Virtue means nothing, nor does it exist aboard the Sea Mirage."

Her hand flew to her throat at hearing his shocking words. Thinking of the man with the scar across his neck, she swallowed deeply. "What does . . . rogered at the rail mean?"

Once again, he chuckled. "Let's just say you'd better not lift your skirts even to relieve yourself because these men will consider that an invitation to take from you any morals or virtues you might have left."

"Oh!" She squeezed her legs together. "And what do you think about that type of conduct?"

She heard the squeak of the nails as the lid to one of the barrels gave way beneath his hands. "Enticing, mouthwatering, and succulent."

"What?" She gasped and suddenly wondered if he'd had thoughts about her that weren't unlike his men. "So are you – going to roger me at the rail as well?"

His head came up out of the barrel. He stalked her from across the room, coming forward slowly, his eyes interlocked with hers all the while.

"Is that an invitation, my lady?"

"Nay!" she shouted. "Don't even think of touching me in this hell hole." He smiled, once again, and popped something into his mouth and chewed as he spoke.

"It hadn't even entered my mind to take you at the rail."

"It hadn't?" She breathed a sigh of relief.

"Nay. I'm the captain of this ship. I do all my rogering in the privacy of my own quarters."

She started to tell him she didn't think it was funny but, before she could speak, he popped something into her mouth. Closing her lips, she tasted ecstasy on her tongue.

"It's a candied fig," she said, chewing slowly.

"That's right. It seems your father sent a whole barrel of tasty sweetmeats. I can't imagine what that cost him. So how does it taste?"

"Delicious."

"Just like I said. Enticing, mouthwatering, and succulent."

"Oh, that's what you meant." Somehow, that amused her and she started to giggle.

"I like the sound of your laugh," he told her, looking into her eyes. "It's been a long time since I've heard the laugh of a lady."

"I'm guessing it's been a while since there's been a female aboard the Sea Mirage as well?"

"You are the first," he told her. That pleased her and frightened her at the same time.

"Who are you?" she asked softly, taking another sweetmeat from him that he popped in between her lips. This time, it was an apricot. Her tongue touched the tip of his finger and she tasted the salty sea on his skin.

"I thought you had that all figured out. I'm the feared and legendary Rowen the Restless. The unwanted, cursed bastard born on the unlucky day of the Feast of the Holy Innocents."

"Bastard?" She looked up in question. "If you and your brothers are bastards, then how is Lady Summer your sister and who is your real father?"

ROWEN COULD HAVE KICKED himself for the slip of his tongue. He'd gotten carried away in the excitement of being with a beautiful noblewoman. Now, he'd gone and spilled his secret.

"Let's see what's in the rest of these barrels," he said, turning his back to continue ripping open his booty.

"There are barrels of the finest wine you've ever tasted in this shipment. My father said he was sending silks, spices, gowns, gold coins and jewels as well."

He stopped with the crowbar and looked back over his shoulder. "Why would you tell me there are gold coins and jewels in here? It's not a good thing to say to a pirate."

"Does it matter?" she asked. "You're about to find out first hand. There is nothing I can do since you've already stolen my only leverage with the king to get what I want."

That got his interest. He stood upright. "What do you mean? What is it you want so badly that you're willing to give all this to the king to get it?"

"Something that someone like you could never understand."

"Try me."

"It's a dowry of sorts."

"Dowry? You told me you're a widow, so why do you need a dowry?"

"I am a widow, but this was going to be used in trade to the king so he wouldn't marry me off to any of his nobles that he sees fit to be my husband, even if they are old enough to be my father."

He put down the crowbar and walked over to hear more. "So, your last husband was old?"

"He was. And sterile."

"What? Are you saying he was unable to sire a child?"

"Almost," she said. "Walter had three wives before me but never had a child. We tried for over four years and when no child came from our union, I thought I would be free of him. After all, a man is allowed an annulment if his wife is barren. But, unfortunately, this arrangement only works in the man's favor to get a new wife and not the other way around."

"So what did he do?" He picked up the bottle of rum he'd brought down to the hold and lifted it to his mouth and took a gulp.

"He rogered me."

Upon hearing this, he spat the liquid halfway across the room. "He did what?" he asked with a chuckle, as she amused him with her choice of words.

"You heard me. He coupled with me as often as possible. When I finally became pregnant, he didn't touch me again."

"God's eyes, that's awful." He shook his head and took another swig of rum. He swallowed, watching her, but she still showed very little emotion at all. "Why are you telling me this?"

"Because you asked. And now that I'm a widow, no halfway decent man will ever want me."

"Then mayhap you should consider lowering your standards and set your sights on a man that's not so decent, instead."

She almost looked to be considering it for a moment when a rat dropped down from the ceiling and landed on her lap. That proved to him that the ice princess was not as emotionless as he thought. Her eyes opened wide and she let loose with such a bloodcurdling scream, he swore his men above deck were going to think he was murdering her. In one quick motion, Rowen reached out and grabbed the rodent by the tail and threw it to the other end of the hold.

Propelling into his embrace, she threw her arms around him. He gathered her up close to him, still holding the bottle of rum in one hand. She trembled and he could feel her heart beating rapidly against his chest.

"Shhhh, my lady, you are safe with me." He reached out his free hand and ran it over her head. Soft spun silk was what her hair reminded him of and he couldn't help himself from reaching down and kissing her atop the head.

"Captain, is everything all right down there?" came Brody's voice. His shadow blocked the light at the door.

"Everything's fine! Now, get back to work," he called out, not wanting his crew coming after him right now.

"Aye, Captain." Sunlight streamed back down into the hold as Brody walked away from the entrance.

Cordelia shivered and glanced up into Rowen's eyes, showing him vulnerability after all. She looked as if she were about to cry. Without waiting another minute, he dipped his head down and pressed his lips gently against her soft mouth. Her kiss held the sweetness of the candied fruit she'd eaten and it intermingled with the rum on his lips, feeling like a fire burning out of control. She affected him in a way that made him lower his defenses and all he could think about was her.

"I . . . liked that," she said, her eyes closing as he put down the bottle on the crate and used both hands to pull her even closer in a hug. She hugged him back and leaned her head against his chest. He cradled her face in one hand and, to his surprise, she did nothing to pull away. "This dowry was to assure me my next marriage would be with a man of my own choosing and not one of the king's," she explained to him. "But now, that will never happen. My only chance is gone."

Rowen wanted that for her more than anything. Not to mention, his hackles rose when he thought of the king commanding her to marry another man that was old and sterile.

"You'll get your chance," he promised. "I'll make certain of it."

"Then you'll bring my dowry back to England instead of taking it to Scotland?" Hope and excitement resounded in her voice and she pulled back to see him, a smile spreading across her face.

He didn't want to ruin the precious moment and had been hoping for another kiss. But he knew with his next words there would be no chance of that happening unless he were to take her by force, which was something he'd never do.

"Nay, I can't do that," he said, and he felt her hands slipping off of his shoulders.

"Why not?"

"I need to bring this to the Scots."

"It's not theirs; it's mine." A shadow covered her face and disappointment shown in her eyes.

"You are a noblewoman and have more than you need and always will. The Scots in the Highlands often go hungry in the winter. They are expecting this and counting on it to help them make it through the harsh times."

"The winter? There is enough gold and jewels in there to support them for more than just one winter."

"There is?" He dropped his hands from around her and looked back toward the bounty. "Why does your father have so much and why in God's name would he want to give it to the king?"

"Because," she said, raising her chin. "My father is Irish and in alliance with King Edward. He will do whatever is commanded."

"I know the king is often in debt, but I still don't understand why you have to give him so much. It isn't right."

"Actually, it was a part of a ploy," she told him. "A lure I guess you could say."

"It was?" This confused him. "How so?"

"The king has been trying to catch the Demon Thief for several years now and hasn't been able to do it. Don't you see? This whole thing was naught but a trap to catch you!"

CHAPTER 5

"A trap?" Rowen felt betrayed. He also felt like a fool. He'd thought he was protecting her during the battle, but obviously not. "So your presence at the docks wasn't by accident," he said.

"Nay. I bribed my guards to take me there because I wanted to make sure my dowry was guarded and I was curious to see the Demon Thief."

"You disgust me!" He went over and started ripping open barrel after barrel. "So I'm sure you planned on me taking you back to my ship all along."

"What? No, I didn't. Why would I?"

"This is still part of the plan. I'm naught but a pawn in the king's devious game, isn't that right? Is he going to attack or are his ships already on my tail?"

"I don't know." Her voice became soft. "It's not like that. You don't understand."

"I understand only too well. Everything you've said or done is a lie. I'll bet you're not even a widow at all."

"I am!"

He threw down the crowbar and sloshed through the bilge water over to the stairs and started to ascend.

"Wait! Where are you going?"

"I don't have time for games, wench. I've got a ship to sail. For all I know, I've got a fleet of the king's ships waiting for me somewhere. I need to find out where since I'm sure you won't be fast to give me information."

"I'll tell you whatever you want to know."

"Really?" He stopped and looked over his shoulder. "Then tell me – what is your game? Why are you trying to destroy me? And why are you working with the king?" He didn't wait to hear her answer. He darted up the stairs and onto the deck, hearing her calling out for him below.

"Don't leave me here! There are rats – and water. Wait. Come back, please."

He ignored her plea for help since that, too, was probably just an act. Pushing past the rest of his crew, he made his way to the sternwalk.

"Captain?" asked Brody, when Rowen came to the take the helm. "I thought you were with the girl in the hold."

"I was," he spat. "Did you know this whole thing was a setup? The king planned a trap for my brothers and me!"

"He did?" Brody stepped aside and let Rowen take control of the ship. "That's not good. If he knew, then mayhap he knows the rest of our plans as well. He could be following or possibly waiting for us in Scotland."

"My thoughts exactly." Rowen searched the waters, looking for any sign that they were being followed.

"Do you think he'll ambush us when we enter the firth?" asked Brody.

Rowen's jaw ticked as he shook his head. "It's possible. Or more likely, he'll stay on English soil."

"So that means he might have his soldiers waiting when Reed

and his men go to the dock to meet Fletcher for their transport home."

"Damn," cursed Rowen, slamming his hand against the till. "They could be walking right into a trap."

"But how would the king know our plans?" asked Brody.

"I'm guessing the same way Lady Cordelia ended up on our ship. She's a spy. We can't trust her."

"That's a shame," said Brody, looking down to the deck. "She's such a beautiful girl. So, I suppose you're just going to let the men have a go at her then?"

"Why would you say that?"

"Because it looks like Muck is already making his move." Brody nodded and Rowen looked down to see that Lady Cordelia had emerged from the hold with the bottom of her gown dripping with bilge water. The men surrounded her and Old Man Muck had her backed against the wall. "Did you want to stop them, Captain?"

It ate away at Rowen's insides that the girl was in danger, not to mention the fact his men had disobeyed him and went close to her after he'd ordered them to stay away. Still, it didn't seem as if any of them had touched her yet. Mayhap, he'd just leave her to fend for herself for a minute until she realized how much danger she'd put herself in playing her little games. Aye, he'd let her feel the fear of facing a band of pirates head-on without having him at her side to protect her. That would serve her right for being the king's informer.

"Take the helm," Rowen told Brody, changing his mind. "I have a feeling I'd better not let this go on too long."

CORDELIA BACKED against the bulkhead of the ship as the old pirate came closer. She'd been trying to tell Rowen that she'd overheard of the king's plan to trap him and that she wasn't a part of it at all. The information came from one of the king's messengers with a loose tongue. It was most likely a deal between the king and her father, and she felt angry that her father had told her nothing about it.

Rowen's anger toward her was misplaced and he wouldn't listen. Something about the king infuriated him so much that just mentioning him made Rowen change from being protective and caring to being a no-good pirate that only cared about himself.

"You shouldn't be here, Wench," said the pirate named Old Man Muck. Spittle ran down his chin when he spoke and it looked like an army of vermin could be living in his long beard. "You're only goin' to bring us trouble."

"Nay, that's not true," she said, reaching for her skirt since she had her dagger strapped to her leg beneath her clothing. Rowen hadn't seen it yet and she liked the fact she had some means of protection, little that it might be. He'd purposely left her alone in the hellhole with the smelly water and the dirty rats. "I'm not trouble; I assure you. You won't even know I'm here."

"The Captain said to stay away from her, Muck," said the tall, lanky man with the eye twitch.

"He left her in the hold all alone didn't he, Odo?" growled the man. "That means we can do what we want with her now."

"Muck, leave her be," said the man's sidekick with the scar across his throat. She thought she'd heard someone call him Lucky Dog. It looked as if he were lucky indeed that he hadn't died when someone tried to slit his throat.

Muck reached out his filthy hand toward her. She leaned over, lifted the wet bottom of her skirts and gripped her dagger in her palm. Quickly swiping it upward, she accidentally drew blood when the tip of the blade grazed the old man's chest.

"You bloody bitch," spat Muck, looking down to his chest. He knocked her weapon away. The dagger flew out of her hand and slid across the wooden planks of the deck.

The men started shouting or cheering, she wasn't sure which. Then they surrounded her while Muck reached out to grab her around her neck. She closed her eyes, thinking she was going to die at the hands of cutthroats and there was nothing she could do about it. It was futile to fight since there were so many of them and she had nowhere to run.

The sound of a blade embedding itself into the wood had her eyes opening quickly. She knew that sound. She'd heard it on the English shores when Rowen had thrown his dagger to stop her. Sure enough, Rowen's dagger quivered back and forth, stuck into the bulkhead right next to Muck's head.

"What part of don't go near the girl don't you boys understand?" Rowen stood atop the sterncastle with his sword drawn. "Get away from her Muck, or the next thing I throw will be my sword, and it'll be aimed right for your heart."

The crew quickly dispersed from their gathering, but the old man just glared at her. It sent a feeling of dread right through her.

"You'll be getting off this ship and soon," Muck told Cordelia. "If not, I will personally escort you off it myself."

Rowen took hold of a dangling line and swung down, landing with bare feet right next to her. "Was that a threat I heard coming from your mouth?" Rowen asked Muck.

"I'm speaking the truth," Muck answered with a scowl. "My brother never would have done something so stupid as to bring a woman aboard. You're going to curse us all."

"I'll have no more talk of the lady being a curse." Rowen's words were dominant and forceful. "Now, I suggest everyone batten down the hatches because I smell a storm brewing."

Lightning flashed in the distance as the winds picked up. The sail billowed and flapped in the wind and the ship glided over the water very fast. Cordelia didn't like storms and certainly not while on a ship in the middle of the ocean. Nightfall was approaching and this whole experience was starting to rattle her nerves. When she was in Rowen's arms, she felt safe, but now she felt as if she were all alone. And being alone was a feeling that scared Cordelia more than anything else.

CHAPTER 6

A storm blew up faster than Rowen's temper. The crew ran around securing the rigging while Cordelia did her best to stay out of the way. Rowen had donned a pair of shoes, but he still wore no shirt. She stood with her back against the bulkhead under the sterncastle out of the rain, watching as Rowen shouted orders to his men and they heeded his command.

"Shorten the main and drop the lateen, and be quick about it," he shouted, looking up to the sterncastle where Brody was doing his best to hold the ship on course. Rain pelted down now and she tried to stay hidden and dry. The ship rocked back and forth, and Rowen's bird screeched from atop the mast.

"Damn, Mya's got her talon caught in the rigging," said Rowen. "Brody, do your best to keep the Sea Mirage steady. I'm going up to get her."

"It's too windy," shouted Cordelia, seeing him reaching up for the lines and starting to climb. The ratlines spun around in the violent wind as he held on with all his might to keep from being blown away.

"Get inside my cabin and stay there," he ordered. "God's eyes, you're going to be blown right off the ship."

She stood there for a second, feeling her heart pounding like a drum. The door to the cabin wasn't that far from her, but fear consumed her and she wasn't able to move.

"Bid the devil, can't anyone listen?" He jumped down from the rigging and hurried over, grabbing her by the arm. Expertly dodging several crewmembers as they hurried about doing their part to secure the ship, he ripped open the door and flung her inside the room. "Now stay here and don't come out until I come to get you." He slammed the door as he left. She hurried back to it, holding on to everything along the way in order not to fall since the boat was lurching back and forth horribly in the storm. Gripping the door, she opened it a crack to peek out.

The storm became even more severe. She had all she could do to keep from falling as she watched Rowen climbing the rigging with his dagger clenched between his teeth, trying to get to his bird. The osprey's talon had tangled in a line that had snapped. The bird flapped its wings and used its beak, trying to hold on to the side of the lookout basket as thunder boomed overhead.

Chaos continued as the crew ran to and fro doing their best to keep the ship from toppling over and being consumed by the storm. Dark, rolling clouds blanketed the sky and cast an eerie green glow over the ship. The waves were getting higher with the swells already half the height of the main mast. A wave splashed down upon them and almost took with it several of the crewmembers. They slid to the opposite side of the ship, frantically grabbing for whatever they could to keep from being washed overboard.

Her fingers ached from holding so tightly to the latch of the door as it swung outward and then back, dragging her with it each time. Wishing for a pair of shoes on her feet right now, she shivered uncontrollably. She wasn't sure if it was from fear or from the fact her gown was soaked from the rain and bilge water, making her feel clammy and cold.

Her wet hair clung to her face and covered her eyes. Bravely letting go of the latch with one hand, she brushed away the wet locks just as another flash of lightning lit up the sky and thunder crashed overhead louder than she'd ever heard it in her life. Her heart jumped in her chest and she almost lost her grip on the door. The taste of the salty sea lingered on her tongue and the thick air filled her lungs. Looking up to the main mast just as another flash of lightning lit up the sky, she spied Rowen holding on to the rigging with just his legs as he reached out and cut the bird free. He was sure not to let Mya loose but, instead, held her securely to his chest.

He swung down on a line with the bird in his hand, landing on the deck just outside the cabin door. The boat leaned to starboard hard. This time, when the cabin door swung open, it pulled her out onto the deck with so much force that she lost her grip and landed on the ground. Using her hands to try to grip the slippery deck as the boat veered back to port, she tumbled over, landing up against Rowen's legs.

"Brody, take the Sea Mirage into the wind," Rowen shouted. "We're just going to have to ride this one out."

She heard Brody shout something back, but his words were lost on the wind.

"Get up, for God's sake," he growled, reaching down with his free hand and pulling her to her feet. He shoved her into the cabin. It was so dark now that she stubbed her toe on something as she entered the room.

"Ow!" she said, tripping and landing on his bed.

"I'm leaving Mya in your care," he said, putting the bird down somewhere but she couldn't see where since everything was black.

"I can't see anything," she cried out.

"Don't worry about it. Just stay on the bed and whatever you do, don't step on my bird. And this time, I'm going to make sure you stay put because I'm locking you inside."

"Locking me in?" she gasped. "What if the ship sinks? The

only window in this cabin is too small to use for escape. I'll go to my death at the bottom of the sea."

"If there's trouble, I'll come to get you. I warn you, don't leave this cabin again because I can't keep saving you while I'm trying to save my damned ship."

She heard him open a trunk or drawer and dig around for something. Then he slammed it shut and left the room, closing the door behind him. The sound of the key turning in the lock told her that he honestly didn't trust her anymore.

She heard the fluttering of wings and covered her head and screamed, curling up into a fetal position on the bed. Mya landed somewhere near her and she decided she'd better do as Rowen ordered. If she accidentally killed his bird, there was going to be hell to pay.

Frightened and curled up into a ball, she started to feel very sick each time the ship swayed. She rolled to one side of the bed and then back the other way. Hopefully, the bird could see in the dark and move out of her way since she couldn't control her actions. In a prone position on Rowen's bed, she found herself wondering if this would be how she went to her death. If only she had never bribed her guards to bring her to the Owl's Head Tavern on the docks in the first place, none of this would be happening.

Rowen didn't trust her and thought she had conspired against him with the king, trying to trap him and his brothers. In reality, she was just as much a pawn in this game as he was, but she'd never get him to believe that.

Longing filled her heart to be in his protective embrace and to feel his lips upon hers once more before going to her death in this storm. Never in her life had she been so scared, without a single soul to comfort her. Her father lived in Ireland, her mother was dead, and she had no living siblings, either. Neither did she have any real ties back in England to care if she should live or die. Only Lady Summer would miss her once she was gone.

A wave of emptiness and loneliness filled her being. Not able to see in the dark, she felt as if she were already dead. She hadn't cried much ever since she lost her mother and siblings to the plague. That harrowing incident had used up all her tears. Or so she thought.

Burying her face in Rowen's pillow, she inhaled his scent and wondered if she would ever see him again. His bird called out for him from somewhere in the dark. That bird was her only companion. Every feeling she'd ever suppressed, every thought she'd ever had throughout her entire life, and every one of her fears rose to the surface at once, causing Cordelia to cry harder than she ever had before. Yes, it seemed she had tears left after all.

CHAPTER 7

Dawn was already breaking by the time Rowen made his way back to his cabin. It hadn't been an easy feat, but he'd managed to lead his crew and weather the storm. As it ended up, he'd secured his ship with no lives lost and very little damage. However, they'd been thrown off course in the process and it took him a while to realize that they were on the west side of the Isle of Man. He'd thought of stopping there, but it was too obvious a place to dock. King Edward might already be waiting for him, so he couldn't risk it.

He'd taken the last shift at the helm while Brody slept. Now, he was so exhausted, all he wanted to do was to go back to his cabin and collapse. Brody would direct the ship to Osprey Island where they'd dock for the day.

He reached for the latch on his door, forgetting it was locked. Never had he needed to bolt his door before, but the girl changed all that. Turning the key in the lock, he opened the door and was greeted by the fluttering of wings. Lifting his wrapped arm, he made a perch for Mya. He quickly examined her foot to make sure she hadn't been injured last night.

Lady Cordelia reclined on his bed, fully clothed, and pushed up to look at him with sleepy eyes as he entered.

"Is it over?" she asked, yawning and rubbing her face. If he wasn't mistaken, her eyes looked red and swollen.

"If you mean the storm, then yes. But other issues are far from over." He ran a hand over the bird's head, seeing she was uninjured. Mya needed to fly and stretch her wings, and she also needed to fish. Opening her beak she squawked out her disappointment at having been locked in the room all night. "I know, Sweetheart, and I'm sure you're hungry." He released his bird and it flew out the door, up into the blue skies.

"You're right, I am hungry," said Cordelia, thinking he was talking to her. "You have no idea how much. I barely ate a thing at all yesterday since I was feeling ill, but my stomach is much better today." She yawned and stretched again, still not realizing he'd been talking to the bird. With a plunk, he dropped the key into the top drawer of his personal chest nailed to the wall. Then he slammed the drawer shut and closed the door to the cabin.

"Link will be by for you as soon as Big Garth prepares the meal. I've instructed Brody to keep an eye on you as well."

"You're not going to be with me?" she asked in surprise, sitting up and putting her feet on the floor.

"Nay."

"Aren't you hungry?" she asked.

"I had some hardtack earlier."

"Hardtack? That doesn't sound appetizing. What is it?"

"You'll find out soon enough."

CORDELIA WATCHED in shock as Rowen stripped out of his wet clothes right in front of her, down to his braies. Sunlight shone through the small open window, the shutter being torn off in the storm last night. She thought he'd stop there, but he didn't. He continued to remove his undergarment, as well, exposing his male parts. Biceps bulged in his upper arms and his chest rippled with toned muscles. Shocked by his manly beauty, she couldn't look away. His skin, kissed by the sun and still wet from the storm, glistened. She found herself fascinated and wanted to reach out and run her hands over it, but didn't. Next, her eyes roamed down past the dark line of tanned skin into the area that was pale and covered with blond, curly hair leading a trail right to his private parts. She caught a glimpse of what was below his waist but turned her head quickly since she was a lady.

Rowen must have seen the blush stain her cheeks because he chuckled slightly and walked over to the bed stark naked with no shame at all. He plopped his body down next to her and she jumped up off the bed at the same time, careful not to touch him.

"Why are you naked?" she asked, keeping her eyes turned in the opposite direction. When he didn't answer at first, she sneaked a curious peek back toward the bed.

He'd reclined onto his stomach with his face buried in the pillow. When he finally spoke, his words were muffled and slurred.

"I'm not going to lay down on my bed with wet clothes, though I can't say you paid me the same respect."

Perhaps she should have thought about that earlier, but it had been dark and in the middle of a storm at the time. She'd cried hard last night, more frightened than she'd ever been in her life. Then, totally spent, she'd fallen asleep with her head on Rowen's pillow, breathing in his scent of woodsmoke and the sea all night long.

"Are you going to sleep now?" she asked him.

"Take off those wet clothes," he mumbled. "Find something to wear for now in my trunks. And mind yourself . . . around the men." His sentence ended with a sudden snore.

"Rowen?" she asked, but he was dead to the world. Her eyes fastened onto his bare, sturdy backside and she felt a stirring within her. She'd seen his manly parts, not able to keep herself from looking, and it excited her. He had a lovely package dangling between his legs. His back rose and fell with his breathing as he slept and, curious by nature, she took a step closer to him. His buttocks looked to be pure muscle and it took all her restraint not to reach out her hand and feel for herself. Never had Walter looked anything remotely close to this. Rowen the Restless had a sculpted body that could compare to any one of the Greek gods. He was so enticing to her that she had half a mind to strip off her clothing and lie down with him.

But she wouldn't. She couldn't. She was Lady of Whitehaven and ladies did not have such ill and wanton thoughts. Besides, she didn't know if he hated her right now or not and nothing was going to change unless she had the chance to talk to him. How could she make him believe that she was not part of the king's plan?

Her body was cold, clammy, and dirty in these clothes and she longed for a hot bath and a cup of warm spiced mead. Unfortunately, she would get none of that here. This was a pirate ship with men who didn't seem to care about comfort and certainly not about a woman's needs at all. They thought her to be a curse and she'd be lucky to receive even bread and water.

Life on a ship had to be tormenting and full of hardships. How could Rowen live this way? And why would he even want to? All she wanted was to get off this wretched vessel and settle her stomach from the infernal rocking. More than anything, she needed to put her two feet on solid ground. Getting back to land and far away from the water sounded like heaven right now.

Holding on to whatever she could to keep her balance, she made her way over to a trunk at the far side of the small room. A board nailed in front of it on the floor kept the piece from moving. She opened the lid carefully, admiring the etched inlaid metal in between the smooth and sanded strips of wood that made up the exterior of the trunk. Looking inside, she saw it filled to the brim with clothes. Carefully, she reached out and dug through her newfound treasure, but it didn't take long to realize there were only men's clothes in there and nothing for a lady. Glancing over to the corner where she'd left her soiled gown, she realized it was gone.

Finally deciding on wearing some of Rowen's clothes for lack of having anything else to wear, she removed her wet, heavy gown and dropped it to the floor.

ROWEN DIDN'T KNOW how long he'd dozed off, but when his eyes drifted open, he saw the most glorious sight. A beautiful angel with milky-white skin and hair of fire stood in his cabin at the other side of the room. Thinking he was dreaming at first, it took him a moment to realize it wasn't an angel but rather Lady Cordelia – stark naked. He had to wrap his head around the fact there was a naked woman in his room while he slept on his bed naked as well. What the hell was the matter with him?

With her back to him, he saw the two womanly moons of her buttocks as she bent over digging through his trunk. He didn't miss the red thatch of hair peeking out between her long and luscious legs. His groin hardened immediately and he was thankful he was lying on his stomach so she couldn't see his erection.

He silently watched as she stepped into a pair of his breeches without an undergarment. With her head down, she looked to be tying the laces at her waist since the breeches were far too big for her. Then she dug around in the trunk again, standing upright with a tunic that she'd chosen. She turned around to don it and when she did, he got an eyeful of her perky, rounded breasts. The hard pink tips of her taut nipples pointed upwards, revealing that she was either cold or possibly excited from seeing him lying naked on the bed.

A slim waist and flat stomach added to her alluring body. Since he hadn't had a woman for a while now, he couldn't stop himself from letting out a moan of delight by what he saw. Her eyes flashed upward and those long brown lashes extended when she opened her lids wide as she noticed him watching her.

"Nay!" she said, moving quickly trying to don the tunic, but she fumbled and dropped it, instead.

"Leave it," he said, sitting up on the bed, no longer able to stay in his reclining position with his engorged manhood aching to have her. He got to his feet. Her eyes fastened to him and she seemed unable to move. "I just want you to see what you're doing to me," he groaned, making it across the room in two long strides, stopping right in front of her. Her green eyes moved down his chest and settled just below his waist. "Like what you see?" he asked her.

"I . . . I . . ."

"I know I like what I see." His eyes raked down her body in much the same manner and he let out a moan of pleasure.

"How dare you look at my naked body as if you have a right to!" She bent over quickly, grabbing for the tunic, but his hand shot forward and his fingers fastened around her wrist. Slowly, they stood up together.

"I could ravish you right now and none of my crew would think less of me because of it."

"You wouldn't do that. Would you?" Her voice trembled when she spoke.

"I'm a pirate, my lady, and you are my prisoner. You don't really expect me to act like a gentleman, do you? If you want a chivalrous and honorable man, you'd better look elsewhere than on this ship."

She angrily pulled the tunic away from him and clutched it to her bare chest. "If you're going to roger me at the rail then I suggest you hurry up and do it. After all, didn't you say this is where you do things like that? In your cabin?"

He let out a frustrated breath. The girl was here for the taking so why was it so hard for him to do just that? "I said I'd protect you and that included protecting you from me," he answered, feeling his thoughts conflicting in his head. As a boy, he'd been raised to respect and see to the safety of women since he lived in a cottage filled with females. But over the last decade, he'd lived his life as a pirate and had gotten used to some very crude ways.

"Do you mean that?" Squinting slightly, she watched him from the corner of her eyes.

"I do. However, I have to admit I like the kisses we've shared. I'd like your permission to try it again, my lady. After all, my lip no longer bleeds from your bite and I'm eager to experience a kiss without the sting this time."

"But you're . . . you're . . . naked." She looked away when she said it.

"I'm willing to bet you enjoyed our kiss as well."

She paused for a second and Rowen watched her tongue shoot out to lick her lips. That told him he was correct in his assumption. If she denied it, he'd know she was lying.

"Well . . . what if I had? Would that make me a wanton woman?"

"Only in your eyes, not mine. I'll leave the decision up to you, but I warn you, if I'm turned down I won't ask again."

"Does that mean you'll just take what you want next time or does it mean you will leave me be?"

"Deny me a kiss and you'll find out the answer for yourself."

She hesitated again as if she were considering it. Then, she finally answered. "I do want to kiss you again," she admitted. "But first I want you to know I was not a part of any trap or conspiracy against you. I found out things only by accident and wasn't even supposed to be on the docks at all at the time of the attack."

"I'm supposed to believe that?"

"Don't you?"

"I'd believe it more if you sealed it with a kiss." He leaned over to kiss her and she didn't object. Their lips met and it excited him so much, he forgot all about how tired he'd been. Her lips were soft and sweet, like a ripe berry kissed by the sun and ready to pluck from the vine. It felt ever so desirable to have the company of not just a woman - but a lady. He couldn't stop himself from taking another kiss. This time, he put his hands on her shoulders. While her kiss was hot, he noticed her bare body felt wet and cold. Beneath his fingertips, he even felt little raised bumps on her arms and he didn't miss the fact her body shivered. He wasn't sure if she shivered from fear, anticipation, or just the weather, but none of that mattered right now.

His tongue shot out and traced her lips. She jerked backward at first. But as he massaged her shoulders, she started to relax. He continued to kiss her, coaxing her lips apart, and when she opened to accept him, his tongue entered her warm, moist mouth. Immediately, he felt himself growing even harder. How he'd like to mimic this action, but with other parts of their bodies, instead. Pulling her closer up against him, he felt the delectable swell of her breasts against his chest. Her mouth opened wider and their tongues danced as he deepened the kiss, wanting to taste every part of her perfect body.

One more kiss and she dropped the tunic completely. She reached up to place her hands on his chest. It felt good. Too damned good. He'd never known the touch of a noblewoman and was finding out quickly that he craved it. Needing to caress her breasts, he slid his hands down her arms, reveling in the feel of silky, satiny skin beneath his fingertips. He slowly ventured inward, his hands cupping and settling over her two perfect mounds as he tested the waters, expecting another storm at sea. To his surprise, there were no waves today. She let him do it and didn't object. He found himself wondering if she was as starved as he for the companionship of each other.

Starting with a light squeeze, he found his action rewarded with the response he wanted when she muttered a moan of passion. Daringly, he traced the tip of one finger around the perimeter of her nipple, delighted when it puckered even more and turned to a rigid peak from his caress. Next, he used both hands and gently rolled her nipples in his fingers as he kissed her deeply at the same time.

"Oh!" she said through ragged breathing, coming up for air.

"Did you want me to stop?" he whispered, nibbling at her earlobe and blowing into her ear gently as he spoke. She trembled at his touch and this excited him even more.

"Nay. Continue," she whispered back, the permission he longed for, springing from her lips.

She'd easily succumbed to his wishes and he could only guess that she enjoyed this as much as he. Relief filled his being. He wasn't sure what he would have done if she had denied him these pleasures. Words spoken could not be retracted and he'd promised to protect her even from him. However, his pirate side was rising to the surface and he was no longer sure he'd be able to deliver on his promise. Not able to restrain himself any longer, he dipped down and opened his mouth, leaning closer and flicking his tongue across one pink nipple. Her back arched from his action and her nipple stood up straighter than a soldier at attention.

"Ooooh," she muttered, arching further, allowing him even more access. Slowly, her eyes closed and her chin lifted as her head fell back and to the side. He used his lips and then his tongue and tasted the sweet essence of a noble that he would never know again in this lifetime. Noblewomen were reserved for knights and lords - not bastards and certainly not pirates. He wanted her so desperately he felt as if he were about to burst. Anxiously, he reached down and his fingers fumbled with the tie at her waist.

"Rowen, mayhap we'd better slow our pace," she said, her spine stiffening at his action. Pressing her hands against his chest, she pushed out of his embrace. Seeming to have changed her mind, this wasn't at all what he expected. It was not going to be easy to stop at a time like this.

"Slow down? Now?" he asked, his lust telling him to take her anyway, but his head warning him that he'd hate himself if he broke his promise to a lady. What was he to do? "Love, you don't know what you're doing to me. I want you so bad it's driving me crazy and I'm not a man who likes to retreat at any cost."

"Part of me wants to continue, but I'm not sure this is a good idea," she replied.

His hands quivered, wanting to reach out and touch her soft skin and rounded curves again. His head ached and he struggled with his decision. Knowing he could never force himself upon a lady because it would haunt him the rest of his life, he took one step backward, making distance between them.

His birth mother had been a noble and probably had been taken against her will by his father – the king. Rage ran rampant through him at this thought and he decided he didn't want to be like his father. Nay, he wouldn't be like Edward, not for anything. Rowen was a bastard, but he still had the blood of nobles running through his veins. Somewhere deep down, there was a blasted chivalrous man buried beneath the legendary pirate he'd become and this made him restless, indeed.

"Damn!" He pulled away and ran a hand through his hair in aggravation, feeling frustrated as all hell. He'd never had to worry about decisions like this until Lady Cordelia showed up. For the last decade, he'd been happy finding his release with whores and hadn't had thoughts clouding his brain of morals, honor, or promises that he might not be able to keep. This was different. Even if Lady Cordelia were willing to lay with him, it would sully her for life in more ways than one. Being a pirate, he was frowned upon and feared by all. Being a bastard would bring about similar results and he had yet to tell her who sired him.

Even after having been raised with pirates from the young age of twelve, he still had some morals and rules he honored. One of them being that he never broke his word.

"Don't be angry with me," she pleaded and he didn't know what to say. He was harder than the hardtack he'd had to break the fast and needed to do something about it right now.

"Just touch me," he whispered, taking her hand in his and bringing it to his hardened form. "I want you to feel what you're doing to me." He wrapped her fingers around his shaft and moaned and closed his eyes at the feel of the warmth of her hand enveloping his engorged member. This only made him wonder what it would feel like pumping into her hot, wet, tight body, with her long legs spread wide and wrapped around him in eager anticipation.

"Nay," she spat, pulling her hand away. His eyes sprang open in confusion. Her words said no, but still, her eyes held want as they focused downward, fixated on his manhood. She was still interested and there was no denying it.

"What's the matter?" he asked, wrapping his own hand around his erection this time. "You seem like you're frightened of this, but yet you said you're a widow and had a baby as well."

"I've never seen a man like you," she told him, turning around and pulling the tunic over her head, hiding her beautiful body from him much too quickly. "You're so big . . . so hard."

"I'm guessing the old man wasn't able to satisfy you?"

"No," she said, glancing over her shoulder and licking her lips, most likely savoring the taste of his essence. He liked that. Then her eyes dropped down below his waist once more. "Many times my husband couldn't get hard at all." She scooped up her short boots from the floor and put them on, finally dragging her eyes away from him. It was over and, to his disappointment, he'd get no more kisses or caresses from her now.

"That's too bad," he growled, thinking of the many ways he had in mind to please her, yet now she would never experience a one of them. It was also too bad he'd have to pleasure himself now, after being so close to coupling with her. He could take her easily but, alas, he wouldn't. His word was important to him and he would not break his promise to a lady. Damn his promise and his noble blood!

"Get out of here, Cordy," he said, using a pet name for her.

"What did you call me?" She stood up and straightened the tunic that was too big for her and, in doing so, it enabled him to see the tops of her breasts. It about drove him out of his mind. He wasn't going to be able to hold back much longer and refused to degrade himself by handling his release with her standing there watching.

"Get out!" he shouted. "Now!"

CORDELIA SHOT out of the captain's quarters and slammed the door behind her, trying to still her rapidly beating heart. Had she just almost made love to a pirate? If her nipples weren't still in nubs and the fire between her legs wasn't burning out of control, she might have thought she'd imagined the whole thing. She'd been so close to allowing him to couple with her and part of her regretted that she had turned him away. The whole idea frightened her and she still couldn't believe he'd left the decision to her, acting more like a chivalrous knight than a black-hearted cutthroat of the sea.

This had been her chance to finally feel the excitement and ecstasy of coupling that she'd never known with the man she'd been married to for five long years. Rowen was a dangerous, rugged pirate and a thief. All the things that should make her despise him but, oddly enough, it excited her and only made her want him more.

What was happening to her to make her feel this way?

No matter, she wouldn't have to worry about it happening again because Rowen said he was a man who wouldn't ask twice and she believed it. The opportunity to couple with a man of her choice was gone now and history wasn't going to repeat itself where this was concerned. She hadn't missed the disappointed look in Rowen's eyes when she turned him away. There was no denying how much he'd wanted her. No man likes rejection, especially during intimate moments, and she was sure Rowen wouldn't forget about this anytime soon.

Grateful she hadn't been ravished, she still felt sad that things between them had to end this way. Why had he been so chivalrous by asking her instead of forcing himself on her? Even her late husband had never asked – just took. It was a common and accepted action for a man to treat a woman this way. Rowen showing her the respect she wished she'd had from Walter only made her decision to turn him away harder. And why had he called her Cordy? She loved his little endearment – an endearment that should be shared only by lovers.

Confused and frightened by what just took place inside the cabin, she was no longer sure Rowen would want to be near her. But at least she'd told him she had nothing to do with King Edward's trap, even if he didn't seem to believe it.

What was left for her now, she wondered? She supposed she'd have to marry a man of King Edward's choosing. The man would probably end up being at least twice her age and have saggy muscles or mounds of fat. Or mayhap, since she'd been aboard a ship full of pirates, she'd be rejected by the king and the nobles altogether. Whatever happened, it wasn't going to make her happy. Right now happiness and companionship are what she longed for, but what she wanted more than anything in life was a baby to call her own.

CHAPTER 8

Cordelia had spent a good part of the morning with Link, avoiding the rest of the pirates aboard the ship as much as possible. After the semi-tryst she'd had with Rowen, it made her realize that the same thing could happen with any of these men. She was sure none of them would retreat like Rowen had. Part of her regretted turning him away, but another part of her was pleased that she'd been able to save her virtue and finish by acting like a lady even if she hadn't started out that way.

Standing atop the sterncastle next to Brody, she watched the first mate sail the ship over the blue waters and toward Osprey Island. She hadn't seen Rowen since early this morning and hoped he would emerge from his cabin soon. Old Man Muck had been eying her up from the shadows and his sidekick, Lucky Dog, had watched her intently earlier as she'd almost choked on hardtack and washed it down with rum that burned her throat and made her cough. The whole thing was unnerving as well as undesirable. She wanted more than anything to sneak down to the hold and get some sweetmeats and fine wine from her dowry but didn't dare venture into the belly of the Sea Mirage unprotected. Besides, she didn't think Rowen had told his crew what the bounty consisted of and neither did she want any of them to know.

The shrill cry of a hawk from overhead took her attention. She looked up and shaded her eyes with her hand to see Mya circling the ship. The bird landed gracefully in the lookout basket atop the mast.

"So how long has Rowen had his pet hawk?" she asked Brody.

The man shrugged his shoulders, looking up to the basket as he spoke. "Not sure. It's been a while. Captain doesn't think of it as a pet. Pets aren't free and he likes his hawk to be able to come and go as it pleases."

"Interesting," she said as a wave hit the side of the ship hard. She grabbed on to the railing to keep from falling. The seas had been quite rough this morning and the sun was no longer shining. Dark clouds blocked the light and only a few rays of sun poked through. She hoped they wouldn't run into another storm. "How soon before we reach the island?"

"Soon," was all the man said. Brody was not very talkative, so when she spotted Link swabbing the deck on his hands and knees, she made her way toward the young boy, hoping for conversation.

"My Lady," said the boy, jumping to his feet, almost knocking the bucket over in the process. "What can I do for you?"

Muck walked by just then and grunted. "She's a prisoner, so stop treating her like a queen." Cordelia didn't say a word until the old man was out of earshot.

"Thank you, Link, for seeing to my needs today," she told him with a nod of her head. The boy had been kind enough that he'd even held up a blanket to shield her while she relieved herself into a bucket earlier, therefore hiding her action from the lusty crew. She wished more of the men were like this boy.

"The Cap'n asked me to watch over you and that's what I did."

"You admire Rowen, don't you?"

"I do," said the boy, wringing out a rag into the bucket and continuing to wipe up the extra rainwater from last night's storm. "I was an orphan and he took me in and cared for me. I consider Rowen and the crew my family. Rowen feels the same way about all of us."

"So how did Rowen get the title of Captain?" she asked.

"The men voted after the death of One-Eyed Ron," he told her, going about his work as he spoke.

"Was One-Eyed Ron Rowen's father?" she asked, hoping to learn more of Rowen's personal life.

"Nay," said the boy, finishing up and taking the bucket over to the side of the ship, dumping the contents into the sea. "One-Eyed Ron was Old Man Muck's brother. I haven't been with Captain Rowen all that long but, from what I hear, One-Eyed Ron raised Rowen from the age of twelve and considered him his son."

"What about Rowen's real parents?" asked Cordelia. "What happened to them?"

"I don't know," said Link, putting down the bucket and untying the cloth from around his head. His blond hair spilled out around his shoulders and he shook the cloth in the air. "The only one who knows for sure is Old Man Muck. Mayhap you should ask him." He nodded toward the old man who was using his very sharp dagger to whittle a piece of wood. His eyes focused on her and a shiver wracked her body. The man scared her.

"Nay, I think I'll just ask Rowen about it, instead. Is he awake yet?"

"He was exhausted, so mayhap not."

"I'll just head to his cabin and find out."

"I wouldn't bother Cap'n Rowen when he's in his cabin, my lady. If you startle him, he might take off your head before he realizes it's you. After all, that's how Lucky got that long scar across his throat."

"It is?" she asked, startled to hear this.

"That's right. Lucky's real name is Stanley. But after that incident, everyone started calling him Lucky Dog since he survived meeting with the end of Rowen's sword."

Her hand went to her throat and she swallowed deeply. "I'll be sure to make my presence known before I take a step inside," she told Link, heading for the cabin.

With her hand on the latch of the cabin door, she purposely made a lot of noise so she wouldn't startle Rowen and end up decapitated.

"Rowen, are you awake?" she asked in a loud voice, opening the door slightly. Cautiously, she poked her head inside, but it took her eyes a moment to get accustomed to the dim light of the cabin. "Rowen, it's me. Cordelia," she said, louder this time. She then made a fist and knocked on the door. "Hello?" Standing at the threshold, she didn't dare to enter.

Finally, her eyes became accustomed to the light and she could see that the bed was empty. Had Rowen left his cabin without her noticing? She didn't think so, but where was he? Pushing the door, it hit something and stopped from opening further. Cordelia took one step into the room and halted.

"In or out, but make up your mind," came Rowen's growl from behind the door.

"Rowen? Are you back there?" She moved forward and the door closed as Rowen pushed it from the other side. He sat on a small stool at a makeshift table that retracted from the wall. On it was what looked like a chess set, with pieces placed in various positions on the wooden board while others were missing. "What are you doing?"

"Don't talk to me, I'm trying to concentrate," he said without even looking at her.

"Are you playing chess?"

"I said, be quiet." His hand hovered above one of the pieces, but he stopped in mid-motion and then pulled his hand back to his side as if he were in deep thought.

"Who is playing the game with you?" She looked around the

room to make sure no one else was present. There wasn't anyone there and she found this to be very odd. After another few minutes without him making a move or saying a word, she sat down on the stool opposite him. "These look heavy." She reached for a piece that was in play, but his hand shot out and grabbed her wrist, stopping her from touching it.

"The pieces not in play are in a box by your feet. If you have to fondle one, use those, instead."

"Fondle?" Her mind raced back to their intimate time together, but he just stared at the board. Bending over, she picked up the smallest of the pieces - a pawn and inspected it. Made from some type of heavy metal, all the chess pieces were either silver or of a copper nature and looked as if someone had taken a lot of time to design them. Intricate patterns were etched into the metal making them elegant and beautiful. "These are heavy," she said, putting the pawn back and looking at one of the ornate kings on the board. It was carved with textures and swirls trailing around the piece. Lines and dots decorated it, as well as diamond shapes on the ornate crown embedded with tiny colored jewels. The queen was just as exquisite and had little flowers etched onto it.

"This is beautiful," she said, reaching out to pick up the king. Once again, his hand shot out and stopped her.

"You never, I repeat never, touch the king. Do you understand?"

"Why not?" she asked innocently, not knowing why he was getting so upset.

"The king is mine to take down and I will!"

"Isn't that usually the object of the game? I do know how to play. Perhaps I can play with you?"

"Nay. He's mine," he spat, moving a pawn one space forward and getting up from his seat. "Up," he said, taking her by the arm and dragging her to her feet. Once she stood, he proceeded to sit down on her stool at the opposite side of the table and, once again, stared at the board intensely.

"*He's* yours?" she asked, settling herself on the stool he'd vacated. It was still warm. "You make it sound as if you think these pieces are real and you have some sort of vendetta against someone."

"Something like that," he said, clenching his jaw and nodding his head. She studied him and started to realize that to Rowen, this was more than just a game used for the purpose of entertainment.

"So if the king is King Edward, then which piece are you?" she asked, taking a wild guess and, once again, coming up lucky.

"I'M THE KNIGHT," said Rowen, cursing himself as soon as he said it. What was it about this girl that she seemed to be able to look into his mind and read his thoughts? She knew things about him and he didn't like that.

"The knight?" She giggled. "You're a pirate. Mayhap you should be one of the other pieces, instead."

His eyes flashed upward to meet hers and her irritating giggling stopped. "I was chivalrous to you when I didn't take you by force or did you forget so soon?"

Her tongue shot out to wet her lips and Rowen focused on the game or he'd be thinking about bedding her again. He hadn't liked having to pleasure himself and would rather not think thoughts that only got him excited right now.

"I didn't forget." She cleared her throat. "So if you are the chivalrous knight, I'm going to guess the bishop is your brother who lives in the church's catacombs, although it seems he should be the rook since his name is Rook." She giggled again, making him very restless.

"I don't like to be talked to when I'm playing the game."

"Well, am I right or not?" she asked.

"Yes, the bishop is Rook and the rook is Reed, not that it's any of your business."

"So your Scottish brother has a castle?"

Rowen couldn't think straight with all the girl's chatter. His hand lifted and wavered above the queen. He had to figure out how to take down the king and this game was going to help him do just that with the right moves. "Reed doesn't live in a castle and he's not Scottish."

"Not Scottish?" she asked. "Well, I suppose if you're triplets and you and Rook aren't Scottish, then he wouldn't be, either."

"Please, be quiet." He changed his mind again and his hand went toward the knight, instead.

"I'll bet one of your parents was English and the other Scottish. Is that right?"

"Nay, you're wrong," he said in aggravation.

"Then why don't you tell me about your parents and how you became a pirate?"

In frustration, he moved the knight and she looked down and shook her head, making a tsking sound with her tongue.

"What is that for?" he grumbled.

"You moved the knight when you should have moved the bishop, instead. Because now the gold queen can take your silver knight like so." She boldly reached out for the queen and slid it across the board, scooping up the knight in her hand in the process. "See what I mean?"

"Damn," he spat, slapping his palm against the table and making all the pieces jump slightly. "Not my knight! Anything but my knight."

"Sometimes, the right move is one you might never imagine. That's the thing about chess – there are so many ways to win."

"And lose," he said, feeling that restlessness churning in his gut again. He needed to do something about his situation. He'd waited for ten years to get revenge on his father and he didn't want his raids to end yet.

"So . . . who sired you?" As she ran her finger in small circles over the table, it only managed to make him think of his own finger not long ago running in small circles over her nipple.

"You don't need to know." He snatched up the king as he spoke.

"My, you seem as if you're going to choke the life out of that piece or perhaps smash it in your palm."

"It has no life and is nothing to me. Do you hear me? It's nothing but a piece in a game." He slammed it down on the board. When he looked up, her mouth was hanging open and her eyes were wide.

"My God, you and your brothers are the English king's bastards, aren't you?"

"I'll kill Brody for telling you," he spat, furious that his secret had been revealed.

She smiled smugly and continued to run her finger in circles atop the table. "Brody didn't tell me a thing, but you just did by your admittance."

"How did you know?" he asked. "No one knows my secret but Brody."

"I just figured it out by the way you grabbed for the king when I asked who sired you. And then you slammed it down with such vengeance, that I knew it had something to do with your life – not the game."

"You know nothing, so don't even think you can figure out what I've been through." He got up and paced the floor.

"Then why don't you tell me?" She stood and walked toward him. "Please, let's sit on the bed and talk."

"I don't want to be on that bed with you unless we're coupling and I think you've already made it quite clear how you feel about that. If you so much as breathe a word of who sired me to anyone, I swear I'll –"

A knock at the door stopped him in mid-sentence. He walked

over and yanked the door open. Link stood there with his hand raised, ready to knock again.

"What is it?" Rowen's words came out angrier than he'd intended and the boy jerked backward in surprise. Link's hand flew to cover his throat.

"I'm sorry to disturb you and the lady, Cap'n. I figured something might be going on and that's why I knocked instead of just walking in."

"Nothing is going on. Now tell me why you're here."

Seeming satisfied his head would remain intact, Link slowly lowered his hand from his throat. "Cap'n, we're nearing Osprey Island and Brody sent me to fetch you."

"We're here already?" Rowen rushed back and grabbed his weaponbelt and started to don it.

"You were in here for hours," said Cordelia, joining him at the door. "I thought you were sleeping, but now I see you were doing something else that is much more interesting." She raised an eyebrow and stepped over the threshold, standing next to Link.

"What was he doing, my lady?" asked Link curiously.

"Playing chess," she said, as Rowen slipped into his boots.

"By yourself, Cap'n?" asked Link. "Or were you playing with Lady Cordelia?"

"I assure you, I was not playing with Lady Cordelia, nor will I ever." He stepped out and closed the door and looked directly into her eyes. "She knows nothing at all about the game, no matter how much she thinks she does."

The air between them thickened and he cursed himself for telling her his secret. "Remember my warning," he said, not sure what he'd do to her if she opened her mouth. He headed up to the sterncastle to bring his ship into port, trying not to think of Lady Cordelia or her ability to figure out all his secrets because it was only going to drive him mad.

CHAPTER 9

Legendary Bastards of the Crown

Cordelia struggled to keep up as Rowen hauled her by the arm down the pier as soon as the ship had docked. Islanders rushed up to greet them. She found herself shocked that they were dressed in rags and had dirt on their faces and bodies. They were barefoot as well.

"Captain Rowen, it's been a while. We're so glad to see you," said a young woman who seemed to be about Cordelia's age. She was petite with dark hair and almond-shaped eyes. A smile spread across her face, but despair could be seen in her expression and Cordelia wondered what was wrong. Three scrawny, dirty, barefooted children followed at her heels.

"Magdalena, where is your husband?" asked Rowen, looking around. "He's usually here to meet me on the docks."

"Our papa died," said the little boy. Cordelia's heart went out to them.

"Oh, how terrible," she said. "I'm very sorry."

"Who is this?" asked Magdalena. "I didn't think you and the crew traveled with women aboard."

"We don't," growled Muck, making his way past them with

Lucky at his side. "She's a curse and has already brought about a storm at sea."

"Muck, hold your tongue and get our things unloaded," Rowen warned him.

"What things?" asked Muck. "Are you planning on leaving our newfound bounty here?"

Rowen's eyes darted over to Cordelia. She didn't like them talking about her dowry in this manner and the only place she wanted it dropped off was back on the mainland where it belonged.

"Nay. Bring ashore only two barrels of ale and one of salted herring," Rowen ordered. "The rest goes to Scotland."

"Thank you, Captain Rowen," said the woman with tears in her eyes. "We've had a horrible time ever since my husband and a half dozen men died in the storm yesterday. We're still waiting for their bodies to wash ashore so we can give them a proper burial. That is, if they haven't already sank to the bottom of the sea."

"What were they doing out in the storm?" asked Rowen. "They should have sought shelter."

"There was a ship out in the storm and they thought it might be in distress. They went to their aid but never returned."

"Was it one of King Edward's royal ships?" he asked. Cordelia didn't miss the warning look to her in his eyes when he said it.

"Nay, I don't think so. It was smaller than one of the king's ships. As far as we could tell, it wasn't flying the crown's colors."

"Good," he answered.

"Good?" repeated Cordelia. "How can you say that when this poor woman's husband might have died at sea, not to mention whoever was on the ship they tried to save?" She walked over and put her arm around Magdalena's shoulders to comfort her.

"I meant it is good that the king hasn't been here." His osprey flew down and Rowen raised his arm to give it a perch.

"It's good to see Mya again, too," said the woman. "She's probably glad to be home."

"Home?" asked Cordelia. "What do you mean?"

"Osprey Island is where I found Mya," Rowen told her.

"That's right," said Magdalena. "This island is home to many sea hawks."

"I will do whatever I can to help you," Rowen told her.

"Thank you. You and your crew are welcome to what little we have," said Magdalena. "There are a few chickens the villagers have been raising for the eggs, but we will slaughter them to celebrate your arrival."

"Nay! Don't let them use the last of their food on us," said Cordelia, looking over to Rowen.

Rowen ran a finger over his osprey's head as he spoke. "Well, how else do you suggest we feed all these people? We are low on provisions as well. Did you want to share your goods with them?"

She knew he meant her dowry, but that was for the king. If she gave it away, with it went her only chance of marrying someone of her choosing. She wasn't ready to give that up.

"What about the bird?" she asked, eyeing his pet.

"No one is eating Mya," he growled, pulling the hawk closer to his body protectively.

"That's not what I meant," she said and flashed a grin, wondering how he could think she would want to eat his bird. "Doesn't that bird fish?"

"It does," he said with a nod of his head. "I see what you mean. Mya, go fish." He raised his arm and the bird flew up into the sky and out over the water. "She'll bring enough fish to supplement our meal," he told Magdalena.

Several men of the island came to join them. Rowen went over to talk to them, leaving the women alone.

"Your clothes – they are the clothes of a man," said Magdalena with question to her voice.

"Aye, they are." Cordelia brushed dirt from her sleeve. "My

gown was soaked from the storm and I hadn't another to wear, so Rowen offered me some of his clothes for now."

"You speak and act as if you're noble."

"I am," she told her. "I am Lady Cordelia de Clare of Whitehaven."

"Oh, my lady! I am sorry, I didn't know." Magdalena bowed and gathered up her children, showing them how to pay proper respect as well. The little one was only about a year old and fell and started crying.

"Hush, Dora," said Magdalena, struggling with her other two children, trying to get to the baby.

"I'll get her," said Cordelia, eagerly scooping the dirty baby into her arms. It felt good to hold a child again and her heart broke for the baby she'd delivered that had died in her arms right after birth. She'd wished she were dead that day instead of the infant and ever since then had longed for another baby. "She is cute but filthy. Do you have a stream or somewhere where the children can wash up?"

"Yes, we do," said the dark-haired woman. "But it's not right for you to be helping. Where is your handmaiden?"

ROWEN HAD ONLY LEFT Cordelia for a minute. When he turned around, he saw her cuddling one of Magdalena's dirty children in her arms. As she smiled at the baby, her whole face lit up in a way that he hadn't seen before. She cradled it and kissed its dirty face, and the baby stopped crying. Cordelia was a natural mother.

Then he heard Magdalena ask where her handmaid was and he decided he'd better get over to her before she said something she shouldn't.

"She doesn't have a handmaiden," he said, walking over to join them.

"What? The Lady of Whitehaven with no handmaiden?" asked

Magdalena. "And why is she on your ship to begin with without an escort?"

"Yes, would you like to answer that?" asked Cordelia, glaring at him. He realized it was no good lying to the Islanders. They knew he was a pirate and they'd often helped him in exchange for the booty he bestowed upon them. They were poor and unprotected. He was able to provide them with goods as well as protection when he visited the island.

"I'm her escort. She's my prisoner," he blurted out, noticing the surprised look on Cordelia's face when he divulged this information.

"Your prisoner?" Magdalena's brows arched in surprise. She picked up the little boy and held him to her chest. "Why would you do something like that?"

"Because she knows too much and I couldn't leave her behind," he admitted. "It could be devastating to me."

"Aren't you afraid you're spilling too many secrets by telling her that?" Cordelia shifted the baby to her other arm and cradled it protectively against her bosom as she rocked her body back and forth.

He chose not to answer. The Islanders didn't need to know about the problems between them. "My men will scan the shores for any flotsam or jetsam from the storm. In the meantime, why don't you women get things ready for our meal? Mya should have enough fish by the time we're done." As if on cue, his osprey swooped down from the sky and dropped a fish at their feet. Rowen threw the bird a salted herring from a pouch at his side as a reward. The osprey caught it in midair, swallowing it whole and then made one more circle above Rowen's head before heading back out to sea.

The children squealed and the little boy squirmed, so his mother put him down. He and his sister ran around trying to catch the flopping fish, only managing to fall and get even dirtier.

"Children, stop it," said their mother, moving them away from the fish. She then reached down and picked up the fish by the tail.

"Magdalena, mayhap you can teach Lady Cordelia to cook," suggested Rowen, sure she didn't know how to do much since she was a lady.

"Cook?" Cordelia looked up in surprise. "Why would I want to do that? That's what my servants are for, although I am very skilled at the chore."

Rowen cleared his throat and motioned to Magdalena with his eyes. Cordelia realized how awful her words must have sounded and was ever so apologetic.

"I'm sorry, I didn't mean anything by that," she told the woman. "I'd love to help you cook the meal just as soon as we get the children washed up."

"Good idea," said Rowen. "After all, I hope you are better at cooking than you are at playing chess."

"Do you know how to play the game?" asked Magdalena excitedly, looking up to Cordelia in awe. "My husband, Fitz, always wanted to learn."

"It's not that hard, perhaps I can teach you," said Cordelia. "After all, women can be very good at the game." She looked over to Rowen and smiled when she said it.

"There's only one rule to remember," Rowen interrupted.

"What is that?" asked Magdalena.

"You always need to remember your goal – nothing else matters."

"To win?" asked Magdalena.

"To get the king." Rowen smiled back at Cordelia and winked. Then he turned and walked back to the dock, already thinking of his next move.

CHAPTER 10

Legendary Bastards of the Crown

The day turned out to be hot and sunny. Cordelia felt herself perspiring profusely – something she hadn't done in quite some time. As the lady of the castle, she'd always had servants to do things for her and barely ever got her hands dirty. Today, however, was a different case. She'd helped Magdalena wash the children in the spring and also cook a meal for the inhabitants of the island as well as for Rowen and his men.

Rowen had added a barrel of apples to the meal. Along with the fish Mya provided combined with the ale and salted herrings, they'd all had food to eat. Cordelia convinced Magdalena not to kill their chickens but rather to keep them for eggs. However, she had to admit that without them, the meal was scarce and she was still hungry afterward.

Back at Whitehaven Castle, a typical meal consisted of stuffed pheasant, rabbit in a savory sauce, venison in rich brown gravy, root vegetables, white bread for the nobles and brown bread for the servants, and a variety of cheeses and sweetmeats followed by tarts and pies. Not to mention, the finest of wine, mead, and two different types of ale. Cordelia had much and these people had little. The children were so skinny that she could see their ribs. They only had one change of clothes and those were nearly threadbare. None of them seemed to wear shoes and she wondered how they survived the cold winters.

The group sat around the outdoor cooking fire. One of the Islanders pulled out a lute and began to play.

"How quaint," she said, taking a sip of ale from the cup she shared with Rowen. "Where did you get a lute?"

"It was my husband's lute," said Magdalena. "Fitz taught himself to play." She cradled one of her sleeping children on her lap and a sad expression washed over her face as she remembered her husband. Magdalena wore a torn and dirty gown. Cordelia wondered how the woman would feel if she ever had a chance to wear a gown like the ones she wore. "He got the lute from Rowen."

"From Rowen?" Cordelia's eyes darted over to Rowen who sat next to her. He took the cup from her before he answered.

"Just a little something, courtesy of our dear old king," he whispered. Raising the cup to drink, he watched her over the rim.

Cordelia wanted to say something to that comment but didn't think it was the proper place or time to do so. So instead, she remained quiet.

"How long will you be staying?" asked Magdalena.

"We'll leave on the morrow," said Rowen, draining the cup and placing it in the sand. "We need to get to Scotland and we've already been thrown off schedule by the storm."

"Yes, we wouldn't want your schedule to be interrupted, would we?" asked Cordelia, disgusted by the way he planned his pillaging, not even considering the fact she was far from home and all alone. He didn't sound as if he were going to be bringing her back to the mainland anytime soon.

"Will you be traveling with them, then?" asked Magdalena.

"I suppose so," said Cordelia, standing up and brushing the

sand off her clothes. "After all, I'm naught more than a pawn in Rowen's game of chess."

She felt as if she needed to be alone and ran off toward the water. It was dark with just moonlight to guide her way, but she didn't fear these people and knew she'd be safe. She stopped at the water's edge, looking at Rowen's ship and also the waves lapping against the shore. They were much too far from the mainland for it to be visible from their position. If she wasn't mistaken, right now they were closer to Ireland than they were to England. She thought of her father and wished she could go to him right now, but it would never happen. She might never even see him again. Her heart was weighted and she felt so isolated on this island. Once they reached Scotland, she would be Rowen's prisoner there and never step foot on English soil again.

Footsteps sounded from behind her and she figured Rowen had followed her. She turned around, intending to tell him to leave her alone. "Rowen, I –" Her words abruptly stopped when she saw Muck and Lucky standing there. Not at all who she wanted to see at a time like this.

"Nice evenin', my lady, wouldn't ya say?" asked Lucky in his deep and garbled voice. He sounded downright scary.

Quickly scanning the area for anyone else, she had hoped to call out for help, but no one was in sight. "I think I'll be getting back to the others." She took a step around them, but Muck's hand shot out and grabbed her by the arm.

"What's yer hurry, wench? I thought we could get to know each other better."

Lucky laughed, but it sounded more like a cross between a horse and someone choking.

"You hold her for me and I'll hold her for you," said Muck, starting to untie the laces on his breeches.

"Nay!" Cordelia tried to pull away, but Muck only held her tighter.

"Wait, Muck. I didn't know you planned on taking it this far," said Lucky, seeming as if he didn't want to be a part of his friend's plan.

"Shut up and do as I say," Muck snapped. Then he spoke to Cordelia. "Did you really think you were going to flaunt your goods in front of a bunch of lusty men and not have to pay for it?" Muck pulled her closer and she could smell the stench coming from the man's body. Horrified that she would be raped, she cried out for help and then raised her leg and brought her knee up hard against Muck's groin. Muck cursed and a whoosh of air left his lungs from the contact. He let go of her arm and bent over, which gave her the opportunity to run. She didn't get far before he jumped her from behind and both their bodies went crashing to the ground. He turned her over and straddled her. Then he clasped one hand over her mouth.

"Not another word, wench, or this will be rougher than I'd intended."

Lucky followed at Muck's heels. "Come on, Muck, let's go," he said, looking around. Then his hand went to his throat. "I don't care to meet with the wrath of Rowen."

"Go if you want, but stop your babbling," said Muck. "This wench needs to be taught a lesson and I'm the one who is going to do it. It won't take long." He reached for the tie on his breeches.

"Get off of her!" A foot shot out from nowhere and kicked Muck in the face. His body rolled off to the side and Cordelia saw blood dripping from his nose. Then the sound of a sword being pulled from a scabbard rang through the air and Rowen stepped forward, holding the tip of his blade to Muck's neck. "What part of stay away from the girl don't you two understand?" Cordelia had never seen Rowen so angry.

"Cap'n!" shouted Lucky in surprise, raising his hands above his head in surrender. "I didn't do nothin', I swear."

"I know, I heard it all. You didn't do anything to help protect Lady Cordelia, either. Did you?"

"It was all Muck's idea," whined the scarred man. "I didn't know he was going to take it this far and I tried to stop him."

"Unless you want another scar across your neck, I suggest you get the hell out of here, Lucky," warned Rowen. "Because when I'm done with Muck, I guarantee he is not going to feel lucky at all."

Lucky lowered his hands slowly, took one last look at Muck, and turned and ran.

"We were just havin' a little fun," said Muck with a chuckle. "I wasn't really going to do anything to your girl." Still prone in the sand, Muck wiped the blood from his nose.

"That's not the way I see it. Now get up!" shouted Rowen.

Muck reluctantly got to his feet. Rowen raised his sword and it looked like he was about to kill the man. Cordelia didn't want anyone to die, no matter how horrible they were. She pushed up to a sitting position and shouted to stop his action.

"Nay, Rowen don't!"

Rowen's blade stopped right under Muck's chin. The man didn't move a muscle.

"Please don't kill him," she begged.

"He deserves to die for what he tried to do to you," said Rowen, scraping his sword against the man's neck and drawing blood. "He disobeyed my orders and now he'll pay."

"I disobeyed your orders, too, when I left your side and wandered off on my own," stated Cordelia. "I'm just as guilty as he is."

"That's right, she is," sputtered Muck.

"Shut up," he said, this time running his blade down Muck's chest. Muck grimaced as the line Rowen traced over to his heart drew blood as well. "I could kill you easily right now. The only reason I'm sparing your life is because it was a request from the lady."

Cordelia saw the anger rising inside Rowen. His eyes bore fire and a nerve in his clenched jaw twitched. There was no doubt he wanted to kill Muck. If she hadn't stopped him, he probably would have done so. This vengeful side of him frightened her. She'd seen him act like a pirate, but not like a cutthroat, and this is one side of him she didn't want to witness.

"Please, Rowen, put down the sword," she begged before he carved into the man anymore. "Nothing happened and that is all that matters."

"But it could have happened, Cordy. He could have had his way with you before I got here and then what would you have done?"

"I'm sorry for wandering off," she said. "I won't leave your side again, but please no killing. Just let Muck go."

He hesitated with the tip of his sword wavering over Muck's heart. She could see the turmoil within him as he tried to make his decision. Then he threw down the sword into the sand and grabbed Muck's tunic in two fists and pulled the man up to him face to face.

"It is taking all my restraint to honor the lady's request because I would have no qualms running my sword through your blackened heart right now you son-of-a-bitch!"

"Sorry, Cap'n, it won't happen again," said Muck, looking like he wanted to kill Rowen as well.

"You're damned right it won't, because if you even look at the girl cross-eyed after this, I'll ram my blade right through your heart so fast, you won't know what hit you. Savvy?"

"Aye, Cap'n," said Muck, not sounding like he meant it.

Rowen released his tunic and the old man stumbled backward. Cordelia breathed a sigh of relief, not wanting to witness a murder. And just when she thought it was all over, Rowen rushed forward and punched Muck straight in the jaw, sending him sprawling across the sand again. He followed up with a kick to the man's stomach. Turning to leave, he changed his mind and twirled around and dove atop Muck, punching him viciously, harder and harder.

"Rowen, please!" she screamed. That was probably the only thing that saved Muck from being beaten to death. Rowen looked over his shoulder at her with his fist in the air and finally stopped.

"God's eyes!" he spat, getting off of Muck and kicking him one last time. Muck groaned and held his wounds. He rolled over and pushed up to his knees. Blood leaked down his neck and chest, and his eye was already blackened.

"You're bewitched by the wench and she's turned you into a lovesick fool," snarled Muck, holding his side and glaring at Rowen. Cordelia hoped they wouldn't start fighting again because she didn't know how much more of this she could take.

"I should cut out your tongue for saying that," spat Rowen, snatching his blade from the ground and holding it out toward Muck again. "Now get out of here before I change my mind and do just that!"

Muck swore under his breath, spit into the sand, and pushed up to a standing position.

Then grumbling to himself, he limped away.

Once he was out of sight, Rowen put his sword back into his scabbard and extended his hand to Cordelia.

"Did he hurt you, Lady Cordelia?" He pulled her to her feet. Cordelia's heart ran rampant and the nerves in her legs shook so much she could barely stand. She threw herself into Rowen's embrace and buried her face in his tunic.

"I – I'm all right," she mumbled. "Just frightened, that's all." She held on to him tightly, not wanting to let go. She'd almost been ravished and if Rowen hadn't come to her rescue, she didn't know what she would have done. "Thank you for saving me."

"From now on, you will not leave my side. Do you understand?"

"I promise." She loosened her grip and looked up to see his mesmerizing eyes staring down at her. "Would you really have killed him if I hadn't stopped you?" she asked, still feeling her heart beating rapidly against her ribs.

"If I had wanted him dead, there would have been nothing you could have done to stop me, Sweetheart."

"Then why did you stop?"

"They're my crew and the only family I have, no matter how rotten they are. Would you want one of your own family killed for trying to relieve a natural urge?"

"Natural urge? They were going to roger me at the rail," she gasped.

He chuckled and ran a hand through her hair. "We're not at the rail or even on the ship, so that is not accurate."

"You know what I mean!"

"Don't worry. I'm far from done with either of them. But there is nothing more I can do tonight. You were to blame as well, just like you said. You asked for trouble by wandering off on your own."

"I wanted to walk on the beach and look at the water in the moonlight," she told him. "What's wrong with that?"

"Nothing, as long as you're escorted."

"Rowen," she said looking back out at the sea. "We're closer to Ireland than England right now, aren't we?"

"Aye," he answered.

"Can't you just drop me off in Ireland? I will go to be with my father."

"Nay. I'm sorry, but I can't do that, Cordy. Now, how about I escort you back to the ship and you can still have your walk?"

"All right," she said, sniffling, as tears fell from her eyes.

"No crying, my lady," he said, reaching down and wiping a tear from the corner of her eye with a quick touch of his hand. It felt good to be touched by Rowen again. "First rule aboard a pirate ship is never to show weakness and especially not fear. The men will see your fear and go into a feeding frenzy like sharks in the ocean surrounding a helpless victim at sea."

"I'll try to be strong," she said, feeling Rowen's arm slip around her waist. The warmth of his body against her stopped her from trembling. "However, I do feel safer with you at my side."

"I told you I would protect you and I'll keep my word. I always do." He led her down the shore and toward the water.

"Doesn't that make you weak in the eyes of your crew?"

"Not the way I look at it. I think it would be weaker to surrender to my manly urges, yet I've kept my promise not to give in unless you agree."

He looked at her in the moonlight and she thought she saw a glimmer of hope in his eyes. He was speaking about coupling with her and being chivalrous as well. Not forcing himself on her like Muck tried to do. "Aye, that is an admirable strength," she said, looking the other way so he wouldn't see the need and want in her eyes.

The waves lapped at their feet and she stopped. She held on to his arm, standing on one foot. "I want to take off my shoes and walk barefoot in the water."

"Take off whatever you like, I won't stop you." His words sounded sultry and she couldn't help but think of the last time his voice sounded like that when they'd almost made love. She slipped off her shoes, rolled up the legs of the breeches she wore and stepped out into the water. The cold waves washed over her feet making her feel cleansed of the dirty, disgusting man who had tried to rape her.

"This feels nice," she told him, looking back over her shoulder. "Why don't you take off your shoes and feel it as well?"

She heard splashing as he trudged out into the water with his boots on.

"What are you doing?" she laughed. "You should take off your boots first."

"In my line of work, we don't take off our boots unless we're bathing, sleeping, or dead. It's always good to be prepared in case I have to go somewhere at the spur of the moment."

"Like escaping a king's army?" she asked, looking up at him as he gazed into her eyes. The moonlight bathed him in a soft glow and he didn't seem like a hardened pirate, but rather like a sensitive, caring lover.

"It's also less temptation if I remain fully clothed around such a beautiful lady such as you." He reached out and cupped her cheek with his hand. She leaned into his caress and closed her eyes.

"Do you really think I'm beautiful?" she asked, having never heard those words from her late husband in all the time they were married.

"Like an angel or perhaps a fae of the forest. You are spirited and vibrant yet at the same time refined and regal."

Her eyes opened quickly. His words were romantic and took her breath away. She loved it. "I'm not sure that answered my question," she said with a slight giggle, feeling nervous every time he touched her.

"Yes, Cordy, I do think you're beautiful. More beautiful than any woman I've ever met."

She loved when he called her Cordy because it struck a note within her. She liked the endearment and felt special when he said it. It caused her to relax in his presence. He stared at her mouth and continued.

"Your eyes are like stars twinkling in the skies and your skin like the virgin new-fallen snow on a winter day. Fire sprites dance in your hair and your cheeks hold the blush of a ripe, juicy berry plucked straight from the vine. And your lips – your lips possess the essence of sweet, ripe plums that I want to taste until I have my fill."

"My, that's lovely," she said, feeling a blush rise to her cheeks. Never had she thought a pirate could speak in this manner. "You should have been a bard."

Then, cradling her chin in one hand, he leaned toward her, staring at her lips and bringing his mouth closer and closer to hers. She closed her eyes again in anticipation and raised her chin, welcoming the kiss of such a chivalric, handsome man. If she didn't know better, she'd think he was a knight. His kiss deepened and she reached up and held on to his shoulders. With her eyes closed, it was easy to forget he was her captor and a pirate of the seas instead of a noble lord.

"You will sleep in my cabin tonight," he said, scooping her up in his arms. Her shoes dangled from her fingertips as he moved toward the pier.

"On the ship?" she asked, remembering him lying naked on his bed. Tonight, they might both be lying naked together. "Is that safe, since your crew will be staying there as well?"

"If I'm by your side, you don't need to fear, my lady. You will be safe on my watch."

He turned and carried her up the beach and onto the dock. Although she thought he'd put her down, he carried her all the way back to the ship. Thankfully, all his crew was still on the island, because she would have been embarrassed to have anyone see this.

Once he got to his cabin, he kicked open the door, entered the room, and laid her down on the bed. Leaning over her, he kissed her ever so gently. It felt like the wisp of butterfly wings against her lips and it tickled.

Then the sound of his hawk outside the door had him standing and walking to the entrance of the cabin. "Sleep in the lookout basket tonight, Mya," he said to the bird and closed the door. Reaching into the chest attached to the wall, she watched him pull out the key to the cabin and lock them inside together.

"You're locking us in here?" she asked, pushing up onto her elbows, trying to see him in the scant moonlight spilling through the open hole used as a window.

"I'll not take the chance of anyone bothering us tonight." She heard him drop the key into the drawer and close it. Then he rumbled around and, before she knew it, he'd lit a lantern. The warm orange hue of the flame encompassed the small room.

"You're staying here as well?" she asked, feeling very anxious.

"Unless you'd rather I go." He proceeded to remove his weaponbelt and she realized he had no intention of leaving. She had half a mind to say yes just because his assumptions were so cocky.

Longing for his companionship, she didn't have the heart to send him away after he'd just saved her from being raped. But she wouldn't trade one ravager for another. She was a lady!

"I'd like you to stay," she said. "But only for company and to keep me safe."

She couldn't ignore the look of disappointment on his face. "Of course." He nodded slightly, pulled out the stool and sat down and studied his chessboard. Not able to bear the thought of him staring at that game all night long instead of at her, she found herself already regretting her comment.

"I was hoping we could talk." She scooted to the edge of the bed.

"So talk," he said, reaching out his hand, letting it waver above a chess piece, not even looking in her direction.

"Tell me something about yourself."

"There's nothing to tell."

She could see this was getting her nowhere and decided he might be more interested if she talked about herself, instead. And she knew just how to entice him.

"I'm sure my handmaid, Lady Summer, is very concerned about me. She is very mature for her young age of four and ten years."

"Lady Summer?" His hand dropped to his side and he turned toward her just as she had hoped. The ploy worked. He no longer paid attention to the game. "How so?"

"Well, she came to me two years ago with her mother, asking

for work at my castle. Her younger sisters, Autumn and Winter were with her."

"Her mother and sisters?" Now she had his undivided attention. He got off the stool and made his way across the room, standing before her. "Tell me how they look. Are they all as pretty as Lady Summer?"

"Aye, just as pretty," said Cordelia, reeling him in. "And it is the oddest thing – Lady Summer has golden hair like the sun, Lady Autumn has red hair like the fallen leaves, and Lady Winter has black hair like the void of color on a cold winter day. Who would have thought three sisters could have three different hair colors?"

"My brothers and I have three different hair colors, too, so it's not that odd at all."

"That's right," she said, remembering him talking to his brothers and seeing this for herself. "And you three are triplets, so that is very rare. Of course, King Edward's graying hair has a red tint to it, and your mother's graying hair seems to have been blond, but where did the black hair of your brother, Rook, come from?"

"She's not my mother," he said, instead of answering her question.

"She's not? But Lady Annalyse is the mother of the girls and you are their half-brother. I know you have different fathers but how could Lady Annalyse not be your mother?"

She watched a sad expression wash over his face. He let out a deep sigh before sitting down on the edge of the bed next to her. "My mother died right after we were born. I've heard her name was Lady Gabrielle and she was Annalyse's twin sister."

"Oh, my! Twins and triplets both in the same family. How lucky."

"Lucky?" He looked over and shook his head. Then he proceeded to remove his boots as he spoke. "Nay, it was the furthest thing from being lucky. Don't you know the second twin is always considered cursed and triplets are feared even more so because they are so uncommon?"

"I do know that, although I'm not sure I believe it at all."

"Well, believe it! I'm living proof that it's so."

"Are you saying it's unlucky because your mother died right after you were born? I had a baby die in my arms as well and there were no twins or triplets involved."

"I didn't know your child was dead." Sadness and concern filled his words. "Cordy, I'm sorry."

"It was a boy," she told him. "A boy that would have inherited my husband's estate had the baby lived."

"That must be hard for you."

"Aye, it is. Not because of the inheritance part, but because I'm afraid I'll never have another baby."

"I'm sure that's not true." He finished removing his boots. "You are young and beautiful and will marry again. You will have many babies."

"Not if the king betroths me to another old man. That's why I need that dowry in your hold. The king will grant me permission to choose my next husband if I give him those things."

"The things that were being used to trap my brothers and me?" He stood up and removed his tunic. Standing before her with a bare chest, he looked like a golden-haired god and it was hard for her to think of anything but reaching out and touching his wonderfully sculpted body.

"Why did you turn to piracy?" she asked, curious as to his motives. "You have royal blood flowing through your veins and could have had so much including a title, lands, and wealth. I don't understand why you'd throw that all away."

"I didn't have a choice," he told her, untying his breeches as he spoke. "The day I was born, my father – the king – ordered the death of my brothers and me after my mother died. So my aunt took us to Scotland to save our lives."

"What?" His words came as a shock to her. "Why would a king want babies of his own blood killed, even if they were bastards?"

"He wanted the first born only, but Annalyse, her mother, and the nursemaid wouldn't tell him which of us was born first. Because of that, he ordered us all killed."

"That is terrible! I'm sorry, Rowen."

"Don't be." He threw his trews to the side and walked over naked and settled himself on the bed. She diverted her gaze in the opposite direction. "I want him dead, too, so we're even."

"Oh, you mustn't say that about your king."

"Edward is not my king. My alliance belongs to King David. I grew up in Scotland."

"So how did you and your brothers get separated?"

"It was on the night of Burnt Candlemas." He looked down and then rubbed his hands over his face and sighed.

"I've heard about that. It was terrible and a lot of people died."

"A lot of Scots, thanks to Edward."

"But you were only a boy then. What could you have done?"

"I was twelve. My brothers and I set out to conquer King Edward, foolishly thinking we could make a difference. We ended up hiding in a monastery, but we weren't safe there."

"That's a holy place and you should have had sanctuary."

"Tell that to Edward. His men attacked. Right before they did, the temple was ransacked by a band of pirates. The pirates ended up taking me with them. A monk helped Rook hide in the underground catacombs. Reed managed to escape and ran back to be with Ross Douglas – the man we had thought was our father."

"How did you find out the truth?"

"Ross was wounded earlier that night and in anger, the truth came out. Then my mother told me everything but only because she had to. She was so upset with Ross that she took my sisters and the nursemaid, and they traveled back to England. She and Ross, as far as I know, haven't seen each other since."

"My, that is some story. Now I know where your vengeance

for King Edward stems from, but I can't say I agree with it. You will be nothing more than a pirate and outcast your entire life if you continue to try to kill the king."

"Who said we're trying to kill him?" He lounged back on the bed and put his hands behind his head, doing nothing to hide his nakedness. Her eyes flashed over to him and once again she looked the other way. "I said I wanted him dead, but I won't be the one to do it. We're only trying to make him as miserable as possible because we feel that is by far better revenge."

"I see." She clasped her hands on her lap and looked down. "So, if the king had known you were the first born, he would have bestowed upon you wealth and riches, probably given you land, and, mayhap, a castle and a title to go along with it."

"Don't forget . . . a lady to marry and bear my heirs as well."

Her eyes shot up to him and he drank her in, making her wonder if his thoughts were the same as hers right now. If only he wasn't a pirate, she could choose to marry him and they could make babies together.

"I'm sure you'll marry someday and have baby pirates of your own."

"I don't want baby pirates; I want my sons to be noble knights and warriors. I want wealth and riches and a title to go along with it. Face it, Lady Cordelia - I'll never get what I want and deserve."

"I don't know if that is necessarily true," she said. "You are already called Captain and lord of your ship. You steal all the wealth and riches you want. I'm sure you'll someday steal land and a castle, too."

"Does any of that matter when I can't have the one thing I want most of all?"

"What is that?" She expected him to say the death of the king, but his words surprised her.

"You, Lady Cordelia. What I want more than anything is you for my wife and as the mother of my children."

"Me?" Her heart sped up and she jumped to her feet and paced the floor. "Why would you want me when you could have any woman you want?"

"I saw the way you handled Magdalena's children today. I could see it in your eyes, as well, that you want a baby more than anything, even if I didn't know the one you'd birthed had died."

"I'm a lady," she reminded him. "I have the opportunity to birth a noble son who will someday be a legendary knight loved by his people and who is loyal to the king. He will be honored and revered by all. Most of all, he will be of pure, noble blood."

"I'm of pure, noble blood," he reminded her. "My father is the King of England and my mother was a noblewoman, for God's sake."

"That's different." She wrung her hands in front of her, trying to talk herself out of actually agreeing to go to bed with the man. He was handsome and seductive. She was sure he would make a much better lover than any old nobleman the king would demand she marry next.

"It's not different, except for the part that I'm a left-handed triplet and considered spawned by the devil. Is that how you think of me?"

"Nay," she said, shaking her head. Why was he making this so difficult for her? "I am a lady," she repeated once again.

"Will the king and everyone else still consider you a lady when I return you to England and tongues start to wag that you've been raped by pirates? Even if you deny it, they won't believe it and you know it. Face it, Cordy; your future was doomed from the moment I brought you aboard the Sea Mirage."

He was right. Her future was doomed because her reputation would be sullied so much that she would never marry a nobleman now. No one would want her since she'd been on a ship of pirates. Everyone back home was sure to know all about it by now since Lady Summer as well as her guards saw her being taken by Rowen.

"You're right," she said with a nod of her head. "But if I lay with you and conceive your child, where does that leave me?"

"With a father who would die for his family and who will teach his son to fight and protect you even when I'm long gone. I know as well as you that I'm not the best choice of a husband, but I've fallen in love with you, Cordy. That is something that I can guarantee you didn't have with your last husband and will probably never have with anyone you marry in the future. Am I wrong?"

She took a minute to answer, weighing out the consequences of her premeditated actions. A pregnant woman without a husband would be scorned in the eyes of the nobles. If she did conceive Rowen's child tonight, she would be banished from England with everything taken from her. On the other hand, she had never felt this way about a man before. She believed Rowen could pleasure her like no other. Like he said, either way, when she returned to England, she would be separated from everything that was her past life. Her fate had been determined the day Rowen brought her onto his ship. It was all her fault since she'd sneaked down to the docks and had been spying on him in the first place.

"I think I've fallen in love with you, too," she admitted. "It is my fault I'm in this position, not yours."

"So what do you want to do about it?"

"I want to lay with a man I love, not despise. And I want more than anything to have your baby, Rowen."

He sat up straight on the bed and a serious expression crossed his face. "Do you know what you're saying?"

"I do."

"Sweetheart, don't do this because of my wants and wishes. I've been doomed from the day I was born, but there is no need for you to go down with me. I don't want you laying with me out of pity."

"There is no pity involved. I still don't agree with your

stealing and killing and going against my king, but I think I've fallen in love with you, Rowen. If I never see you again, I won't go to my death never knowing how it felt to make love with a man of my choice."

"So . . . you choose me? Are you saying you want to lay with me of your own accord?" he asked as if he couldn't believe what she was saying.

"I do. Now, are you going to give me the pleasure you promised or are you going to turn me away the way I did to you when your want and desire for me was consuming your every thought?"

"I would never turn you away, Love. Now take off your clothes and come join me on the bed."

CHAPTER 11

Cordelia found herself undressing at Rowen's suggestion. He sat and watched. Although she wanted him to help, she also knew he wanted this to be her decision. Was she making a mistake? Would she curse herself in the morning? Somehow, right now, none of that mattered.

Rowen's story had touched her heart, helping her to decide. Everything about him, all his thoughts and beliefs, seemed to stem from having had such a hard life. She couldn't even imagine someone wanting to kill a baby – especially a baby of their own blood. Now, Rowen didn't seem like the vile creature she'd first thought him to be. Instead, it was her king who took that title.

She finished undressing and dropped her clothes to the floor, standing in the flicker of the firelight naked. The ship gently rocked as if it were trying to comfort her like a mother rocking a baby.

"Come here, Cordy," he said in a sultry voice, his eyes hooded and the corners of his mouth turned slightly upward with a satisfied grin. "You are a princess and I don't deserve you."

She sauntered over to the bed. His manhood stood straight up, anxiously awaiting their union.

"You deserve more in this life than you'll ever see. I'm sorry things have been so tough for you," she told him. She let him take her by the wrists and pull her toward him.

"I'm tired of thinking about what I don't have. Tonight, all I want to do is think about what I do have, even if it only lasts for one night." He reached up and kissed her. When their lips met, all her inhibitions slipped away. With his second kiss, she reached for his shoulders as his hands slowly slid down her back and caressed her bottom.

"Shall we lie down?" she asked.

"Nay," he said, trailing kisses down her neck and to her chest. "There are other ways to couple. I'm guessing you've never tried any of them but the one."

"You're right," she said. "But what do you mean?"

His mouth roamed freely to her breast. His tongue flicked across her nipple. A spiral of excitement shot through her and caused her to gasp. Then his tongue curled around her nipple causing it to go taut. He used both hands to hold her breast as he suckled her like a baby.

Her womanhood pulsed deep within her core. She quivered as he repeated this action to her other breast as well. Involuntarily, she arched her back, trying to hold in her moans of desire.

"Let it loose, Cordy. Don't hold back. I want you to know passion in every sense of the word."

Her legs became weak when he took her torso in two hands, running his tongue slowly down her chest and to her navel. His tongue swirled in circles as he tasted her there.

"My knees are weak and I fear my legs will give way beneath me," she said through ragged breathing.

"Then you need to sit down, Love." He grabbed her hips and pulled her closer, taking a thigh in each hand and spreading them to encompass his waist. His hardened form throbbed and pushed up against her and, daringly, she let her hand slip down his chest until it rested on his engorged form.

"Ah, that feels good," he said in a breathy whisper. "Grip me harder." When she hesitated to do so, his fingers wrapped around her hand and he squeezed. His eyes closed and his lips pursed together as she reveled in the feel of satin over steel. He released her hand and she used her fingers, working them up and down his shaft. The size and length of him compared to her late husband was extraordinary. She felt excited yet apprehensive, thinking she might not be able to take in all of him.

He pushed her hand away and let out a breath. "We'd better slow down or I'm going to finish before you even begin."

"Tell me more about these different ways to make love," she said, placing kisses on his face and blowing gently into his ear.

"Oh, you have no idea what that is doing to me," he mumbled. She felt good to be able to excite him the way he excited her. In her marriage to Walter, she'd felt like a failure when it came to making love. But with Rowen, she felt like the Goddess of Seduction. It felt glorious and oh, so right.

His hand snaked in between them. His fingers played with her womanly folds and her nub of pleasure. Then he slipped a finger into her, using his thumb at the same time to arouse her unbridled passion.

"Oooooh," she called out. "I think something is happening, Rowen."

"Then it's time, Cordy." He used his hands to lift her hips upward and, slowly, he lowered her over his hardened form. At the same time, he continued to suckle her breasts, nipping and pulling playfully with his mouth. She felt him enter her as he gently slid into her deeper and deeper, igniting a fire within her core that burned out of control.

They imitated the motions of coupling from a sitting position, although she never thought it was possible. And then Rowen grunted and fell backward onto the bed, pulling her atop his body in the process. The ship rocked more now. She wasn't sure if the rocking was from the waves slapping against the side of the ship or from their bodies slapping together as he slid in and out.

"Rowen, flip me over. I cannot be on top."

"Why not?" he asked, never stopping to put her in the proper position.

"Because, I'm supposed to be the one on my back, not you."

"Not on my ship, you're not. I rather like it this way. In this position, there is more of you to taste."

His tongue continued to make magic at her breasts while his hips moved in rhythm with hers, creating magic below the waist. And just when she thought it could feel no better, his love-making triggered off something inside her that she'd never felt before. Unable to hold back her cries of passion, she heard herself making noises she never heard before as she found her release. Her world exploded behind her closed lids in colors of vibrant pink and purple.

Rowen seemed to anticipate her every emotion. When he knew she had reached the precipice of her desires and lifted up over the edge, he no longer restrained himself. With both his hands on her hips, he used them to move her back and forth. His hardened length slid in and out guided by their liquid passion. Then he moaned once more and she felt his seed spill into her. The thought they might be creating a baby excited her so much that she found herself surprised when she reached her peak yet another time.

Finally sated and spent, she rolled off the top of him. They lay in each other's arms, not saying a word. All was peaceful and quiet except for the sound of waves hitting against the side of the ship that rocked the back and forth.

Then she thought she heard a noise outside the open window, but when she tried to get up and look out, Rowen pulled her back into his arms and held on to her possessively. Enjoying it, she closed her eyes, letting the rocking of the ship lull them both to sleep wrapped in each other's embrace. This had been the best night of her life and no matter what happened in the future – she didn't want this part ever to end.

* * *

THUNDER AWOKE Cordelia from a sound sleep the next morning. When she opened her eyes, she saw lightning flashing in the distance outside the open window. Memories flitted through her mind from last night's coupling with Rowen and she smiled until she realized the bed next to her was empty.

"Rowen?" She shot upright to see him sitting in the corner with the light of the lantern illuminating the chessboard and its pieces. He moved the copper rook and captured the silver knight.

"Damn," he said, shaking his head, still staring at the board. She scooted to the edge of the bed, totally naked. Feeling uncomfortable in this position since he was fully clothed, she wrapped the bedcovering around her. Still, he didn't even look in her direction.

"What are you doing?" she asked, jolting in surprise as a crash of thunder shook the ship and it rocked back and forth like a helpless pawn in the angry sea.

"There is a rag and water in a bucket next to the bed. I'd suggest you use it if you need to, before it spills all over my floor. The weather is getting rough."

She felt and saw the evidence of their lovemaking on her body and smiled. Although her muscles ached, it was in a good way, from taking all of Rowen into her when she wasn't used to a man that size. She reached over for the bucket and cleaned herself as he suggested.

"I'll be sure to have a bath prepared for you once we reach Scotland."

"Thank you. I'd like that." She hurriedly dressed in his clothes again, although she noticed her gown and the gown he'd given her both dry and spread out across a trunk.

"Your gown is dry if you'd like to wear it. I had Link clean it and hang it out to dry."

She pulled one shoe and then the other onto her feet and walked over to him, holding on to whatever she could since it was so rocky she thought she'd fall. Making it to the chessboard, she could see it was secure with the rim of boards nailed to the table holding it in place. The pieces were sturdy and unless the ship rocked uncontrollably in a storm, they looked like they'd stay in place.

She heard a slight squawk and looked over to a perch Rowen had set up that was sticking out of the wall. Mya was atop it, holding on with her talons.

"Rowen, if you don't mind, I think I'd like to leave my gown as well as the one you pilfered with Magdalena. I'd also like to leave some food and coins from my dowry for her and her children and the people of the island as well."

"Really?" This announcement caused him to look up from his game. "I thought your dowry was important to you so you could give it to the king and marry the man you want. If you give it away, you'll lose your edge."

After last night, she wasn't sure why he was saying this. He'd told her he loved her and wanted her to be his wife. This morning, it almost seemed as if he were trying to talk her out of the plans they'd made together.

"I don't want to leave all of it, just a small part to help them out. Magdalena and her children have so little and I have so much."

"How noble of you to give away my bounty that I'd intended to use to help the Scots make it through the winter."

"What's the matter?" she asked, sensing something was wrong. Mya squawked from the perch behind her, seeming to agree with her observation.

"You were right about the bishop," he said, still surveying the board.

"What?" She almost fell when the ship rocked, and hurried to sit down on the stool across from him. "What are you talking about?"

"Yesterday, you said it was the bishop's move and you were right. Today, the rook took out my knight. My knights are all gone and yet the king survives. I was never any good at this game, although I always wished I could play as well as my brothers."

She chuckled. "Rowen, you're not even playing the game with anyone other than yourself. You can move wherever you want. If you wanted to save your knights, you could have done so."

"Nay." He shook his head, seeming very disturbed. "This tells me that my brothers are in danger and need to make a move against the king."

"What about you?" she asked, looking down to the board void of all the horses.

"It's too late for me. I think we both can see that. I am doomed no matter what move I make."

She studied the board, thought of his last move, and shook her head. "You didn't have to lose your knight. Look! Your queen could have come to your rescue." She demonstrated, moving the piece and reaching for the horse to put the knight back on the board.

"Nay." His hand grasped her wrist. "What's done is done. I can't go backward no matter what mistakes I've made."

"What does that mean?" she asked, slowly putting the queen back into place. Somehow, she was getting the feeling he regretted their lovemaking last night.

He jumped to his feet and started pacing the floor. "Something is wrong. I feel it in my bones." He seemed so restless that she wanted nothing more than to gather him into her arms and lay him down on the bed with her so they could comfort each other like they had last night.

"You seem jumpy for some reason. There is nothing wrong,

now just relax." Odd that she should be telling him this when it should be the opposite way around. She was his prisoner, yet he acted like he was the one who was trapped.

"Captain Rowen, are you in there?" Someone pounded on the cabin door, startling her, and she almost fell off the stool as the boat shifted again. Rowen stayed surefooted and didn't even waver. He headed over to the door and pulled it open. It wasn't locked like last night. By the evidence of the bucket of water and the bird in the room, she realized he must have left the cabin and returned while she'd slept right through it.

"What is it?" he growled. Cordelia stretched her neck to see Link and Brody standing outside the door.

"I think you'd better come at once," said Brody. "Something washed up on the shore in this morning's storm. You're not going to like it."

"There is wreckage," added Link. "Lots of it, just wait until you see it all."

"Stay here," Rowen said over his shoulder to Cordelia, grabbing his weaponbelt and strapping it around his waist. "I don't want you out in the storm."

"The rain is starting to let up," said Link. "From up in the lookout basket, I saw blue skies on the horizon."

"Good." Rowen wrapped a leather binding around his forearm and whistled for his bird. Mya flapped her wings and flew across the small room, landing on his arm. "Mya will be able to spot anything that we miss. Let's go collect our bounty."

CORDELIA STOOD at the door with her mouth open, not sure what to think. The pirate in Rowen was coming out this morning if the first thing he thought of when he heard about a shipwreck was how much bounty he could collect and pilfer for himself. What about passengers or possibly crew? If there was a lot of wreckage, then that most likely meant a ship went down in the storm. She needed to go with him in case someone required her help.

With one step outside the cabin, she was promptly stopped by Link blocking her path.

"Step aside, Link. I need to go see if anyone was hurt."

"The captain knew you'd not listen to his orders and told me to stay at your side."

"Fine. Then you come with me."

"That's not what he meant. He wants you out of the way in case there's trouble."

"Well, if there's trouble, then I think I'd be safer at his side." Cordelia walked back to gather the gowns. She opened up a trunk and chose a pair of shoes as well. "Link, can you have some of the crew bring a few of my things to the island?"

"Your things? I don't understand."

"I'm speaking about the cargo in the hold. Have the men bring one of the crates of smoked meat, one of pickled vegetables, and two barrels of wine. And also the big hump-backed trunk, as well, since it's filled with clothing."

"My lady, I do believe we're leaving today. Wouldn't you want the things to stay on the ship, instead?"

"Not at all. I'm giving these things to Magdalena to share with the residents of the island. Did you see how poor they are? Oh, that reminds me. There is a small square chest with an X on it. Have them bring that to shore as well."

"What's in that one, my lady?"

"Coins. I want to leave enough so that Magdalena can survive and raise her children herself now that her husband is gone."

"I don't think the captain is going to like this."

"I assure you, he won't mind. I mentioned my plans to him this morning. He knows all about it." She didn't have to stress the point that Rowen hadn't agreed to her idea. Then again, even though he knew about her plans, neither did he tell her not to do it, either. She would be doing a service to the people of Osprey

Island and this made her feel proud since she had more than she needed.

"If you're sure, my lady."

"I'm sure." She stepped outside and noticed the rain had let up and the sun was starting to peek through the clouds. Up in the sky was a beautiful rainbow. "There you go," she said to herself. "Nothing is wrong. There is a rainbow to prove that everything will be all right after all."

CHAPTER 12

Rowen's jaw twitched and he shook his head, looking down at the dead body of Fletcher, the tradesman who had drifted ashore in the storm. Next to him were some of his crew and all around them were pieces of his ship. Rowen had thought the man was on his way to pick up Reed and the Scots to take them back to Scotland, but it wasn't so.

"Damn!" he spat, hunkering down, feeling the side of the dead man's neck. His skin was blue and his body cold and stiff. This couldn't have just happened. "Fletcher's ship must have gone down in the first storm. Last night's storm just pushed the wreckage to shore."

"Your brother and the Scots are expecting him to show up in Maryport today," Brody pointed out.

"With no ship there to carry them back to Scotland, they're nothing more than sitting ducks," spat Rowen. "If the king got wind of our plan, he might already be laying a trap for Reed and his men."

"What are we going to do?" asked Odo, bending his tall frame over to look at the body. The sight only made the man's eye twitch more than usual.

"It's too late to try to set up another pick up," said Spider, crowding in to see the body and crossing his hairy arms over his chest.

Rowen stood up and looked out to the sea. His eyes narrowed in thought. He was supposed to bring the bounty to Scotland, but they'd been thrown off course and were closer to the shores of Maryport right now than they were the Firth of Lorne. "We're going to do the only thing we can," he told his crew. "Brody, get everyone aboard. We leave immediately."

"For Scotland?" Brody questioned.

"Nay, for England. I'm not going to leave my brother and his men stranded. We're going to Maryport to get them and take them back to Scotland with us."

Brody gave the orders and the men started to scatter about, making preparations to cast off.

"What about the bodies and the bounty from the wreckage?" asked Brody, following Rowen as he walked down the shoreline, examining one dead body after another, searching for survivors. There looked to be a good dozen bodies washed up on the beach as well as wooden boxes and barrels that could hold a substantial amount of wealth. He would like nothing more than to collect it all and claim it for himself, but to do so would take time. And time was not on his side at the moment.

"Leave it," he said, walking toward a dead man that was face down in the sand. "The Islanders can collect the bounty and keep it, instead."

He saw residents of the island running toward them. Magdalena led the way with her youngest child in her arms. He bent down and flipped the dead man over to see his face bloated with chunks missing as if fish had taken bites out of the man's flesh. It wasn't a pretty sight. "It's Fitz," he told Brody, just as Magdalena ran up to join them. She looked down to her dead husband, screamed, and dropped to her knees crying, clutching her child to her chest.

"Magdalena, what's wrong?" came Cordelia's voice from behind him. Rowen just shook his head, knowing this was the last thing he needed at the moment.

"My husband," cried Magdalena, covering her child's face and keeping the little girl from looking. The woman started to wail and so did her child. Her other two children ran up followed by more adults, saw their father, and began to scream and cry as well.

"Come here," said Cordelia, pushing past Rowen, holding two gowns in her hand. She reached out with her free hand and herded the children off to the side, away from the dead body. "I have things for all of you. If you're good, I'll let you look in the trunk."

"What?" Rowen turned to see two of his crewmembers carrying one of the trunks that was part of the king's shipment. They threw it down in the sand, followed by another two men who rolled several barrels down the pier, followed by two more of his crew carrying a crate. Link threw down a small square chest marked with an X at Rowen's feet. The chest burst open and coins spilled out into the sand. The children squealed and ran over excitedly to pick up the coins.

"Nay, get away from that. It's not yours," Rowen said, trying to stop the children but they just kept on coming.

"It's not yours, either. It's mine," retorted Cordelia, handing the gowns to one of the women and rushing over to Magdalena. She bent down and put her hand on the woman's shoulder to comfort her.

"Why are we giving away our bounty?" growled Big Garth, running over to see what was going on.

"Aye, the wench is calling the shots and I'll have none of it," said Muck. Rowen hadn't even known he was standing there. If he didn't make it seem like it was his idea, there was going to be mutiny. It was important right now that Rowen maintain control of his men and ship if he planned on sailing back to England to pick up his brother and the Scots. Without a crew and ship, they would all be doomed.

"That's right. I am leaving these things for Magdalena and the occupants of this island," he told his men, receiving a lot of groans in return. "Magdalena, you and the others will take all of the bounty that washes ashore to live on to help you get back on your feet. You've lost a lot of good men and I won't leave you with nothing."

"Thank you," said the woman through teary eyes. She reached out one trembling hand to touch her dead husband's cold body. Cordelia collected the baby from her and proceeded to help her to her feet.

"We're leaving now, Cordy," Rowen told her. "Give her back the baby and get on board where I told you to stay in the first place."

"We can't just leave these dead bodies on the shore," Cordelia protested.

"They can bury the dead. If we don't move quickly, I'm going to have a lot more to worry about than just a dozen corpses."

"How can you be so cold and cruel at a time like this?" she asked, comforting the crying baby in her arms. "I want to stay until the bodies are buried and we've had a funeral for all of them."

"Give me the baby," said Rowen, reaching out his hands. Cordelia smiled, thinking he wanted to comfort the child. Instead, he took it and handed it over to its mother. "Magdalena, you'll have more than enough to live on with the coins and the bounty. I'm sorry we can't stay to bury your dead, but I have another important matter to attend to."

The woman took her baby from him, wiped a tear from her face and reached up and kissed Rowen on the cheek. "I know you would do whatever you can to help me. You already have. Go. Take care of your own business. I will forever be grateful for everything you've done."

"Let's go," growled Rowen, taking Cordelia by the arm and dragging her along with him. "And next time I leave you in the cabin, I'm locking you in since you can't seem to follow orders."

CHAPTER 13

Rowen ran a finger over Mya's head, talking to the bird as if it were an old friend. "I need you to find Rook and Reed," he told the bird, knowing she understood his brothers' names. Whenever they wanted to send messages to each other, they sent their birds up into the sky. When they saw the birds, they knew their brothers were close. "Go," he said, sending Mya up into the air. She flew toward the mainland.

"Do you think they'll see her, my lord?" asked Brody, directing the ship toward the shores of Maryport.

"They'll see her," he said, staring across the water. "I'm sure they'll understand I'm coming for them. I just hope King Edward doesn't see the bird or he'll be alerted of my return."

"I'm sure the king doesn't even notice the birds, my lord."

"Cordelia did. She also overheard more than she should have and I'm not comfortable with it."

"So are you going to keep her as your captive or set her free when we dock in Maryport?"

"I'm not sure." His heart ached to think of possibly never seeing her again. After they'd made love last night, he realized that all he did was make it harder for both of them. "I said some things to her that I wish I hadn't now." He stayed focused on the water, trying to use the tranquil vision to soothe his restless soul.

"Like what?" asked Brody. "Surely it couldn't have been anything of importance."

"I told her I loved her and wanted to marry her and sire her babies."

"Ouch!" Brody made a face and shook his head. "She's getting to you, isn't she? I haven't seen you enamored with any woman the way you are with her."

"She's not only beautiful, but smart and witty. But she's a noblewoman and, alas, I'm naught but a lowly pirate. You know as well as I that this can never work."

"You're not just a pirate. You've got the blood of nobles running through your veins and that of the king himself!"

"Shhh." Rowen's eyes scanned the deck and his crew. "I don't want anyone to know."

"Why not?" he asked. "Mayhap you can use it to your advantage."

"Not after what my brothers and I have been doing for the last few years. The king would never pardon our actions."

"We'll be approaching land soon," said Brody. "You'd better decide what to do with the girl and fast. Do you think she'll spill your secrets if you let her go back to Whitehaven?"

"I'm not sure. But either way, I'm sure nothing good will come of it. I feel in my bones that my brothers are in trouble. I just wish I could think clearly." He turned and headed down the steps of the sterncastle, smashing into Muck who was making his way up the stairs.

"Muck, what do you want?" he asked. The crew usually stayed on the deck and didn't come up to the sterncastle unless needed.

"Just wanted to tell you the wench is looking for you."

"Do you mean Lady Cordelia?" He looked down to the deck to see Cordelia talking with Link who headed up the rigging to the lookout basket atop the main mast.

"Of course I mean her. Is there another bloody wench on board?" growled Muck.

"Use her title when you speak of her and show some respect. To both of us," he added as an afterthought. Walking away from Muck, he came up behind Cordelia, putting his hands on her shoulders. She turned her head and smiled at him.

"I'd like to go up there," she said.

"Up where?" he asked.

"Up there." She pointed upwards. "To the lookout basket where Link goes every day."

"Nay. That is no place for a lady."

"But I know how to climb. When I was a child, I acted more like a boy than a girl. My father never said anything about it, but it worried my mother. That's why she sent me away to be fostered to learn how to act like a lady."

"Lady or not, my answer is still the same. You'll not go up there and I don't like you out on the deck with the crew when I'm not by your side."

"I'm starting to get to know them and I like most of them. I don't think they're that dangerous."

"Assumptions like that are going to get you into a lot of trouble. Or have you already forgotten one of them almost raped you?" He reached out and brushed a stray hair from her face, tucking it behind her ear. "We'll be approaching Maryport soon and we need to talk."

"Oh, good! I can't wait to be back on the mainland. I have so much to tell Lady Summer."

"You'll tell her nothing! I can't set you free unless I know you will not endanger me, my crew, or my brothers and their men."

"But Lady Summer is your family. She needs to know about you."

"Nay! You'll say nothing about where you've been, what you've heard, or what you've seen, do you understand me?"

Her smile turned into a frown and she crossed her arms over

her chest. "You forgot about what I've done. Or is it permissible to tell everyone I've slept with a pirate?"

Rowen noticed his crew looking over and he needed to silence the girl. There was only one place to take her to enable his privacy. "Come with me," he said, taking her by the arm and leading her to the cabin.

"I just came from the cabin. I want to watch as we approach shore," she complained. "Are you sure I can't go up in the lookout basket with Link?"

"You'll be safer here if something should happen once we reach land." He opened the door and hauled her into the room.

"What do you mean if something happens? Are you expecting trouble?"

"I'm not sure, but I need to make the right move." He looked down to the chessboard as he said it. "Things aren't always as they seem, Cordy. Now I know I should never have bedded you last night. It was a mistake on both our parts."

CORDY'S HEART dropped in her chest when she heard Rowen's words. "Bedded me?" she asked. "We made love. Or do you consider what happened between us naught more than a fast relief like you have with whores?"

She saw him rub the back of his neck in frustration and look to the floor. "We're too different in status. You know as well as I that we can't be together. It won't work."

She didn't cry often but felt the tears welling in her eyes. She'd thought she'd found the man of her dreams. While she had hoped there was a future with Rowen, he didn't seem to feel the same way.

"Why didn't you decide this before I gave myself to you?" she spat in aggravation. "You made me think you loved me just so you could roger me in your cabin, didn't you?"

"Nay. It's not like that, Cordy. You don't understand."

"I opened my heart to you and this is how it's going to end? Fine! Just drop me off on the mainland and forget all about me. I think I'd have a better conversation with King Edward than with you, so we are done talking." She started toward the door, but he gripped her wrist hard and kept her from going.

"You have to promise me you won't say a word about anything you've heard. Not to Lady Summer, not to your guards, and certainly not to the king."

"Why do I have to promise you anything? You're just a pirate, remember?" She taunted him and saw the anger rising in his eyes. If she hadn't been so furious at the moment, she would probably be frightened, instead. Immediately, she regretted saying anything at all.

"That's right, I am a pirate," he ground out. "And pirates don't let girls with loose tongues run to their enemy with all their secrets. You're staying here."

"Staying here?" Her heart raced. He couldn't mean he was keeping her as a prisoner and not letting her go back home, could he? "I'm going back to Whitehaven. Now leave me alone. I'm sorry I ever thought you were anything but a black-hearted rogue in the first place." She shook her hand loose from his hold and ran to the door but didn't get far. He grabbed her from behind and scooped her up off her feet and carried her toward the bed as she struggled in his arms. Somehow, she didn't think he was taking her there to make love. He threw her down on the bed and headed back to the door.

"I'm sorry, Cordy, but you give me no choice. I didn't mean for things to happen this way, but I just can't take the chance." He reached over and opened his chest of drawers by the door and pulled out a key.

"Rowen?" She shook her head. "What are you doing?" He turned around, holding the key in the air. "You're not going to lock me in here, are you?" she asked him, horrified by the thought.

"It's for your own good. Once my brother and his men are safely back in Scotland along with the cargo, I'll send you back to England, but not before."

"Nay!" She jumped off the bed and ran to the door. Before she even got there, he closed it and turned the key in the lock. "Let me out!" She pounded her fists on the door, shouting at the top of her lungs. "You can't do this! I hate you, Rowen, and I wish I'd never met you."

ROWEN LEANED his back against the door and closed his eyes, listening to Cordelia shouting that she hated him. Her venomous words cut through him like a sharp blade. They'd shared intimate moments as well as private stories with each other. He'd thought he could trust her until now. He did love her and that was the problem. Any other pirate would see her as the hindrance that she was and would kill her rather than to keep her or set her free. He could do neither.

Never would he raise a finger to hurt her, because he truly did want her for his wife. But neither could he set her free. She was so angry right now that if he set her free, she would run right to King Edward and tell him everything she knew. Mayhap she'd cool down in a few hours. On the way back to Scotland, they'd try to figure things out between them.

"Land ho!" shouted Link after a while from the lookout basket overhead. Rowen looked up and saw Mya landing and perching on the edge of the basket. He hoped the bird had alerted his brothers that he was here. They were arriving later than Fletcher was scheduled to be there and he hoped all hell hadn't already broken loose because of it.

"Crew, we'll only be docked long enough to collect Reed and his men. So don't get off the ship and go inland. There is no time."

"Not even for a quick drink, Captain?" asked Spider.

"Nay. I'm not sure Edward won't be waiting for us. We can't take the chance."

"I'm going to disembark and have myself a drink," complained Muck, rubbing his hands over the scabs at his neck from Rowen's blade. "Our provisions are running low since the wench gave away so much to the Islanders, so we'll need to replenish our goods as well."

"Her name is Lady Cordelia and it was my call to leave the provisions, not hers," said Rowen. "The trip back to Scotland won't take that long. We'll be fine."

"We're adding another two dozen men to the ship. That's a lot more mouths to feed," complained Big Garth, waving his cleaver in the air.

"I'll not have anyone question my decision. Now, you'll do as I say and if anyone dares to leave the ship, you'll be left behind."

"What about the girl?" asked Muck. "What are you going to do with her?"

"She's locked in the cabin, safe from curs like you. That's where she'll stay until I return."

"She's bad luck," said Muck and several of the crew agreed with him. "We need her off this ship. She's already been the cause of us almost getting caught, two storms at sea, and now she's commanding the ship as well."

Rowen grabbed the old man by the tunic and pulled him closer, face to face. "You say another word about her, old man, and I'll slit your throat this time since there's no one here to talk me out of it. Savvy?"

"Aye," Muck choked out. Rowen pushed him backward and he landed on his butt on the deck. The rest of the crew laughed at him and Muck didn't like it.

"Prepare for docking," Rowen called out. "Furl up the main and man the lines! We've got a job to do, so be quick about it."

CHAPTER 14

Cordelia paced the room for what seemed like hours, tears flowing from her eyes. How could things end this way between her and Rowen? Why had she let herself fall in love with the man? She'd foolishly believed somehow that since he had noble blood, as well, they could plan a future together. She thought she could change him, but now she could see that it wasn't so. He held such animosity toward the king that he was blinded to anything else.

Mayhap, he deserved the life he lived or, mayhap, she was the one who deserved the predicament she'd gotten herself into once she decided to lay with him in the first place. She wasn't sure of anything right now.

Hearing a key in the lock, she turned around. Rowen was coming back to get her after all. "Rowen?" She ran to the door but stopped in her tracks when she realized her mistake. It wasn't Rowen standing in the doorway, but Old Man Muck!

"Leave me alone," she said fearfully, remembering the last time she'd encountered him and Lucky. Rowen had come to her rescue. But now the ship was docked and he wasn't here. Nor would he come to her rescue since he thought she was locked in the cabin.

"I'm not here to hurt you." Muck threw the key down onto the chest next to the door.

"How did you get that key?"

"Your lover didn't give it to me if that's what you're thinking. I stole the extra key years ago."

"My L – lover?" Could he possibly know the truth?

"I know all about you and Rowen since I was listening at the window when he took you to his bed. Now I see why he didn't want me to take you - because he wanted to ravish you himself."

"How dare you!"

He took a step forward and she took one backward, holding up her hands to protect herself from him.

"Don't worry, wench. I'm not here for pleasure this time. I'm here to help you escape."

"You are?" She looked at him from the corner of her eyes. "Why would you do that? You'd be going against your captain's orders."

"I don't take orders from anyone," Muck said, spit flying from his mouth as he spoke. The man was truly disgusting. "I should be captain of this ship and everyone knows it. My brother was once captain and I curse the day he ever brought Rowen aboard the Sea Mirage."

The hatred this man held for Rowen was intense and it scared her. It wasn't unlike the vengeance Rowen held in his heart for the man who sired him. She didn't know what to do.

"Lucky, get in here," ordered Muck. The pirate with the scar across his throat came to join them.

"The captain's off the ship now and the Scots haven't boarded yet," reported Lucky.

"Quit calling him Captain! Give me the bag." Muck ripped a large burlap bag out of his sidekick's hand.

Suddenly, Cordelia had the feeling they meant to put her in it.

Muck reached out and grabbed her by the arm and yanked her toward him. She tried to knee him in the groin again, but he was wise to her tricks this time. He dropped the bag and used his hand to push away her knee.

"Try that again, wench, and I might just decide to slit your throat, instead. You're making me angry."

"What are you going to do with me?" she asked, trying not to sound frightened although her legs were shaking. She remembered Rowen telling her to act strong or they'd feed on her like sharks.

"I told you. We're helping you escape."

"He wants you off the ship," said Lucky, running a hand over his scar. "He thinks you are bad luck."

"She *is* bad luck!" spat Muck. "Now put her in the bag and let's throw her into the water."

"You're not here to help me escape, you're going to drown me!" She struggled against them harder, fighting for her life. "Let me go," she shouted, managing to pull away and run out the door. She made her way over to the hull of the ship and when she heard someone coming, she hid behind a barrel. Not sure who she could trust at this point, she just wanted to stay out of sight.

"Big Garth, did you see the wench?" asked Muck.

"Nay," Big Garth answered. "And I hope I don't. You're right that she's brought us nothing but bad luck. The captain went ashore to get the Scots but Link is up in the lookout basket and just reported that he saw a band of English soldiers sneaking up on them. Someone's got to warn the captain."

"We'll go," said Muck, nodding to Lucky.

"It's dangerous," said the cook.

"We'll be fine," answered Muck. "I'll tell Brody so he can be ready to cast off if he has to, in order to keep the rest of the crew from being captured."

"Are we really going to warn the captain?" asked Lucky as soon as the cook had walked away.

"Nay," answered Muck, spitting on the deck. "I just didn't want anyone else to warn him. As soon as the attack starts, we will leave here and the Sea Mirage will be mine."

"That's mutiny!"

"Aye, so it is, Matey." Muck laughed so hard he ended up coughing and gagging. When he bent over, Cordelia used it to her advantage and ran toward the boarding plank of the ship.

"Hey, she heard us," said Lucky.

"Get the bitch," ordered Muck, and they both took off running after Cordelia.

* * *

ROWEN WAITED AT THE DOCKS, watching Mya make a lazy circle in the sky. His brothers were nowhere to be seen and he'd started wondering if they'd gotten his message. Then Reed's red kite flew up from a tree and the caw of Rook's raven sounded from a nearby roof.

"Good," he said, making his way down the wharf, seeing Reed emerging with the Scots from their hiding place. Rook looked on from a distance, surrounded by his men in case they should need his help.

"Rowen, what the hell happened?" asked Reed, coming to shake hands and backslap his brother. "We were here early this mornin' like ye told us, but Fletcher ne'er showed."

"Fletcher and his crew are dead. Taken by the storm," said Rowen, his eyes scanning the busy docks and his surroundings. Something didn't feel right and the fact all his knights had been captured in his game of chess made him even more restless.

"Guid to see ye, brathair." Reed's long, red hair lifted in the breeze. He and his men had their plaids hidden under plain brown robes that looked like those of monks, trying not to be noticed.

"You're all wearing monks' robes?" asked Rowen, shaking his

head. "You should have just worn your plaids in plain sight because this is a horrible disguise."

"It's all Rook could come up with on such short notice. So tell me, how did ye get all the way to Scotland with the goods and back again so quickly?"

"I didn't. I've had a few distractions. The cargo is still on the ship."

"Edward's soldiers have been searchin' for us for the last two days. If Rook hadna hidden us underground in the crypts of the monastery, we might no' be here right now. Edward is determined to find us. I think that the last shipment was a trap."

"I know it was a trap. If I ever find out who talked, I'll kill them myself. We're not safe here. Now get your men on the ship, anon," Rowen ordered.

"Aye," said Reed, directing his men down the pier and to the ship. Rowen shook his head again. If over two dozen monks boarding a ship all at once wasn't suspicious, he didn't know what was. He'd have to have a talk with Rook about finding better disguises next time.

Rowen heard the sound of running footsteps on the wooden planks behind him and turned to see Cordelia escaping from the ship with Muck and Lucky close behind her in pursuit.

"Rowen!" she called out. Looking over her shoulder as she ran, she ended up crashing into Reed's chest.

"Och, lassie, be careful," said Reed, his hands going around the girl's shoulders to steady her. "Ye need to watch where ye're goin'."

"You're in danger," she said, before she realized he wasn't Rowen. "Wait! You're not Rowen."

"Nay, I'm no' lassie."

"Cordelia, what are you doing?" snapped Rowen, tired of the girl always disobeying his orders.

"They're coming for you. They know you're here."

Muck stopped and grabbed Cordelia by the arm. "We got her,

Captain," he said. "She escaped your cabin and we ran after her like we knew you'd want us to do."

"Everyone, just calm down. You're going to draw attention to us," said Rowen, noticing the horrified look on Cordelia's face.

"I wasn't escaping from you," she cried. "They wanted to kill me and they're planning mutiny as well."

"This one is a troublemaker with her lies," said Muck.

"Don't believe a word of it, Captain," Lucky added.

"Get your hands off of her, Muck, or haven't you learned your lesson? Now get back on the ship, anon. All of you," ordered Rowen, not wanting this kind of distraction. Just the fact that a woman was on the pier was going to raise suspicion with the dockworkers and merchants. Muck let go of Cordelia's arm.

"I'm trying to tell you that you're in danger," she said again.

"You are the one going to be in danger if you don't heed my orders right now," spat Rowen. His eyes scanned the docks to see people looking in their direction. The girl was already attracting attention. "Cordy, get yourself back on that ship and in my cabin immediately. I don't want to have to tell you again." He wasn't sure how she'd managed to get out of his cabin when he'd locked the door but he had no time to ask her about it now.

"Why I tried to help you after the way you've treated me is beyond me," she said. "I never want to see you again as long as I live, Rowen the Restless." She shot away so fast that she slipped right past all of them. Instead of heading back down the pier to the ship, she headed inland.

"Damn," cursed Rowen.

"Shall we go after her?" asked Lucky.

"Nay, get back to the ship. I'll get her myself."

Muck and Lucky left. All the Scots loaded quickly, leaving just Reed and Rowen on the pier. Rowen turned to go after Cordelia and noticed English soldiers emerging in the distance. Shouts went up as they saw Rowen and the ship. Their weapons lifted into the air as they rode forward atop horses.

"Nay!" shouted Rowen, realizing now that Cordelia had been trying to warn him and that he should have listened to her.

"We need to cast off now, brathair," said Reed, starting down the pier. When he noticed that Rowen was still standing there, he hurried back to get him. Rook and his men appeared from their hiding spots and held the soldiers at bay, giving them time to escape.

"They'll be slaughtered. We've got to help them," said Rowen.

"Nay, brathair. If we do, the English will take the ship. Rook will distract them long enough for us to get away and then retreat. We need to go!" Reed grabbed Rowen's tunic and dragged him along with him, while Rowen looked back over his shoulder at Cordelia. She'd stopped and was standing there staring at them. Their eyes met and he could see the turmoil on her face. If he wasn't mistaken, she was crying.

"I'm not going," he said, pulling out of his brother's hold and unsheathing his blade from his side. "I'm going after her."

"Ye fool!" shouted Reed. "Just let her go. She'll bring us nothin' but trouble."

The next time Rowen looked up to Cordelia, she was heading toward the soldiers, waving her hands in the air to flag them down. It was too late. She'd gone to King Edward's men for help and it was evident she wanted nothing more to do with him. She was a lady and he was a pirate. He needed to remind himself of that, once more.

"The ship is castin' off. We've got to go. Now!" shouted Reed. Mya flew overhead, followed by Reed's red kite. The birds headed toward the ship together, calling out their warning cries as if to tell them to hurry.

Rowen watched as a soldier on a horse pulled Cordelia up behind him. Her arms wrapped around his waist and as they turned and headed away, she looked back over her shoulder with no expression at all on her face. Her fae-like red locks trailed out behind her as they rode. His heart ached as he watched her ride out of his life. It was over between them and he would never see her again. It pained him like a knife to the heart. But it was her choice and she hadn't chosen him. There was nothing more he could do about this. He only hoped she'd keep her tongue from wagging and spilling all his secrets.

"Let's get the hell out of here," said Rowen, turning and running for the ship with Reed at his side.

CHAPTER 15

Looking over her shoulder one last time, Cordelia saw Rowen and his brother, Reed, jump aboard the Sea Mirage and cast off while their triplet, Rook, risked his life and that of his men to hold the soldiers at bay. Once the ship was out of reach, she saw Rook signal his men to retreat and they disappeared without a trace.

Right as she turned around, a raven swooped past them shrieking and almost hit her. The guard pulled back on the reins and the horse reared up causing Cordelia to fall to the ground.

"My lady. I'm sorry," said the guard, jumping off the horse and coming to help her. The raven swooped past her, once more, as if it knew she had defied Rowen and was about to betray him, too. It cawed a guttural sound that sent a chill through her body and made her think of the dead. She didn't want Rowen or his brothers to die. It had looked as if Rowen was contemplating coming after her, but yet he hadn't. Her head clouded with confusion. She got up and brushed off her clothes – Rowen's clothes - already missing him desperately.

"I'm unharmed," she told the soldier.

"I'll take you straight to the king and you can tell him all about your capture by the pirate," said the guard, helping her mount the horse. "I'm sorry you were naught but a pawn in this game between the legendary Demon Thief and the king. That man is a horrible creature."

Cordelia realized the man thought one person was tormenting the king and no one knew it was look-alike triplets. However, she knew and could tell them so, and had half a mind to do just that. When the man called her a pawn, she flashed back to Rowen playing his game of chess by himself. He'd been so sure he was doomed since all the knights that depicted him on his chessboard had been captured during his game. It was true, he would be doomed if Cordelia told the king all she knew. But what if she didn't tell him? Would that be considered treason to the crown?

Her stomach churned and her head swarmed with unsettled emotions that confused and clouded her mind. How could she love and hate a man at the same time? She needed to think about all this and wasn't ready yet to go to the king.

"Take me back to Whitehaven," she commanded the soldier.

"Whitehaven?" he asked in confusion. "My lady, the king is in London. You should go to talk to him about all that has transpired."

"I am Lady of Whitehaven, and I've left my castle unattended for far too long. My presence there is required and that's where I need to go."

"Aye, my lady, but the king won't be happy with your decision."

"If the king wants to talk to me, then he can pay me a visit," she said boldly, knowing she should never be speaking this way. Perhaps Rowen's hatred of the king had started to rub off on her as well.

"He can order you to appear before him," the soldier reminded her.

"Then I'll wait for that to happen. Right now, back in Whitehaven is where I want to be."

* * *

ROWEN STORMED INTO HIS CABIN, restless and frustrated by what just happened. How the hell had Cordelia managed to get out of a locked room? She'd upset everything and, in the process, he lost her. Nothing was working out the way it should lately. For all he knew, Rook could be dead right now. He should never have left Maryport in that situation and already regretted doing so.

His eyes fell upon his chessboard and he thought of Cordelia telling him twice he'd made a wrong move. She'd been right, although he hated to admit it. The room felt so empty without her. Her scent of rosewater and lavender still filled the air. He'd had everything he'd ever wanted in the palm of his hand, but now, in one quick moment, he'd lost it all.

"Damn!" he spat. With one swipe of his hand, he sent the pieces of the chessboard clattering to the floor.

"Captain, is everything all right?" Link stood in the doorway watching him.

"Nay, it's not," he said, running his hands over his face and letting out a growl.

"I'm glad I saw the soldiers from the lookout basket or we might all be dead right now."

"What did you say?" He slowly removed his hands from over his face.

"I spied them and told the others. That's why Muck and Lucky came to warn you before it was too late."

"Are you telling me that they knew we were in danger?"

"Of course. We all did. That's why the two of them ventured off the ship after you and told everyone to stay put. They came to warn you."

His eyes fell on something atop the chest by the door. It was his key to the cabin. He walked over and picked it up to inspect it. Then he put it down and reached into his pocket and pulled out an identical key.

"Oh, that's how Lady Cordelia escaped," said Link. "You had two keys to the door and she must have found one."

"Aye. I had two keys," he said, picking up the other one and comparing them. "But a few years ago, I lost one of them. Or should I say it up and disappeared. Everyone claimed to know nothing about it, but I can see now that someone lied to me. Who opened this door, Link?"

"I can't say for sure since I was up in the lookout basket," said Link, shrugging his shoulders. "But I did see Muck, Lucky, and Cordelia come out of the cabin earlier."

Rowen's mind flashed back to Cordelia running down the pier. Fear had shown on her face, but he knew now it wasn't fear of him. Muck and Lucky had been chasing her, plus she kept saying that Rowen was in danger. He hadn't listened to her, but mayhap he should have. His eyes dropped down to the chess pieces rolling in half circles on the floor as the ship leaned one way and then the other. Aye, she'd been right about his moves and he should never have doubted her. He'd been wrong again and should have protected her, but he hadn't.

"Cordelia was trying to warn me and they were trying to stop her," said Rowen, throwing both the keys down on the chest together.

"Who are you talking about?" asked Link.

"Where are Muck and his scar-throat sidekick now?"

"They're with the others under the main mast."

Rowen stormed from the room with Link following at his heels. "Muck! Lucky!" he called out, stomping across the deck. He felt the veins bulging in his neck and anger rising in his blood.

The Scots and Rowen's crew parted and gave Rowen room as he walked up and grabbed Muck by the neck and started to choke him. Muck's hands went around his throat and he sputtered.

"I should have killed you on the island when you tried to rape my girl," shouted Rowen, no longer able to control his temper. He truly wanted to kill the bastard now, even if he considered the man his family.

Shouts came from the crew as the fight broke out. Muck sputtered, not able to breathe. Lucky drew his dagger and ran toward Rowen.

"Behind you, Captain!" shouted Link. Rowen released Muck with one hand and turned and grabbed Lucky's wrist with the other. Using his foot, he kicked Lucky in the gut and twisted his wrist until the man dropped his dagger to the plank floor. The men shouted and gathered around to cheer him on. Muck managed to grab his dagger and lashed out at Rowen, but he moved his hand quickly, only getting nicked in the process.

Lucky ran at Rowen, but Rowen turned and punched him in the face, sending him sprawling across the deck. Then Muck came at him with a sword and Rowen met him with his blade, and they dueled. Blood dripped down Rowen's arm and fueled his fire even stronger. Spying a whip on a nail nearby, he commanded his crew to help him.

"Hold them for me," he called out. Spider, Odo, Ash, and Big Garth hurried to do as ordered. The two traitors struggled, but his crewmembers were able to hold them with their arms spread to the sides and facing away from Rowen. Rowen raised his whip and lashed it forward, stinging one of them and then the other until their clothes were shredded and blood ran down their backs. His anger grew stronger and stronger. He whipped them for trying to rape Cordelia as well as for disobeying his orders and trying to start a mutiny aboard his ship. They finally stopped moving and fighting, and fell to their knees, but he wasn't finished. Once more he lifted his whip, but his brother reached out and grabbed him by the wrist to stop him.

"That's enough," said Reed. "I think ye've made yer point to everyone on this ship."

"Stay out of this, Reed," Rowen warned his red-haired brother. "This is a personal matter. I should have killed these bastards long ago."

"I see the one already has a scar across his throat," said Reed, releasing his wrist.

"Who the hell do you think gave it to him?" asked Rowen. "Rumor has it, he surprised me in the dark and I almost took off his head. The truth was I caught him stealing from me. That's why he's got the scar."

"I should have raped the wench and thrown her overboard. We would never have had any problems," said Muck, barely able to speak. "She was bad luck and everyone knows it."

Rowen could hold back no longer. He wouldn't have anyone speaking ill of Cordelia, even if he'd already lost her forever. "You'll die for that comment," spat Rowen, throwing down the whip and unsheathing his sword.

"Are ye sure ye want to do that, brathair?" asked Reed. "They're unarmed and near death."

"You heard what he said about Cordelia," said Rowen, his anger out of control. "Besides, the two of them were trying to take my position and my ship. They both deserve to die. It's nothing different than One-Eyed Ron would have done."

"Ye sound like a true pirate, laddie," said Reed under his breath. "That's no' how mathair and faither raised us."

"I'll kill them, I swear I will," said Rowen.

"Then do it already," growled Muck from the ground. Lucky sat silently with his head down and his body shaking like a leaf. "You already stole everything that was supposed to be mine, so why not take my life as well?"

Rowen hesitated. Muck was right. When One-Eyed Ron died, Muck, who was the man's brother, by right should have inherited his ship and his position of captain. But the crew liked Rowen better and he'd been granted things that Muck only wished he had. Suddenly, Rowen realized he was not that different than the old man.

Rowen and his brothers were of the king's blood and, by right, they should have titles, wealth, and noblewomen to marry. Being the first born, it bothered him that he'd been denied the things that first born sons inherited from their noble fathers. He wanted those things more than ever now. If he'd had them – he might not have lost Cordelia. He couldn't blame her for leaving and not wanting a poor and restless bastard. Especially since he'd told her he'd made a mistake by bedding her when he didn't feel that way at all.

"Arrrgh," he growled, grudgingly returning his sword to his scabbard. "Tie them up and throw them both in the brig," he ordered.

"I'll do it," said Reed. "I wouldna want ye to take a chance of havin' more of yer crew turn mutinous."

"Does anyone else feel as if Muck should be your captain?" shouted Rowen. Everyone stayed quiet. "If you do, speak now! If not, I'll hear no more about it and the next one to speak of it won't be so lucky as these two today." He stormed off, going to his cabin where he could be alone and think of how to change things because he didn't know how he was going to go on without Cordelia in his life.

CHAPTER 16

Cordelia sank into the hot water, savoring her bath. Every one of her muscles ached from being on the ship and her body still hadn't fully recovered from the rigorous love-making with Rowen. She'd dreamed about a bath for the last three days and found herself thinking most of the men on the ship could do with one as well.

When she'd returned to Whitehaven, she'd been greeted enthusiastically by her people and it felt good to know she'd been missed. Everyone was excited to hear about her capture by the Demon Thief and were eager to know how she'd escaped. Not wanting to say anything until she thought about things further, she told them she would need some time alone before she was ready to talk.

"Oh, Lady Cordelia, I was so frightened for you." Lady Summer sprinkled more rose petals into the hot water as she aided Cordelia with her bath. All the other servants had been dismissed. "When I saw that man from the tavern take you with him on the cart, I told your guards, but it was too late. They said they couldn't fight off all the Demon Thief's men to save you and needed to protect me while they still could."

"Remind me to have those two flogged or hanged for that," she said with her eyes still closed. The scent of roses filled the room, intermingling with the odor of the harsh tallow and wood ash soft soap that was scented with musk and cloves.

She found herself wondering if Rowen had ever had the opportunity to experience a hot bath in a wooden tub and then her mind drifted to fantasies of sharing one with him. He was gone now and she'd most likely never see him again. As she'd watched him hesitate on the dock, for one fleeting moment, she had thought he'd come after her. But he hadn't, and she found herself heartbroken when he'd turned and boarded his ship, instead. She'd been angry at the time and now regretted her words, knowing it was her fault she'd never see him again. He'd planned on taking her with him to Scotland and she should never have left his cabin.

"You don't mean that, do you?" asked Summer.

Cordelia opened her eyes to see the girl staring at her.

"Mean what?" she asked, her mind so filled with thoughts of Rowen that she'd already forgotten what she'd said to the girl.

"You said you were going to flog or hang the guards. You are starting to sound like that bastard pirate who abducted you."

She heard the word bastard and sat up straight in the tub. The droplets of water clinging to her hair ran down her neck and shoulders, making a trail back to the water from which it came. It wasn't unlike the way Rowen made his way back to the sea. "Lady Summer, what do you know about the bastard brothers?"

"Brothers?" asked Summer, collecting a large drying cloth and holding it out for her. "I'm not sure what you mean. I'm sorry I said bastard, but I suppose it's because I've heard my mother say the word more than once when she didn't know I was listening."

"She did?" Cordelia stood and the water sloshed slightly over the rim of the cloth-lined tub. The tubs were often lined with cloth to ensure the nobles wouldn't incur slivers from the wood rubbing against their bare body. "Are you sure it wasn't your father who said something like that?"

"Nay," she said, helping Cordelia from the tub and wrapping the cloth around her wet body. "I don't remember much of my father. I was very young when we traveled to England with my mother and handmaid and left my father behind. I'm not even sure he's still alive."

Cordelia remembered Rowen talking about that night and how terrible it had been. "The night of the Burnt Candlemas," she said in thought, tying the cloth around her.

"That's right," said Summer. "It was very frightening."

"What do you remember about that night?" asked Cordelia, collecting her clothes and heading over to the bed to lay them out.

"Lady Cordelia, those are the filthy pirate clothes," said Summer, laughing when she saw what Cordelia had done. "You will want to wear one of your gowns now that you've returned." Summer's smile was broad and bright. With her blond hair, Cordelia could see a lot of Rowen in her. They were surely from the same blood. The only difference was that the girl's eyes were green instead of the bright, blue bird-like eyes of the triplets.

"Yes, I suppose they are the clothes of a pirate," she said looking down to Rowen's billowy white tunic and brown breeches that she'd had to tie around her tightly in order not to lose them. Her heart ached for him. She reached out and ran her fingers over the tunic, pretending she was running her hand down his strong, sturdy chest.

"You need to dress in the proper attire of a lady. Here, wear this." Summer placed one of Cordelia's gowns atop the bed and quickly scooped up the dirty clothes, holding them far from her body and with just her fingertips. "I'll make certain to have these burned right away. Who knows what type of vermin are living in them from that rugged, filthy pirate." She headed for the door.

"Nay!" Cordelia held out her hand to stop Summer from

leaving the room. "I want to keep those clothes. Just have them washed and returned to me at once."

"Keep them?" Summer looked at her as if she were addled.

"Rowen is not what you think at all."

"Rowen?" she asked, putting the clothes down on a chair and heading back across the room. "You are speaking of the Demon Thief, yet you are calling him by his Christian name? And you're telling me he's not a dirty pirate?"

Summer was asking too many questions and Cordelia wasn't sure she wanted to answer them. "He's not dirty," she said, knowing she couldn't deny the fact he was a pirate. "And everyone deserves to be called by their Christian name."

"You fancy the man, don't you?" Summer giggled and held on to the bedpost, leaning out and throwing her head back. "You, Lady of Whitehaven, were abducted by a pirate and now you're enamored with him."

"Stop it! I am not enamored with him and I did not couple with the man."

"Couple?" Summer stopped twirling around and her eyes opened wide. "I said naught of that, my lady. I said abducted only. Why would you say that unless he . . . he raped you, didn't he?" Her eyes opened even wider in fear. She gasped and slapped her hand over her mouth. Then she slowly removed it. "Oh, I'm so sorry, my lady. I had no idea." She put her arms around Cordelia to comfort her but Cordelia pushed the girl away.

"Hush! He did no such thing and I won't have you starting such gossip."

"I'm sorry, my lady." Summer put her head down and picked up Cordelia's shift. "Shall I help you get dressed now?"

The disappointment in Summer's eyes only reminded Cordelia of the way Rowen looked when she'd turned him away. Summer was a young girl and also Cordelia's best friend. Cordelia needed to talk to someone about how she was feeling and mayhap she should give her a chance.

"Nay," said Cordelia, gently touching the girl on the arm. "Please, sit down on the bed and talk with me."

"Of course." Summer moved the clothes to the side and sat alongside her. "What would you like to talk about? The weather? Or what we'll be dining on for supper?"

"Neither. I want to talk about –" Cordelia cleared her throat, released a breath she hadn't been aware she was holding and tried again. "I want to talk about me . . . and Rowen."

"You do?" Summer's eyes lit up and that mischievous smile was back on her face that reminded Cordelia too much of the man she'd left on the docks. "Do tell."

Cordelia leaned in toward her and spoke in a soft voice. "I will tell you something, but you need to promise me that you will never repeat a word of what I say to anyone. Do you understand?"

"I do, I do," said the girl excitedly, bouncing up and down slightly on the bed, making the bed ropes that held the down-filled pallet creak with her action.

"Well, first of all, Rowen is a very handsome man." Cordelia wrung her hands on her lap, looking at them rather than at Summer because she was afraid a blush might stain her cheeks with what she was about to reveal next.

"He *is* very handsome. I noticed that in the tavern," Summer agreed. "Something about him seemed so familiar. Mayhap it was because he was friendly and not gruff."

She wanted to reveal to the girl that Rowen was her long lost brother, but not now. It was too soon and there would be time for that later.

"Yes, he's very nice. And gentle."

"You laid with him, didn't you?" Summer asked excitedly.

"Aye." Cordelia's lips turned up into a smile and she nodded. "I did, but it was my choice to do so. He never forced himself on me in any way."

"A pirate that has manners and morals?" asked Summer in surprise. "He sounds more like a knight than a bandit."

"Yes. Yes, he does," she agreed, her heart soaring just thinking about him.

"So what was it like to couple with the Demon?"

"Oh, you mustn't call him that, please. And it was wonderful. I would do it again if I could."

"You would?" Summer giggled. "Oh, Lady Cordelia, you are not acting like a lady at all."

"Nay, I suppose I'm not." Neither did she care. The past few days had been terrifying, exciting, and mesmerizing all at once and she had never felt so alive as she did when she was with Rowen.

"Tell me how he disappears and appears in different places without being caught," the girl begged. "I heard a rumor that he takes innocent maidens down to his sea cave and another rumor that he eats their flesh raw. He can change his hair color from blond to black to red and has many disguises. Did you know he can even talk and act like a Scot if he wants to?"

"Now you're just being silly," said Cordelia, giggling, too. "Rowen is no sea monster, nor does he eat young maidens. His hair is blond. The red-headed Scot and the dark-haired man are his brothers."

"His brothers?" Summer stopped giggling and batted her eyes. "I've also heard his face and eyes are always the same."

"Yes. That's true." She looked back down to her hands, cursing herself for saying too much already.

"If they are three brothers with the same face and eyes, do you think they are triplets like the brothers I once had?"

Cordelia shot up off the bed, not knowing how to answer that question. If Summer discovered the truth, she might go to her mother and sisters and tell them. The story could get back to the king and the truth might come out that the babies were never killed as the king ordered. She didn't want Summer and her family to get into trouble, nor did she want any harm to come to Rowen and his brothers.

"It's time for supper, now help me dress. No more talk of legendary pirates and monsters."

Summer bounded off the bed. "Lady Cordelia, tell me more about triplets. Triplets like my brothers. I was so young that I don't remember my brothers, but in my heart, I miss them every day."

"There are no triplets, no monsters, and no secrets to reveal."

"Is it a secret?" asked Summer. "Do they not want anyone to know they are triplets?"

"Stop it!" she ordered, not knowing how to keep the girl from figuring out more. Cordelia had already divulged too much information and now regretted telling her anything at all. "You will not say another word about any of this to anyone and neither will you ask me any more questions. Do you understand?" She heard herself reprimanding the girl and thought she was starting to sound like Rowen. She'd never spoken so harshly to Summer before and the girl looked frightened and confused. But Cordelia couldn't comfort her or she might slip up again and tell her something she shouldn't.

"I understand, my lady," said Summer in a soft voice, picking up Cordelia's shift. She kept her eyes downward and did not meet Cordelia's gaze.

What had she just done? How could she remedy this situation? Turmoil filled Cordelia's heart and a knot formed in her throat. This wasn't the first of all the questions that she'd been bombarded with since her return. And they would only get worse. Everyone would want to know what happened on the legendary Demon Thief's ship. People would bother her day and night. Alewives would soon be gossiping about the lady who spent three days in the hands of a rogue. Worst of all, if the king ordered her to come to London and reveal to him everything that happened with the man's nemesis, she would have to go. If so, what would she say?

How could she tell Summer that Rowen was one of the triplets that she remembered as her brother? And how in the world would she tell the king the triplets that he'd sired and ordered to be killed were the ones who had been stealing from him for the last three years? She couldn't. Not when they were now legends, making their own father - the king of England, look like a fool!

CHAPTER 17

"Rowen, I'm talkin' to ye," said Reed, waving his hand in front of Rowen's face to get his attention. "Did ye want some more ale?" He held out a tankard, but Rowen just shook his head.

They'd been back from England for over a fortnight now, and Rowen couldn't stop feeling like he'd made a mistake by leaving Cordelia behind.

"Och, stop it," said Reed, sitting down next to him at the outdoor fire. Reed, his father, and their Uncle Malcolm and his wife and children had been living at the MacKeefe camp since the night of Burnt Candlemas. Most of the Douglas Clan had gone back to live in the Lowlands years ago, but they'd decided to stay here with the MacKeefes. Ever since Ross became physically challenged and his wife and children left him and went to England, the man had not been himself. Once a confident and strong warrior, now Ross hid away in the longhouse and barely even showed his face.

"Stop what?" asked Rowen, leaning forward on the wooden bench and getting lost staring at the flames. It was nighttime, and most of the Scots had retired for the evening. They went to sleep in either the longhouses or the cottages that dotted the camp, made from wood, stone, wattle and daub. They had two longhouses that could hold many families. One of the big buildings was used as a hospice.

Sheep and cattle covered the hillside and most of the animals would be slaughtered come winter to feed the clan. The MacKeefes shared the bounty brought to them with neighboring clans that were more in need. The MacKeefes had a camp in the Highlands and also had secured Hermitage Castle on the border.

"Ye ken what I mean. Ye're still pinin' o'er the girl, are ye no'?"

"I am not." Rowen stood up and walked away. Reed threw his tankard to the ground and rushed after him. "Don't follow me," warned Rowen, wanting to be left alone. Every day since their return, he'd thought about Cordelia. And every day, Reed reminded him that the English were no good.

"She's a Sassenach," spat Reed. "Ye dinna want someone like her."

Rowen stopped in his tracks and Reed almost crashed into him. Slowly turning around, Rowen faced his brother. "Our parents are both English," he said in a low voice so as not to be overheard. Or do I need to remind you?"

"Nay! We're Scottish," Reed disagreed.

"You probably really believe that." Rowen headed down to the water, wanting to sit on the banks of Loch Linnhe. The loch was one of the only sea lochs and connected to the Firth of Lorne that opened to the sea. Rowen had been able to sail his ship almost up to the shores of the MacKeefe camp. "You need to stop talking like a damned Scot. Why did you even start that to begin with?"

"We lived in Scotland all our lives," Reed pointed out. "So, I dinna ken why ye and Rook talk like ye're English."

Rowen stopped again and turned around. "You always did admire Ross, but you don't have to imitate everything he's ever said or done."

"Ross is the only family besides ye two that I have. Of course, I admire him."

"You were lucky, that's all," said Rowen. "The night of Burnt Candlemas, you ran back to him and didn't have to endure what Rook and I went through."

"I'm sorry ye were taken by pirates and that Rook lives with the dead, but ye both coulda come home if ye wanted."

"Home?" Rowen lifted a brow. "I was aboard a pirate ship being raised by bloody cutthroats. They were the only family I knew for a good part of my life. That was home to me. And Rook lived with the monks when they saved him from our father's wrath. He's lived like a mole in the dark catacombs for the last ten years and that is all he knows. So don't talk about family and home to either of us because we didn't have it as good as you, Reed."

"Faither would have taken ye back. Both of ye. Just like he did with me."

"Ross is not our father and yet he pretended to be for the first twelve years of our life," said Rowen, softening his voice when he thought he heard a noise in the brush. "I don't like that."

"He only did it because Mathair made him promise. It was her sister's last wish on her deathbed that we never ken who our real parents were. Ye canna blame him."

"Annalyse is not our mother, she's our aunt," said Rowen. "Besides, she was no better for keeping the secret from us."

"Wasna she?" asked Reed softly. "We were happy when we thought Ross and Annalyse were our parents and Summer, Autumn, and Winter were our sisters. It's only when we found out the truth that we all became miserable. I can see why Gabrielle didna want us to ken."

"Mother, not Gabrielle," said Rowen. "You have your mind muddled and still can't accept it, can you?"

"Faither has been miserable ever since Mathair and the girls left him. For a decade now, he just sits and mourns them as if they're dead. I think we should go to England and look for Annalyse and our sisters," said Reed. "It's time someone brings them back together so they can be happy the way they were when we were just lads."

"Nay! Neither of them deserves it."

"Dinna ye miss Mathair?" asked Reed. "I ken I do. And I often wonder how our sisters look today."

"They're beautiful," said Rowen, staring out over the water, thinking about seeing Summer in the tavern.

"Ye've seen Summer and I want to, also," said Reed. "Do ye ken where to find her?"

Reed knew exactly where to find her – at Whitehaven with Lady Cordelia. He longed to see her again, as well as Cordelia, but to do so would only open more wounds for something he could never have.

"Nay, I don't know." Rowen stared out at his ship on the water, bathed in moonlight. The Sea Mirage had been his home for the last ten years. He lived on the water and that was all he knew.

"Brathair, I think mayhap I was wrong."

"What do you mean?"

"About Lady Cordelia. I didna want ye to go to her because I didna want the three of us to go our separate ways again after finally findin' each other after so long. I like workin' with ye and Rook again and dinna ever want to lose that. I'm sorry I was so selfish."

"You weren't," he said, feeling sadness encompass him. They'd only found each other again three years ago. Instead of bonding and doing things together that brothers usually did in their lifetime, they only talked about vengeance and how to steal from the king. That was no relationship, even if they were brothers. Cordelia was right, once again, saying their vengeance was blinding them to what was really important in life. He didn't want to lose his brothers, nor did he want to lose his life. But he was miserable without Cordelia and didn't want to lose her, either. "Nay, I was the selfish one," he said. "It wasn't you, Reed."

Rowen walked down the shore, leaving Reed behind. He needed time to think things over.

"A lassie can make every decision harder," came a voice in the night. The laird of the clan, Storm MacKeefe, walked out of the brush.

"How long have you been there?" asked Rowen.

"Long enough to ken that ye have some important decisions to make."

"I didn't mean for anyone to overhear our conversation."

Storm chuckled and nodded his head. The long, blond braid at the side of his hair swung as he hunkered down on the shore and looked out over the water. "I willna tell anyone yer secrets, Rowen." He picked up a rock and turned it over in his hand as he spoke. "I ken all about secrets, as I've had many of my own."

Rowen hunkered down at the water's edge next to him. Storm was a fair and honorable man in his mid-forties who had married an Englishwoman years ago. They now had a family of four children and had no qualms about having English stay with them. That was one of the reasons Ross had fled to the MacKeefe camp with Reed to begin with. Storm welcomed them with open arms.

"I don't know what to do," said Rowen, picking up a rock and throwing it into the water. It landed with a splash, making ripples in the placid water.

"I'll tell ye one thing, laddie. I was miserable when my wife, Wren, left me before we were married. I cursed myself for not goin' after her. If ye care for this lassie – then dinna let her go. If ye do, ye will always regret it."

"Thanks," said Rowen, getting to his feet. "I need to think about it."

* * *

CORDELIA HUNG her head over the merlon of the battlements and retched. She'd come up here in the first place to clear her head in the fresh air, thinking it would also help her upset stomach to feel better, but it had done neither. She thought her sea sickness would have left by now, but in some ways she still felt as if she were aboard the ship. From up so high she could see the water clearly and found herself visiting the battlements every day, waiting and watching for black sails on the horizon as Rowen sailed his ship back to get her. But he didn't and that made her sad and lonely.

"My lady, you shouldn't be up here." Sir Kenton, her steward, walked up with a cloak in his hands and wrapped it around her shoulders.

"Why not?" She forced a smile although it was the last thing she felt like doing right now. "I like the fresh air. It makes me feel better."

"Excuse me for saying, but if you like it so much, then why do you vomit every time you walk the battlements?"

She didn't know and neither did she need to explain anything to him. "I prove my point! I come up here to retch and now I feel better."

Sir Kenton cocked his head and shot her a wry grin.

The sound of the straight trumpet echoed through the courtyard, announcing the arrival of a noble. "I'm not expecting visitors," she said, her heart racing, hoping it wasn't the king. She'd gotten a missive saying he wanted her to come to London to speak with him about the pirate attack and she'd scheduled two trips now. Thankfully, each time she prepared to go, she'd gotten sick and stayed at Whitehaven and managed to dodge the king's questions about Rowen.

"It looks like Lady Summer's mother and sisters," said Kenton stretching his neck to see down into the courtyard. A small entourage of guards escorted a woman on a horse and two girls in a cart. There were trunks and barrels in the cart as well.

"Oh, good," she said, taking off at a near run, eager to see the woman who raised Rowen. She wanted to know more about him and, mayhap, Annalyse Douglas was the one who could tell her about Rowen.

She hurried down the stone stairs of the battlements, running to greet the woman and her daughters. They'd only met a few times since Lady Summer came to work for her and Annalyse hadn't stayed long on any of her visits. This time, Cordelia hoped to convince her not to be in such a hurry to leave. Cordelia's mother was deceased and she didn't have any living siblings. Her father was in Ireland, remarried to a woman she didn't like. Cordelia barely ever saw her father. This only added to her loneliness and she longed, more than ever, to someday have a family of her own.

"Mother," Summer called out, running across the cobblestones. Lady Annalyse was helped from her steed by one of her guards. Her daughters, Winter and Autumn, climbed out of the wagon and ran to greet their sister. Summer was the eldest of the siblings at fourteen years of age and her sisters were eleven and twelve.

The sisters embraced and laughed giddily, happily jumping around in the sunshine. Cordelia almost felt jealous. She wondered if Rowen and his brothers had played with their sisters while growing up and if the girls even remembered them at all.

"Lady Annalyse, we are happy for your unannounced visit," said Cordelia, walking over to greet the woman.

"Do you mean you didn't know we were traveling here?" Annalyse's blue eyes looked confused.

"Nay, I had no idea," said Cordelia. "What brings you to Whitehaven?"

"My daughter said it was of utmost importance and that you needed me. So I came right away."

"She did, did she?" She glared over at Summer who just shrugged her shoulders and threw her an apologetic grin. "Did she say why I needed you?" Cordelia wondered how much Summer had told her mother.

"Nay, not really," said Annalyse, removing her riding gloves. "However, she did mention it had something to do with a man."

"Lady Summer," Cordelia scolded under her breath. Summer just smiled and ran off with her sisters toward the keep.

"I see you brought your things," said Cordelia, eying a number of trunks and barrels in the back of the cart. "Were you planning on staying longer this time?"

"I wasn't sure. Summer's missive said something about you losing your dowry that was going to be given to the king in exchange for you being able to choose your next husband. I'm sorry I didn't have much to bring, but since I'm not married, I'm only allowed to live in a small manor house. I brought what I could."

"Not married?" Cordelia raised a brow, knowing better.

"Nay," said the woman, looking down to her hands. "Where would you like my men to put the things?"

"My steward will handle it," she said, calling Sir Kenton over.

"Yes, my lady," he said with a bow of his head.

"Please take Lady Annalyse's things to the ladies solar. Also, have the chambermaid prepare the chamber in the east wing for Lady Annalyse and her daughters."

"Aye, Lady Cordelia," said the man, leaving to do as instructed.

"Once you and your daughters are settled, I'd like you to join me in the great hall, Lady Annalyse. I'll order my cooks to prepare a meal, anon."

"Thank you, Lady Cordelia, you are so kind," said the woman. "If I can do anything at all for you, don't hesitate to ask."

"There is something you can do, if you don't mind."

"Of course," said the woman, her eyes soft and kind. "What is it?"

"Tell me why you lied and said you are not married when I know your husband is alive and resides in Scotland."

Cordelia had been blunt and, possibly, a little too harsh because Annalyse's kind eyes changed and the brightness she'd seen there a moment ago turned dark. "I don't like to talk about my past, Lady Cordelia. I hope you'll forgive me for not answering."

"Of course," she said, wondering if she would get any information from the woman at all. She wanted to ask her about Rowen but decided she needed to approach the subject gently. Mayhap after a day or two, she'd try again. For now, she'd do all she could to see that Annalyse and her daughters were comfortable. To do this, they would start out with a good meal and some spiced, mulled wine. Cordelia needed to approach the woman with more caution to her words because she didn't want Annalyse to turn her away. Right now, she needed to talk to someone about Rowen and his brothers, and this woman was the only one who would be able to help her.

CHAPTER 18

Rowen felt restless the next morning, having stayed at MacKeefe camp for the last few weeks, leaving his ship anchored off shore. Never had he been idle for so long and his crew was eager to get back to the sea as well. He'd been sleeping out in the elements instead of the cruck-framed cottages that the MacKeefes generously offered. The longhouses held many people, the curved timbers supporting the thatched roofs and running all the way to the ground. Some of the huts were dug right into the ground and the roofs rested atop them. It would have been nice to seek shelter, but he wanted some space. So he'd ended up laying on the ground by the fire staring up into the star-filled sky. The nights were lonely without Cordelia next to him curled up to his chest and in his arms.

Lucky and Muck had been transported to the dungeon at the MacKeefe's Hermitage Castle on the border until Rowen decided what to do with them. He would have killed them by now if his brother hadn't stopped him and he wished he had – after what they'd almost done to Cordelia. Without them on the ship, hopefully, no more of his crew would be thinking of mutiny.

"Guid mornin'," said Reed, walking from the longhouse that

housed many of the families as well as the single men. "We've been lookin' for ye and I almost thought ye set sail in the night without even sayin' guidbye."

"We?" asked Rowen, yawning and rubbing his eyes. Then he saw just who Reed meant as Ross hobbled out of the keep with a crutch under his arm and Laird Storm MacKeefe at his side. He hopped more than walked and looked gaunt and pale. It disgusted Rowen to see him like this after so many years of seeing him act so fierce and strong.

Ross Douglas had, at one time, been a man that Rowen and his brothers had admired, but Rowen didn't like a man who gave up. Especially one who let his family walk out of his life without putting up a fight to keep them.

"Rowen," said Storm. "Are ye leavin' us so soon?" Storm held the hand of his seven-year-old daughter, Heather. His nine-year-old son, Hawke, and oldest daughter, Lark, who was twelve, were at his side. "The bairns wanted to show ye the carrier pigeons we use that have been carryin' messages between yer brothers, Reed and Rook. They were also hopin' to go for a ride on yer ship."

"That's not possible since I'll be leaving with my crew immediately," Rowen told them, not wanting to disappoint the children, but not wanting to stay here any longer, either. "Mayhap next time."

"Come on children, let's go down to the loch," said Storm, heading away with his family.

"Rowen, where are ye goin'?" asked Reed. "We havena received a message from Rook about the location of King Edward. I dinna think we'll have another raid so soon."

"It's never too soon to raid that bastard," stated Ross, shifting uncomfortably against his crutch. "Get everythin' ye can from the man because he owes it to us – to all the Scots."

"Funny to hear you call him a bastard when we're the bastards," said Rowen.

"It's been over ten years and not once have ye or Rook come

to see me or even speak to me," Ross said, surprising Rowen with the tinge of sadness he held in his voice. It was true Rowen had never gone out of his way to see the man because he never forgave him for keeping such a huge secret.

"I was being held prisoner aboard a pirate ship against my will for seven of those years," said Rowen. "Or didn't Reed tell you that?"

"I told him the night of Burnt Candlemas, that I saw a pirate take you away," said Reed.

"So you knew and yet you didn't come to look for us?" asked Rowen. The man stayed silent and looked to the ground. "Oh, mayhap it was because you were hoping we'd be killed since we were naught but bastards of your enemy king. Is that it?"

"Stop it!" shouted Ross and he stood up straight. Rowen saw a glimpse of the man he used to know who raised them and ruled with an iron fist. It was Ross who'd taught the boys to fight and given them their first swords. He was also the one to teach them how to play the game of chess, always stressing how important it was to get the king. "I couldna come after ye or havena ye noticed because of that bastard and his army I've been left as half a man?"

"If you want to pity someone, pity me," said Rowen. "After all, I'm naught more than a black-hearted pirate and thief. I'm never going to get all that I deserve."

"Ye deserve to be put o'er my knee and whipped for talkin' like that," spat the man, coming to life even if it was only out of anger.

"I'm not a child anymore and I have no idea why you even came to talk to me. We have nothing to say," growled Rowen. "You lied to us and tricked us. I want nothing to do with you ever again."

"He's also the one who told us the truth," interrupted Reed. "If it wasna for him tellin' us, we might have never heard the truth."

"Too little, too late," Rowen grunted. "He only did it because of his anger. What is it you want?" he asked again.

"I heard ye saw Summer," he said. Rowen thought Ross' eyes looked wetter than before.

"I did."

"How did she look?" he asked, sounding like a father pining over a lost child. "Is she pretty like her mother?"

"Why do you care about it? You let them walk out of your life and once again – you never tried to get them back."

"I agree, and it was the biggest mistake of my life," Ross shouted. "If there is one thing I wish I'd learned was never to let a woman walk away if ye truly love her."

"Love her," Rowen repeated softly, realizing that he'd let Cordelia walk out of his life, too. It would have been risky and he could have been captured or killed if he'd gone after her, but it would have been worth it because he was miserable without her. Storm had told him the same thing last night and Rowen didn't need to wait around for anyone else to say it.

"I'm going back to Whitehaven," he said and turned on his heel, heading to his ship.

"Rowen, what are ye doin'?" called out his brother.

"I'm not going to let the woman I love walk out of my life forever," he said, making his way to the water. "That is one mistake I will never make again!"

CHAPTER 19

Cordelia waited two days before she asked Annalyse any more questions. She'd managed to keep busy and had kept to small talk with the woman, trying to decide what to do. Annalyse thought she'd been called there because Cordelia wasn't feeling well, so she tended to her ministrations and acted like a mother. It seemed Summer didn't tell her about Rowen after all.

That relieved Cordelia as well as made her even more anxious. If Annalyse knew nothing about the situation, then Cordelia would have to be the one to tell her because she couldn't keep this a secret any longer.

A messenger appeared at the gate and Cordelia stretched her neck to see clearly. "Nay," she said to herself when she realized it was a messenger of the king.

"I'm here for our stroll through the gardens," said Annalyse, coming across the courtyard being followed by Summer and her sisters.

"Just a moment." Cordelia held her hand in the air and flagged down the messenger who was speaking with one of her guards.

"Lady Cordelia, widow of the late Walter de Clare of White-haven?" he asked.

"Aye," she said holding out her hand. "Do you have a message for me?"

"It is from King Edward. I've ridden ahead of him to bring you this missive." The man dug the missive from his travel bag and gave it to her with two hands. She took it from him and nodded her head. He bowed in return.

"Thank you. You are dismissed." She didn't open the sealed parchment until after the messenger had gone.

"What is it?" asked Annalyse with concern in her voice. Her curious, bright blue eyes that looked just like Rowen's lowered toward the letter.

"I think I have a pretty good idea what it is and it isn't anything I'm going to like." Cordelia ran her hand over the stamped, wax seal with the impression of the king's signet ring pressed into it. Breaking the seal carefully, she opened the vellum parchment with shaking hands and scanned the words written inside. A knot formed in her stomach and her throat tightened as well. The king was announcing that he would be there on the morrow to speak to her about her abduction. He was stopping there on his way to bring money and goods to Blackpool. It also said he was bringing with him a man who had agreed to marry her despite the fact she'd been prisoner aboard a pirate ship.

"How much did you have to bribe him to agree to that?" she mumbled to herself, folding up the parchment and shoving it into the pouch hanging from her side.

"What did you say, my dear? Is something wrong?" Annalyse watched and waited for her answer.

"'Tis naught to worry about right now." She took a deep breath and released it. "Now, how about that walk in the garden?"

Moments later, she strolled through the gardens with Annalyse at her side. Summer and her sisters followed. It was a chilly fall day and she wrapped her cloak around her for comfort, wishing it were Rowen's arms, instead.

"I do admire your gardens," said Annalyse as they strolled through an archway covered with a flowering climbing vine. She'd had her gardener construct a cobblestone path that curved and meandered through her herb garden and vegetable garden, ending up at a wooden bench carved with forest animals and butterflies.

Summer followed, chatting and giggling with her younger sisters. It only made Cordelia think of how she never had the chance to enjoy her childhood since she'd already been betrothed at Autumn's age and married when she was just a year older than Summer. If only she could have had the chance to be so carefree and happy.

"Thank you," said Cordelia. "I often work in the gardens myself since I find it very relaxing."

"I am sure you must still be in turmoil after being taken by a pirate," said the woman.

Summer looked up. The girl nodded, urging Cordelia to tell her mother. Still, Cordelia said nothing.

Annalyse continued. "That is the reason I came. I knew that you needed comforting and had no mother to talk to. I've been patient, but you've yet to tell me what happened when you were on the ship."

Cordelia glanced over to Summer for help, but she just shrugged and turned back to her sisters. "Come along, Autumn and Winter. I'll show you the practice yard next," said Summer and, to Cordelia's dismay, she headed away.

"Stay away from the men in the practice yard," Annalyse warned her daughters. "Men are no good and I don't want you girls anywhere near them."

Cordelia felt her stomach flip. For some reason, she didn't want to be alone with Rowen's surrogate mother.

"Lady Annalyse, why would you say such a thing?" asked Cordelia, figuring animosity toward her husband might have something to do with it. Perhaps she'd be able to get Annalyse to talk about her husband and family now. Instead, she surprised Cordelia by what she said next.

"It's the truth. All men want is to bed women. Just like what happened between you and that pirate."

"What?" Cordelia blinked and laid her hand on her stomach. "Why would you think the pirate bedded me?"

"Because, my dear," she said, laying a hand on Cordelia's stomach as well. "You are with child and we both know it is a bastard of the pirate."

"I need to sit down," she said, feeling her face flush. She hadn't even considered she could be pregnant. But now that the woman mentioned it, she had been ill a lot since she returned to Whitehaven. She'd just figured it was part of her sea sickness and that it would take a while to get over it.

"Yes, let's sit," said Annalyse, settling atop the ornately carved bench in the center of the garden. "Did you want to tell me about it?"

Cordelia didn't know what to say. She had to say something since this was her opportunity to find out if the woman knew the pirate was Rowen.

"His name is Rowen the Restless and he didn't force himself on me," she blurted out, peeking from the sides of her eyes to see the woman's reaction. Annalyse stiffened, then forced a smile.

"Go on," she said, laying her hand over Cordelia's.

"Does that name mean anything to you?" she asked.

She saw Annalyse swallow deeply. "I've heard rumors that the pirate's name is Rowen, if that is what you're asking."

"He has two brothers who help him raid. They are triplets. Their names are –"

"Rook the Ruthless and Reed the Reckless, yes, I know." Her hand slipped off of Cordelia's and she looked down as she spoke.

"I know they are your sons – your late sister's sons," said Cordelia.

Annalyse's eyes shot up to hers. "Whatever do you mean?"

"They are the bastards of King Edward and he ordered them killed at birth."

Annalyse jumped up off the bench, her eyes filled with fear. "You're wrong," she said, shaking her head. Tears streamed down her cheeks. "You don't know what you're saying."

"I do know. I know all about Burnt Candlemas and how the boys were separated for years. Rowen told me everything."

"It wasn't my fault," she said wiping away a tear. "Ross was the one who told them. If he had just kept his promise to my sister, then none of this would have happened."

"That's why you left your husband, wasn't it?"

The woman wept and Cordelia held out her hand. It was her turn to do the comforting now. "Please, sit back down, Lady Annalyse. I do not plan on revealing the secret, but I want to talk about it with you."

The woman hesitated, then nodded and sat back down. "How is Rowen?" she asked in a small voice. "I've longed for the boys every day for the last ten years. It broke my heart to leave them, but I had the girls to think about and I needed to protect them."

"Then why didn't you stay with your husband?"

"Nay," she said, wiping another tear from her face. "I couldn't. He never accepted the boys and he's the one who taught them to hate Edward. I didn't want him influencing the girls as well. It was better this way."

"Don't you love Ross? I couldn't even imagine walking away from someone I love."

"I do. I never stopped loving him," she said, half-smiling and crying at the same time. "He was everything to me. I loved him from the day he first kissed me under the kissing bough."

"Kissing bough?" asked Cordelia. "How exciting. Tell me about it."

"I don't want to talk about it if you don't mind. It is too hard to bear. But please, I do want to know about the boys."

"They are fine – just filled with vengeance toward the king," relayed Cordelia.

"The king must never know it is them causing him so much trouble. He would have them executed."

"They are of the king's blood. How could anyone ever want to do away with a baby that is of his own making? Is it because they are bastards?"

"Nay." Annalyse shook her head. "King Edward has many bastards. It is because they are triplets. Three babies with the same face, yet all with different colored hair. Edward feared them, just as twins are feared. But this time, it was worse than what I went through with my sister."

"What do you mean?"

"My sister, Gabrielle – the boys' mother, was my twin."

"I know, Rowen told me." Then Cordelia had a horrible thought and her mouth opened wide. "Did the king have her killed because of it?"

"Nay." Annalyse laughed and shook her head. "Edward loved Gabrielle. She was his mistress – and also a good friend of the queen. But I was sent away to an abbey and had only returned at my sister's request."

"Aye," she said with a nod. "I know that the second born twin is always considered evil. Tell me – did you ever resent the boys since your sister had everything you ever wanted? Rowen talked about being the first born and he sounded as if he resented the fact he'd missed out on all the privileges that went with it."

"I can't speak of this anymore," said the woman. "I need some time alone."

"Of course," said Cordelia, not understanding what she'd said that upset the woman so much. Annalyse ran across the garden with her cloak billowing out behind her in the breeze. Suddenly, Cordelia realized she was no different than Annalyse. After all, Cordelia had walked away from the man she loved, too. A shiver went through her and she laid her hand back on her belly, wondering what she was going to do.

CHAPTER 20

Rowen could see Whitehaven Castle high atop a cliff as his ship sailed to the shores of Cumbria. It was a huge castle that sat like a proud sentry overlooking the turbulent sea. Cordelia was in there and it was where he needed to be. He would have to be careful not to be seen, because for all he knew, the castle could be filled with the king's men.

"Prepare to dock," Brody shouted to the crew as they approached the wharf. Several ships were already docked and the sun was just peaking on the horizon. Merchants, tradesmen, and dockmen could be seen swarming about, tending to their business of the new day.

"Nay," shouted Rowen to his crew. "We will anchor here. I will take a shuttle boat to shore. We can't risk docking when it is so busy."

"Captain, wait," said Link, climbing down the rigging. "You can't go by yourself. Let me come with you to row the boat and wait for you."

"Fine," said Rowen, heading down the steps of the sterncastle. "But at the first sign of danger, you get back to the ship. Brody, you will leave without me if need be, because I want you to see to the crew's safety first. Do you all understand me?"

Mya shrieked and flew down from the sky, landing on the side rail of the ship. Then the bird took off and headed toward shore.

"Will there be another raid on the king while we're here?" asked Spider.

"The provisions are running low and we need to bring back more since the wench gave the Islanders part of our booty," added Odo.

"Her name is Lady Cordelia," said Rowen, securing his weapons in the belt around his waist. Then he reached for the lines attaching the shuttle boat to the ship and with Link's help, they lowered it into the sea. "I told you, it was my decision to leave provisions with the Islanders, not hers," he lied, not wanting them to think of him as weak. "Now, I will not hear another word about it. We aren't here to raid. I am here to pay a visit and that is all."

"You're not going to bring the wench back on the ship, are you?" complained Big Garth.

"What I do is my business," snapped Rowen. "Now, keep alert. If there is trouble, collect Link and head for Osprey Island. If I'm stranded, I'll meet you there in a few days' time."

"Aye, Captain," said Brody, taking charge and keeping the men from complaining more. "Give our regards to Lady Cordelia," he said with a smile.

"I'm not giving anyone's regards when I'm not even sure she'll want to see me." He put his leg over the side of the ship and descended the rope ladder. Link already waited for him in the shuttle boat. The sky clouded up overhead and a storm looked to be brewing. He just hoped it was nothing like the storm he was about to cause sneaking into Whitehaven to see Cordelia.

* * *

"WHAT DID MY MOTHER SAY?" asked Summer, following Cordelia back into the keep. "Did she want to see Rowen again? And what about Father? Will we be able to see him again after all these years? Will we return to Scotland?" Summer's sisters stood in the distance out of earshot.

"She . . . said I was pregnant," said Cordelia, not able to think of anything but that.

"Pregnant?" Summer's voice was louder than it should be and Cordelia turned around and put her hand over the girl's mouth.

"Shhhh." Cordelia scanned the courtyard. The sisters were talking to some of the other children and the servants went about their duties. The guards were at their posts and, thankfully, no one seemed to have heard her. "Don't talk so loud," she scolded. "I don't want anyone to hear this."

"I'm so excited for you," said Summer, continuing to follow Cordelia toward the keep. "You've got to tell Rowen."

"Nay." She stopped and turned around again. "I'll never see him again. Even if I did, I wouldn't tell him."

"Why not?"

"Because it doesn't matter. He is a pirate and I'm a lady. We can't be together. He's made sure to tell me that and there is naught I can do about it."

"But . . . what about the baby?" she asked in a whisper, talking behind her hand. "You will need to be married."

"I will be. I've received a missive today from the king. He will be here in person on the morrow and is bringing with him a man I am to marry. I will marry him quickly and no one will need to know the child is not his."

"Nay!" She stopped in her tracks and put her hands on her hips. "You can't do that to Rowen."

"I don't have a choice," she said, holding back the tears threatening to spill forth from her eyes. "Rowen is not here and I am in need of a husband. The king has convinced someone to marry me, knowing I've been on a pirate ship and could have been ravaged."

"Why would anyone agree to that, if you don't mind me asking, my lady?"

"I'm sure the man is being paid well. Everything that was my late husband's will be his – and probably more."

"You have to tell my mother."

"Tell her what?" asked Cordelia. "There is nothing she or anyone can do once the king chooses my husband. Now, if you'll excuse me, I'd like to go to my chamber and lie down."

"I'll come with you to help you undress."

"Nay!" She could see the hurt on the girl's face and needed to explain. "Please, don't think you've done anything wrong, Lady Summer. I just need to be alone and think about things, because everything has happened so quickly that it's made me feel restless inside."

"Like Rowen the Restless?" asked the girl.

Just hearing his name made Cordelia want to cry. She turned and ran into the keep. Then she headed for her chamber where she could cry without anyone watching or hearing her. Slamming the door behind her, she hurried over to the shutter and pulled it open, letting in the crisp autumn air. Waves washed upon the shore from the sea below and the smell of salt air filled her nostrils. Gulls cried out from overhead and a ship pulling into port sounded a whistle.

"Rowen," she said, rubbing her belly, wondering if their baby would be a boy or a girl. She'd tried for such a long time to have a baby with Walter, but with Rowen, it happened so easily. Thoughts surfaced about her last baby who died in her arms just after birth. She'd been so distraught that she'd never even named the child. What if this baby died as well? It was the only memory she had left of Rowen and she didn't want to lose it, too.

Cordelia threw herself down on the bed and hid her face in the pillow and cried harder than she'd ever cried in her life.

CHAPTER 21

Rowen gripped the vines tightly as he climbed the wall of the tower with his dagger clenched between his teeth. The bloody castle was heavily guarded and he'd had to shimmy over the postern wall just to get inside. Not an easy feat since the castle hung over the edge of a cliff. He'd risked his neck hanging on to rocks while pebbles and earth gave way beneath his feet.

When he'd first seen the open window it didn't look so far up. Now he wondered if he was just plain out of his mind even to attempt this at all. If he could get inside, he'd stay in the shadows or disguise himself while he looked for Cordelia. He had no idea what he was going to say once he found her, and if his life wasn't hanging by a thread at the moment, mayhap he'd be able to figure it out.

Thorns ripped into his fingers and he cursed the fact these clinging vines were mixed with wild rose vines. Thankfully, his arms were covered. But if he didn't get to the window soon, he was going to throw himself over the edge of the cliff so that he didn't have to climb anymore with thorns ripping into his skin.

His bird circled the air above him, watching him, and he didn't want Mya to give away his presence.

"Mya – go 'way," he said, his words garbled from trying to talk with the handle of a dagger in his mouth. The bird tried landing on him and he reached out with one hand to swish it away, almost falling in the process. His eyes focused downward at the craggy rocks and water far below. Taking a deep breath, he silently told himself to keep going and look upward only.

Finally managing to make it to the window, he put his hands on the ledge and was getting ready to pull himself up when someone from inside slammed the shutter. Pain seared through his fingers and he almost let go. His mouth opened and the dagger fell, and he screamed out in the process. His eyes followed the dagger falling . . . falling . . . and clinking against the stones on its way to what seemed like a bottomless pit.

CORDELIA FELT TORMENTED by the sounds of the sea and had even thought she heard Rowen's osprey. She just couldn't take it anymore. Jumping off the bed, she headed to the window and slammed the shutter, wanting to block out anything and everything that reminded her of Rowen.

The shutter stopped as something jammed it and she thought she heard someone cry out. Then she heard the call of the hawk again and she ripped open the shutter and looked out to the sea.

"Down . . . here," came a small voice. Looking downward, she saw Rowen hanging onto the vines that hugged the castle walls. He only used one hand, the fool. Blood trailed down the window ledge and his feet dangled in midair.

"Rowen!" she shouted, her heart beating rapidly against her ribs.

"Not so loud," he growled. "You're going to alert every guard on the battlements that I'm here."

"Well, why didn't you come in through the front gate like

most visitors?" As soon as the words left her mouth, she felt foolish.

"Think of what you're saying, Cordy. But do it later. Right now, I could use a hand or I'm going to join my dagger at the bottom of the cliff."

"Of course!" She reached down and used both hands to grab on to his arm. He kicked his feet, finally managing to secure his footing on the vines again. One of the vines snapped and his body jerked, almost pulling her out the window.

"Be careful. I don't know how secure those vines are," she warned.

"You're telling me?" He grunted and groaned, and finally gripped on to the ledge, his hands bleeding from the thorns.

"You're bleeding," she said, running a finger over his hand.

"Cordy, get out of the way. I need to swing my legs up and I don't want to hit you."

She did as told. Rowen managed to haul his body in through the opening, barely fitting since the window was very narrow.

He fell into the room and landed on the floor with a thud. His sword still secured at his waist had twisted on the belt and now lay over his backside.

"What were you thinking?" she spat, angry that he could have been killed.

"It's so nice to see you again, too," he mumbled, getting to his feet and brushing off his clothes.

Emotion welled up inside Cordelia and it wasn't all happiness, either. Angered by the fact he'd locked her in the cabin to begin with and then that he hadn't listened to her warning on the dock or come after her, she reached out and slapped him across the cheek. His head turned in the process and his eyes closed slightly. Then he looked at her with a side glance.

"So I guess that means you're not happy to see me?"

She didn't answer because she was too choked up that he'd risk his life to come back to her after all. He'd returned when she didn't think he would. Throwing herself into his arms, she covered his face with kisses.

"All right, so mayhap you are pleased," he said in confusion.

She pulled out of his hold and stepped away. "Where have you been and why didn't you come after me on the docks?"

"Cordy, calm down. Don't get so excited. Now, how about something for my bloody hands?"

She grabbed his wrist and dragged him over to the wooden tub filled with water. She'd used it for bathing this morning and the servants had yet to remove it.

"Put your hands in here," she said, sticking them into the cold water.

"Oh! That's cold, Love," he said, looking down into the tub. "Do you usually take cold baths or just when you're thinking about me?" He grinned, but she didn't appreciate his sense of humor.

"The water was warm at the time and I am surprised you even know what it is. After all, I didn't think pirates knew about things like bathing."

"I wasn't always a pirate," he reminded her.

A knock at the door startled them and they looked at each other with wide eyes. Rowen quickly reached for his sword, splashing water onto the floor in the process.

"Who is it?" she called out, hearing the voice of one of her servants answer.

"We've come to remove the tub, my lady. Were you finished with it?"

"Not yet. Come back later."

"Aye, my lady, we will."

She turned back to talk to Rowen and was surprised when he pulled her into his arms tightly and kissed her so passionately that she considered making love with him right there. Then as he released her just as quickly, she dizzied and had to hold on to him to keep from falling.

"What's the matter, my lady?" he asked with a chuckle. "Still getting your sea legs about you?"

"Rowen, why are you here?" she asked in a half-whisper, glancing back at the closed door.

"Isn't it obvious?" he asked. "I came back for you."

"To abduct me again and take me back as your prisoner?"

"Nay. I want you not as a prisoner, but as my wife."

Her heart soared to hear this, but it saddened her at the same time. What kind of life would it be, married to him if they were on the run all the time? She had a baby to think about now. Her child would be raised in the castle and trained as a lady or a knight – not as nothing more than a bandit. But how was that ever going to happen in this situation?

Trumpets sounded from the front gate and Cordelia's head snapped up. "Someone is here," she said, wondering who it could be. She couldn't see the front gate from her chamber window, because she'd chosen this chamber purposely since it overlooked the sea.

She walked back to Rowen standing next to the tub. He grimaced as he pulled a thorn from his hand with his teeth and spat it across the room.

"There are a lot of things we need to talk about," she told him.

"Aye, I agree." He pulled her back into his arms. "However, it's nothing that can't wait for a little while. I've missed you, Cordy."

He kissed her again. Just when she was mellowing from his embrace, she heard the sound of the chamber door open. Turning around with a jolt, she knocked into him, and he fell over the tub and landed in the water with a loud splash.

"Lady Cordelia, are you sleeping?" Summer peeked around the edge of the door and then opened it wider and motioned her sisters into the room as well. She walked over toward Cordelia while her sisters giggled and ran over to sit on the bed.

"What do you want, Lady Summer?" Cordelia asked, leaning back against the edge of the tub, using her hand behind her back to feel for Rowen. She'd heard him go into the water, but hadn't heard him come back out and she needed to keep him hidden for now.

"I came to ask you if you've decided yet what you're going to do about being –"

"Nay!" Cordelia cut her off, knowing she was about to say pregnant. She didn't want Rowen to know yet. Not like this. "I suggest you and your sisters go down to the kitchen and find something to eat."

"Whatever for?" asked Summer coming closer. "We've already broken the fast and the next meal isn't for hours yet."

ROWEN POPPED his head up out of the water and spit a stream of water from his mouth into the air. Cordelia stood blocking his view of the door, but he was sure he'd heard a woman's voice. Peeking up over the edge of the tub, he saw Summer talking to Cordelia. The girl was even prettier than when he'd seen her in the tavern.

Dressed in a green gown, her blond hair twisted around into a braid that hung down and trailed halfway to her waist. Then he heard giggles from across the room and stretched up a little higher to see two younger girls sitting on the bed.

"Autumn and Winter," he whispered to himself, barely able to believe these were the girls he'd last seen as babies. He knew they were his sisters by the red and black colors of their hair and the fact the girls were playing a hand game that he'd made up and taught Summer when she was only four. She'd always loved the game and it made her giggle, just like the girls were doing now. He wanted to see them better and get to know them. Rowen started to get up from the tub, but Cordelia reached back with her hand and pushed his head down under the water again.

The next time he came up for air, someone else had entered the room.

"Lady Cordelia, you have guests," said the newcomer.

He peeked up over the edge of the tub to see the lovely vision of Annalyse – the only woman he'd ever known as his mother. His heart softened and a pain shot through him. It had been so long since he'd had a mother.

"Guests?" asked Cordelia. "Whoever could it be?"

"King Edward and his queen have come to your courtyard. You must hurry to greet them," said Annalyse, always being proper even though she'd lived with a rugged Scot who hadn't cared about such things.

"They're here now?" Rowen heard the panic in Cordelia's voice. "They weren't supposed to arrive until tomorrow."

"That's not all," said Annalyse.

Rowen noticed the slight wrinkles around the corners of Annalyse's eyes and the dark circles beneath them that made her look drained and tired. She was still the vision of loveliness, but the years seemed to have taken a toll on her. The happiness he used to see in her eyes and the smiles and laughter were no longer there. She'd looked much happier when she was with Ross.

"Oh, please tell me they didn't bring –" Cordelia stopped short her sentence and looked back at Rowen over her shoulder without the others noticing.

"Yes, dear, the king has brought the Earl of Leicester with him. I've just heard the word that you and the earl will be married on the morrow."

Rowen couldn't hold back his gasp of surprise.

"Is there something in the tub?" asked Annalyse, coming closer. "I thought I heard a noise."

"Nay. Let's go - all of us," said Cordelia, directing the women out of the room. The soft thud of the door closing led Rowen to believe they'd all gone. He sat up straight, dripping with water, confused by what he'd just heard. If Cordelia already knew she was getting married, why had she kissed him with so much passion? He had to find out more.

Spying a cloak on a hook on the wall, he exited the tub and wrapped it around his shoulders. Covering his head with the hood, he followed the women down to the courtyard, leaving a wet, soggy trail behind him. Staying hidden in the shadows, he took his position behind a cart of hay where he could see everything clearly.

Dear old dad had an entourage of men and servants around him, creating a grand show as always. Sitting high on his white steed that was draped in trappings embroidered with the royal crest, the man kept his back straight and his chin tilted upward. A slight reddish-brown tint of his hair was mixed with mostly gray, making him look even more regal for his old age of mid-fifties. His hair hung down to his shoulders and his beard was halfway down his chest. An ermine-lined cloak billowed out behind him in the breeze as he dismounted.

Queen Philippa was helped from her horse by several guards and looked beautiful and too good for such a cheating man. Her hair was coiled around each ear and covered by a headpiece that strapped under her chin. She was adorned with jewels, same as the king, and her necklace sparkled from across the courtyard.

"King Edward, Lady Philippa, I am honored by your presence and am sorry I wasn't here to greet you when you rode into my courtyard. I wasn't expecting you until the morrow," said Cordelia holding out her gown and curtseying. A man whom Rowen guessed to be the Earl of Leicester dismounted and walked toward her. He was about as old as the king and had gray hair and looked like he'd seen quite a few battles.

"Lady Cordelia," said Edward after clearing his throat. "I am not happy you have failed to come to me as instructed. I need to know everything that happened when you were abducted by the Demon Thief. Now that I'm here, we will have our little talk."

Rowen's ears perked up. So the man was here to ask about him. Why wasn't he surprised?

"I'm sorry, Your Majesty," said Cordelia, curtseying again, "but I've been feeling ill lately and was not able to travel."

"That is no excuse!" shouted the king. Rowen got the feeling he was speaking loudly for show. "I have half a mind to –"

"My good king," came Philippa's calm voice, interrupting her husband. "It no longer matters since we are here now. Wouldn't you like to introduce the earl?"

"Oh, yes," said Edward, nodding toward the older man. "This is Earl Benedict Egerton of Leicester. He has agreed to marry you even though you are now an undesirable woman in any man's eyes."

Rowen's fists clenched when he heard this. It angered him that anyone would say such a thing about Cordelia. It wasn't true at all.

"So happy to make your acquaintance," said the earl, bowing slightly to take Cordelia's hand and kiss it. "After tomorrow, you will be my wife and I will be the new Lord of Whitehaven. Things will be different with a man in the castle again. I want you to know that I expect my wife to be silent and obedient."

"As a woman should be," agreed the king, getting a glare from his wife.

"Of course," said Cordelia, bowing her head to the wretch. "Whatever you desire, my betrothed." This infuriated Rowen even more. He couldn't believe she agreed to not only the marriage but also his absurd terms.

"I have brought my best guards with me because I'm transporting some of my riches to Blackpool where I am having a new castle built," said the king. "I have the goods and gold in this wagon." He nodded to a covered wagon surrounded by his men. "I trust the protection of Whitehaven is just as strong as when Walter was alive?"

"Yes, of course," said Cordelia, glancing over her shoulder, looking for Rowen. "Just as strong. You have naught to worry about."

"I am hungry," complained the king.

"I invite you to feast with us, Your Majesty." Cordelia curtseyed to the nobles. "Please, everyone join me for a meal in the great hall."

Rowen had heard enough. When a stableboy passed by with the king's horse, he knew he had to make his move. He shot out and yanked the reins from the boy, jumping atop the horse, keeping covered with the cloak as he sped away.

"My horse!" shouted the king, and commotion filled the courtyard. Guards chased after him, but Rowen made his way under the portcullis and over the drawbridge before they could stop him. His anger had made him act irrationally and now he had the king's army on his tail. There was only one place he could go for help and he hoped he remembered how to get to Rook's secret crypts because he was going to need not only somewhere to hide, but also someone to talk to right now.

CHAPTER 22

Rowen headed through the woods trying to lose the soldiers on his tail. He had to shake them before he made his way to the ruins of Lanercost Priory or he'd lead them right to his brother. Thankfully, the king's horse was fast, but the ornate, colorful trappings with the king's crest were much too easy to spot.

Winding through the woods, he made his way farther from town, coming across a peddler with a horse and cart and one horse in tow as well. The old man veered backward when he saw Rowen, almost falling from the seat.

"Your Majesty!" The man bowed his head.

"I'm not the king, you fool," grumbled Rowen, quickly dismounting and taking the extra horse that was tied to the cart.

"What are you doing?" asked the peddler.

"I need your horse. Now make sure you throw the king's guards off my trail and I'll make this all worth your while." He dug into his pouch and threw the man a half-crown. The man caught it and his eyes opened wide.

"Who are you?" he asked, turning his face upward, squinting one eye.

"Just call me the Demon Thief," he said, racing off toward the monastery.

His change of horses worked beautifully. Or perhaps it was the half-crown he'd thrown to the old man that did the trick, but Rowen managed to lose the soldiers that were following him. He traveled all day, heading for the border being happy that the weather held out. His osprey had spotted him and flew in circles high above him in the sky. When he heard the caw of a raven, he knew he was getting close to Rook's home.

Something moved in the brush off to the side and he saw the flash of a horse. He was about to take off at a run when he noticed the raven swooping down and saw Rook appear through the trees with the bird on his shoulder.

"Rowen. I saw your bird and knew you'd returned," said Rook, riding to his side. Three of his men traveled with him.

"Good to see you, Brother. I need a place to hide for a while. The king's guards are on my tail, but I believe I lost them for now."

"Of course." Rook looked over to his men and nodded. "Check the surroundings and make sure no one follows us," he instructed. The men headed off and Rook continued to ride at Rowen's side.

Rook's black hair fell past his shoulders and he wore chain mail and leather gauntlets with the padded gambeson of a knight. He carried his sword proudly at his side.

"You never told me where you got that chain mail," said Rowen, longing for some for himself. A knight's attire was expensive and hard to come by – especially when someone was not a wealthy noble.

"I took it off of one of the last victims who tried to remove my head," said Rook.

"The king's men," said Rowen scoping the woods as they rode.

"That's right. So, I heard about the king being in Whitehaven with another shipment of gold and riches that he's taking to Blackpool."

"How did you know?" asked Rowen. "I only just heard about it myself."

"Brother Everad's informant told him. I heard about it two days ago and sent a message with one of the homing pigeons to Reed. Didn't he tell you?"

"I must have left right before the message arrived."

"Reed should be here by the morning with his men. We need to discuss how we'll take the bounty."

"Rook, I don't care about that right now. I have other things I need to discuss with you. Can we speak in private where I won't have to keep looking over my shoulder?" He looked over his shoulder once more as he said it.

"Aye. We'll go to the crypts where we won't be disturbed. Just follow me."

* * *

THERE WAS no way Cordelia could concentrate on the meal when she worried for Rowen's safety. What had made him do such a foolish thing as to steal the king's horse? If he wanted to die, then he was doing a good job trying, because he had a dozen angry soldiers on his tail.

"Tell me about the Demon Thief," said the king who sat next to her at the trestle table atop the dais. She'd had her servants prepare something to eat as the king requested, but had she more warning that he would be coming for a visit, she would have had a meal better suited for a king. The king stabbed a big hunk of venison and slapped it onto his platter. Since a trencher wasn't something a king would use, she'd given him a silver platter along with a silver spoon and he shared his cup with no one.

"Your Majesty, the meat hasn't had enough time to cook

properly," she said, seeing the blood leaking out of the venison. "Perhaps I can have it returned to the kitchen."

"Nonsense," said the king with a wave of his hand. "I like my meat bloody. Now stop stalling and tell me what happened aboard the pirate ship. Where did the Demon Thief take you, and how many times did he force himself on you?"

"What?" Shocked by his question, she grabbed her cup and downed some wine. His queen sat next to him, watching intently. Next to her was the earl and next to Cordelia was Lady Annalyse. Summer and her sisters sat at the ends of the long dais table.

"I think what my husband means, is are you all right, Lady Cordelia?" interrupted the queen. "It must have been such a harrowing experience for you and he is concerned for your safety and well-being."

The king scoffed at his wife. "Nay. I'm not asking of her well-being, I want to know about this bloody monster that I can't seem to catch."

"Rowen is not a monster and neither did he force himself on me," she spat before she could think it over. Once the words left her mouth, she realized she'd said the wrong thing, but it was too late to take it back.

"Rowen?" asked the king, chewing his meat. "You're on a first name basis with the Demon?" He held out his tankard, waving it in the air, angry it took the serving boy so long to fill it again.

"I'm sure you've heard he's called Rowen the Restless," said Cordelia, knowing she had to tell him something at this point.

"Aye," answered the king, raising his tankard and taking a swig. "I've also heard him called Rook the Ruthless and Reed the Reckless. The Demon has many names."

She longed to tell him the Demon Thief was not one man but instead his bastard sons who were stealing from him, but being frightened, she said nothing. Discussing this with someone else first to get an opinion would be beneficial. And it needed to be a woman. She turned to Lady Annalyse.

"Lady Annalyse, I am feeling quite ill and wonder if you'd take me back to my chamber."

"Of course, but shouldn't Lady Summer do that?" asked the woman in surprise. "After all, she is your lady-in-waiting."

"Nay, I want you to do it."

"You're not going anywhere before you tell me about the Demon Thief," said the king. "Why does he steal from me and where does he take my riches? How can I catch him and put his head on a pole to show my people I will have no more legendary demon making a fool of me?"

"His head on a pole?" Just the thought of it made her queasy. She turned and retched on the floor between them.

"Your Majesty, I need to take Lady Cordelia to her chamber," said Annalyse jumping to her feet.

The king looked down at the floor and shook his head. "Get her out of here before she spoils my meal. But we will talk," he told her. "And tomorrow morning you will marry the earl at St. Mary's at the edge of town. I will take my cart and men with us, so I know my riches will be well protected."

Cordelia wondered why he kept telling her about his gold and riches but, at the moment, she didn't care. The vision of Rowen's head on a spike was stuck in her mind and she needed to go lie down before she swooned. Once she and Lady Annalyse made it to her chamber, she entered the room and closed the door behind them.

"Lie down on the bed, dear," said Annalyse, taking her by the shoulders and guiding her to the raised dais that held the pallet. "You need to sleep."

"Nay, I don't want to sleep," she said, sitting down on the bed but remaining upright. "Lady Annalyse, there is something I need to tell you that I should have told you when you first arrived. But I was frightened and didn't know what to do."

"Lady Cordelia, you have been through a lot lately. Mayhap it is better that you sleep now. We will talk later." She put her hands on Cordelia's shoulders, but Cordelia pushed them away.

"Nay! You need to know that I love Rowen the Restless - your son."

Annalyse stopped and stared and didn't say a word. Then she wrung her hands in front of her and sadness shown in her eyes. "I know," she said, sitting on the bed next to Cordelia. "I've also suspected for some time that the Demon Thief was three men and not just one. When I heard the descriptions of men with black, blond and red hair, all having the same faces, I knew it was more than just a coincidence. Then I started hearing their names and there was no denying my suspicions were correct. Rowen, Rook, and Reed were the names my sister gave her sons on her deathbed. She also said they would be legendary someday. But if Gabrielle knew her boys were legendary for stealing from the king, she would be turning in her grave."

"Why is that?" asked Cordelia. "After all, the king ordered her babies to be killed."

"She never knew the king's order," said Annalyse, "and I'm glad. If she had known, it would have broken her heart since she was in love with King Edward."

"You were fond of the boys, weren't you?"

"I have to admit, at first I was jealous that my sister had three children and I had none. But when my daughters came along, my feelings changed. I was married to a wonderful man and had three healthy daughters. What more could a woman ask for? I considered the boys my own sons, but Ross always held resentment in his heart for the English king and it was hard for him to keep the secret that he was raising King Edward's bastards."

"You never told me who saved the boys from being killed," said Cordelia.

"I did it," came a voice from across the room. Cordelia looked up in surprise to see Queen Philippa standing in the open doorway, as she'd never even heard her come in. There was a guard behind her in the corridor. She dismissed him and entered the room by herself.

"Your Majesty," said Cordelia, jumping up. Annalyse did the same.

"Sit down, both of you," she said, elegantly gliding across the room with her long gown of blue velvet sweeping across the floor behind her as she walked. Gold fabric slippers peeked out from under her dress. Rings of emerald, amber and ruby covered her fingers. After she had settled herself on a chair, she continued. "Gabrielle was my husband's mistress, but she was also my good friend."

"I'm not sure how you could forgive her for being with your husband," said Cordelia, sitting back down on the bed. Annalyse did the same.

"I know my husband all too well. He has had many mistresses and bastards through the years," admitted Philippa. "I don't hold anger in my heart against the women that he orders to his bed."

"That is very kind of you," said Annalyse. "My sister always spoke well of you and also of Edward."

"I couldn't let my husband kill babies – no matter how superstitious he was that they were spawns of the devil."

"Does he know they still live?" asked Cordelia.

"Nay. He believes I had them killed. He never knew the babies' names or else he would have figured it out. But I think he is starting to suspect. He's determined to trap the Demon Thief and kill him."

"Like the trap he had set up the day Rowen took me?" asked Cordelia.

"Yes," answered the queen. "I came with Edward on this trip to warn you that my husband has set another trap. He plans on using this excuse of talking to you and bringing you someone to marry to lure the Demon Thief closer and catch him this time. That is why he has been announcing freely that he has riches and gold with him and why the wedding will be in town instead of inside the safety of the castle walls. He is trying to lure him out."

"I need to warn Rowen!" Cordelia shot up off the bed. "I can't let him walk into a trap. And I won't let anyone put his head on a spike!"

"I will do what I can to help you," said Philippa in her calm and collected voice. "But I fear that the king's mind is made up. This time, it might be too late to do anything to help Lady Gabrielle's sons."

CHAPTER 23

Rowen paced the cold stone floor of the crypts under Lanercost Priory, hating the feeling of being so confined in the cold and dark. He longed for the fresh sea air filling his lungs and the splash of the ocean waves against his face. "How can you live in such a morbid place?" he grumbled, eyeing all the tombs around him. Some of the caskets were stacked up in the walls and others were adorned with stone coverings carved with bodies and faces of the nobles or clergymen who had died. There were crosses everywhere; big ones, small ones, plain ones, and even ones carved of stone with jewels embedded in them. The floors were dirty and dusty, and the whole place smelled musty.

Then again, they were deep in the bowels of the earth. He was sure some of these graves were from hundreds of years ago.

"You'll get used to it after a while," said Rook, lighting another tallow candle. The stench filled the air and made the musty area smell even worse. Rook's raven, Hades, hopped around the top of one of the tombs pecking at something. Rowen thought the dirty bird was perfect for a place like this. However, while this was, indeed, a place of the dead, the fact his brother had named his bird after the Greek god of the underworld was a little disturbing to Rowen.

Water leaked down in spots through a crack overhead, echoing the continuous sound of dripping that about drove Rowen mad. Then a rat nibbled at Rowen's feet as if this place weren't bad enough without it. He kicked it away. Rook's right hand man, Brother Everad, lingered in the shadows hidden beneath his long, black robe.

"This is disgusting," spat Rowen. "I can't think in these conditions. Can't we go somewhere else?"

"Of course," said Rook, as if his surroundings didn't bother him at all. "Why don't we go into my personal chamber? Mayhap, it'll be more to your liking." Rook walked over to a large stone door and pushed a lever. The door creaked open, revealing another chamber. "Brother Everad, I'll be in my chamber. Do keep a watch and let me know if there is any trouble."

"Of course, my lord," said the monk, bowing and scurrying away not unlike the rat that had inspected Rowen's feet moments ago.

"My lord?" Rowen raised a brow at hearing what the monk had called his brother. "Lord of the Underworld, mayhap, but that's about it."

Once inside the chamber, Rook lit a lantern. The room brightened up in an orange glow. The raven flew in after them and settled atop Rook's shoulder.

Rowen's jaw dropped when he saw the difference in this chamber compared to what he'd just seen in the antechamber. It didn't look like an underground crypt at all, but more like the solar of a king.

A large, four-poster bed sat atop three steps. From black iron bars above the overstuffed pallet hung deep purple velvet bed curtains tied back with golden brocade woven ropes with tassels on the ends. The ceiling was supported by thick wooden beams and there was a warm wooden-planked floor beneath their feet instead of cold stone. The walls had been painted in whitewash and an ornate scene of knights jousting at a tournament was depicted on one.

Colorful woven tapestries lined the rest of the walls. There were several trunks around the room and a painted wooden wardrobe to hold clothes, standing tall in the corner. Beeswax candles instead of those made from animal fat burned in little niches carved right into the walls.

He even had a table complete with ornate legs and four chairs that were carved and looked like they were painted with gold leaf across the backs. On the table was a chessboard made of polished, marbled stone.

It was dry in here and very accommodating, nothing at all like the outer crypt. There were barrels of food and drink stacked against the wall. It smelled like cinnamon and cloves instead of must and tallow.

"What the hell is this?" asked Rowen in shock.

"You'd know it was my living quarters if you had ever taken the time to come see where I lived at least once in the last three years."

"Had I known you lived like a king, I would have hurried to get here. I've been telling Reed how horrible you have it living in a crypt and how lucky he was, but now I can see I've had my facts a little confused."

"Nice, isn't it?" asked Rook, pointing to the painting on the wall. "Brother Everad was a scribe here before King David decided to desecrate the place two decades ago. He painted the scene for me. I'm going to be a knight jousting in a tournament someday."

"You keep dreaming, Rook."

"The monks have been trying to rebuild and recover from their losses ever since the attack, but very few are housed here now. My men stay in some of the buildings on the premises and have been helping to fix things up. We all hide down here whenever we see anyone coming. Everyone thinks it is abandoned and leaves us alone."

"You have it all figured out, don't you?"

"I think I do a pretty good job," said Rook with a satisfied nod.

"If the priory has been ransacked, where did you get all these fine things? I've been bringing my share of our booty to the Scots and so has Reed since they are poor and need it. I thought you'd been doing something of the same nature, but now I see you've had another idea of what to do with your share."

"Close the door," said Rook. "If you leave it open, the rats will come in and I don't fancy sharing my food with them." He opened a barrel and dug out an apple and then closed up the top again.

Rowen shut the door, wondering if they were sealing themselves into a tomb.

"Is there enough air in here?" he asked.

"Look up." Rowen pointed to the ceiling with his dagger, then used the blade to slice off a piece of apple. He handed the food to Rowen. Rowen just shook his head, looking upwards to see vents of some sort embedded into the ceiling.

"Where does that lead?"

"I've built a system of vents that lead out into the monastery and flow back here. There is always fresh air flowing in, so you don't need to worry about suffocating."

"I'm not sure I'd call this air fresh," he commented, walking over and picking up a golden chalice on a shelf. "Is this from the church?"

"Brother Everad has seen that I get whatever I can't provide for myself."

"I guess so," he said with a puff of air from his mouth. Something ran by his feet again and he stepped backward quickly.

"Another rat," he said.

"You didn't close the door fast enough," commented Rook

with a chuckle. "Don't look so disturbed by it. I'd think you'd be used to rats on that ship of yours."

"Rats on a ship that is regularly docking at different ports can't be helped. And while you might find some vermin in the hold, I assure you you'll never find a rodent in my sleeping quarters. My crew is good about keeping them under control."

"Even the king's castle has rats, Brother. If I could have a fire down here, they'd stay away, but since I can't, I have to live with it. However, I have a little help controlling them."

"How so?"

"Hades, do your job," said Rook, putting the apple and dagger on the table and walking over and opening the door. The raven squawked and made a fuss, flapping its wings and pecking at the intruder. The rat ran in circles and hissed at the bird. Before Rowen knew it, the rodent ran out the door being chased by the bird. Rook closed the door and brushed his hands together as if he'd done something of importance. "I might not have a crew, but I have a little help, too. Hades knows I prefer he kill the rats outside of my chamber."

"If only rats were my biggest problem." Rowen plunked down atop the bed and ran his hands over his face.

"What's bothering you, Brother? Does it have something to do with that girl?"

"Yes," he admitted. "I came back to Whitehaven to get Cordelia. I'm in love with her. But she's going to marry an earl on the morrow."

"That's a shame." Rook sat down at the table, slicing off another piece of apple and looking over the chessboard. "How about a game of chess? I've been playing against Brother Everad, but why don't you take his place, instead?" He popped the piece of apple into his mouth and chewed as he surveyed the board for his next move.

All three of the brothers played chess and were very competitive about it. Ross had taught them to play the game when they were boys. The winner had always gotten out of chores for the day. Reed was the best at it and, of course, Rowen was the worst. He never liked playing the game with his brothers since he was usually the one ending up doing all the work.

"I don't want to play chess." Rowen got up and walked over to the table and began to pace the floor. "I want to talk about Cordelia. What do you think I should do?"

"What can you do?" asked Rook, his hand wavering atop a pawn. "She's just a pawn in this whole game and has no chance at all of marrying you. For that matter, why would she even want to? You have nothing to offer and the earl has everything she needs. Forget about her, Rowen. That is one game you can never win." Rook moved the pawn, seeming pleased with his move. "I know you were never good at chess, but are you sure you don't want to play?"

"You're wrong about Cordelia," said Rowen, feeling restless and pacing the floor faster now. He let his brother's words upset him. "I don't believe this is the way things should be. I've seen Mother as well as Summer, Autumn, and Winter. They are all at the castle."

Rook's eyes moved upward slowly, but no expression showed on his face. "She's not our mother and the girls are only our cousins," he reminded him.

"Aren't you even curious to see them?" asked Rowen.

"Why should I be?" He still stared at the chessboard. "We were lied to for the first twelve years of our lives. I don't want to be around liars."

"The girls were just children and I'm not even sure they know the truth. Don't be so ruthless, Rook."

"You'd better not get any silly notions of trying to talk to them. It'll only bring trouble. Just forget about them and forget about Cordelia as well. You'll be better off."

"Nay, I won't forget about them, and I will have Cordelia for my wife." He continued to pace back and forth. "And you're going to help me do it."

"Nay, I'm not," said Rook. "Tomorrow, Reed will get here and, together, the three of us will raid dear old dad once more." He chuckled. "The king will be so busy with the wedding that he won't even notice us. We'll be in and out of there before he knows what hit him. My, this will be a prosperous month for us. Now, come on Rowen, just move one piece. Try a pawn or something and let me have my next turn," he said, studying the chessboard. "I have it all worked out."

"You don't have it all worked out and we're not going to raid the king," said Rowen. "I want Cordelia, even if I have to abduct her again to get her."

"God's eyes," said Rook, smiling and shaking his head. "I've never known you to have to force a woman to go with you, Rowen. You must be losing your touch."

"I'm not losing my touch. I'm sure she wants to come with me, but she is being forced to marry by order of the king. She told me herself that it was her dowry we took on our last raid, not the king's goods. She intended to use it to bribe Edward to let her choose her next husband. We've gone and ruined that chance for her and I don't like it. I'm going to go back and get her and make things right, with or without your help."

"Then it'll be without me because I'm not about to risk my neck for your personal problems."

Rowen glared at his brother.

"Besides, you're going about it all wrong," Rook said. "You'll never be able to pull it off and you know it. Even if you abduct her again, then what happens? Are you going to live with her on your ship with a few dozen lusty men for the rest of your lives? You'd never get a free minute because you'd have to be watching her over your shoulder constantly. Think about it, Rowen. We're doomed to live as bandits in the night because of what happened to us in the past and there is nothing we can do to change that."

"We're nobles, dammit," spat Rowen, kicking at the table leg and shaking all the chess pieces. "I'm the first born of the king and deserve good things in my life."

"Not when you're a bastard and especially not when you're a triplet. Face it, Rowen; we were deprived of everything the day we were born. Now take your move, will you?"

Rowen stopped pacing and slammed his hand down on the table, causing the chess pieces to wobble once more. "I'll never give up, do you understand me? I'll get what I deserve no matter what I have to do to get it." He reached over and snatched up the white queen and slid it across the board, knocking his brother's bishop off the table and to the floor. "Check," he said and headed out of the room, leaving Rook sitting there with his mouth open just staring at the chessboard.

CHAPTER 24

Morning came much too fast. Before Cordelia knew it, she was dressed in her finest gown with flowers woven into her hair and was riding atop her horse being escorted by the king and his entourage as they made their way to St. Mary's church for the wedding. Her stomach turned and her eyes kept darting around, as she watched for Rowen and his brothers. She wondered if they were going to fall for the king's trap. She had to warn Rowen somehow, but couldn't do that when she didn't even know where he was.

Lady Annalyse and her daughters rode beside her. King Edward, Queen Philippa, the earl, and a half dozen of the king's men led the way. The cart was behind them, still covered, and she wondered just what was inside. Whatever was in there, it wasn't worth dying for.

They stopped in front of the church where a crowd of people covered from head to toe wearing long cloaks were waiting for them. She couldn't see their faces since they seemed to all be looking downwards as if they were praying.

There'd been no time even to post the wedding banns, so she

didn't understand how so many villagers knew about the wedding.

"Get down from your horse and let's get this over with," growled the earl, walking to her side and all but yanking her to the ground. She almost twisted her ankle when she landed.

"I don't want to marry you," she bravely spoke out, but it only made the man laugh.

"Who else is going to want you, whore? Now get up to the stairs of the church because the priest awaits us."

Cordelia struggled against his grip but went with him. The king and queen stayed mounted atop their horses, and she noticed the look of helplessness in Queen Philippa's eyes. The woman had tried all night to convince her husband to wait and post the banns, hoping to stall for time while they figured out what to do, but Edward wouldn't hear of it.

A cry of a bird caught her attention and she looked up to see Rowen's osprey circling overhead.

"He's here," she said to herself, turning and searching for Rowen, but didn't see him.

"Who's here?" asked the earl.

"No one," she said quickly, but unfortunately it was too late. He knew exactly what she meant. The earl signaled the king and the king motioned to his guards standing around the cart. Only a dozen men were guarding the king's riches and she hoped that Rowen's brothers came with him. If so, they might have a chance of escaping, even if this were a trap.

"Let's start the wedding," said the earl, pulling her up the stairs to the church where the priest waited with an open book. She looked back to see Lady Annalyse gathering her daughters around her protectively. They all looked as if they were about to cry.

As the priest started the ceremony, she didn't miss the shriek of a red kite and the guttural call of a raven from somewhere behind her. Then when it came time for her to say her vows, a lone rider atop a horse shot out from the trees. Rowen headed toward her.

"Wait for it," she heard the king say under his breath and her heart beat anxiously.

"No one is going to marry Lady Cordelia, but me," shouted Rowen, riding with his sword drawn and stopping at the foot of the stairs. "Come on, Cordy." He motioned with his head for her to join him.

The earl drew his sword, but the king's command stopped him.

"Wait!" The king rode over with his sword in hand, eyeing up Rowen. "You are the Demon Thief, aren't you?"

"I'm Rowen the Restless," he answered, instead.

"Why have you been stealing from me? And what do you want with this girl?"

"I love her and want her for my wife."

The king chuckled and shook his head. "Why would you think that you – a mere pirate – could ever have a noblewoman as your wife?"

"Because I am noble," he said. Cordelia held her breath, wondering what Rowen would say next. Should she warn him now? It didn't seem as if he'd come for the king's goods, only for her, so mayhap she should stay silent and wait to see what happened. Or at least until his brothers arrived. She hoped they were coming to his aid.

"You are no noble," growled the king. "I should behead you right here for even saying such a thing."

"I'm not surprised you want to kill me again . . . Father."

"What?" That took the king by surprise and he didn't like it. "I've had enough of this fool. Kill him," he ordered with a wave of his hand to a guard mounted atop a horse next to him.

"Wait!" shouted Cordelia and the king lifted his hand in the air again to stop his guard.

"What do you want, Lady Cordelia?" he asked.

"Your Majesty, with all due respect, I cannot marry the earl."

"Why not?" Edward scowled.

"Because I am in love with Rowen the Restless . . . and I am pregnant with his baby."

ROWEN ALMOST DROPPED his sword when he heard Cordelia's announcement. Surprise, elation, and fury swept through him all at once to hear that he was going to be a father. Now, more than anything, he knew he would get Cordelia out of here, even if he lost his life in the process. He had to protect her and his unborn child.

"Pregnant by that pirate?" shouted the earl. "I didn't know that. No one told me! I won't marry her now, no matter how much you pay me."

"I can't expect you to want a bastard spawned by a pirate," the king told the earl.

"That's right," said Rowen. "After all, they might be triplets spawned by the devil and you'll have to kill them someday."

"What are you talking about?" the king growled.

"You tried to do that to me when I was a baby," said Rowen.

"And me, too," came a voice. Rowen looked over to see Rook riding out on a horse, making his presence known. He was happy to see him since Rook had denied Rowen's request for help and he didn't think he'd show.

"And me," added Reed, appearing from the shadows on foot. Rowen nodded to them. So his brothers were there to help him after all. The king's eyes opened wide when he saw the three of them together. His face paled and he looked like he'd seen a ghost.

"Bid the devil, tell me this isn't so. There is no way. You three are dead!"

"Nay, we're not," Rowen told him. "Now, I'm taking Cordelia with me."

"And we're taking whatever is in that cart," added Rook. Rowen groaned inwardly. So that's why they were here.

"Attack!" shouted the king. All the people who Rowen thought were villagers dropped their robes to reveal they were armed soldiers of the king. Mya's cry split the air as the men rushed forward. He saw his brothers wave their arms through the air signaling for their small armies that appeared from the brush and started to fight the king's men. Rowen fought from the top of his horse, but it reared up, and he fell to the ground, dropping his sword. Two of the king's soldiers approached and he grabbed for his weapon, being helped as someone shot out with a sword drawn. He looked up to see Brody, Link, and his crew coming to his rescue.

"Sorry we're late," said Brody. "We left England as you instructed, but turned back when we saw your brother's hawk."

"Thanks," said Rowen, getting to his feet and fighting as well.

"Summer, get your mother and sisters into the church where you'll be safe," Rowen shouted to the girl he still considered his sister. The women took off at a run as swords clashed all around them. He turned back to try to get to Cordelia. His heart almost stopped when he saw the earl holding a blade to her throat.

"Call them off or I'll slit her throat," shouted the earl. Cordelia whimpered in his hold, her frightened eyes wide as she silently looked to Rowen for help.

"Stop!" Rowen shouted to his brothers, but they didn't call off their men. He then shouted out once again. "Rook, Reed, stop! Do you hear me? If not, he's going to kill Cordelia."

"Dammit, Rowen, I told you something like this would happen," shouted Rook, waving his arm to signal his men. "Retreat," he called out and Reed did the same.

"Go back to the ship and get out of here," Rowen told Brody.

"But, Captain – what about you and the girl?" asked his first mate.

"I'll figure something out. Now go!"

"Aye, Captain."

Rowen's brothers, their armies and Rowen's crew, hurried away with the king's men chasing them. Once they left, Rowen jumped atop the horse and headed toward Cordelia. The earl still held the blade against her throat.

"Let her go," Rowen told him. "I did as you said and the men have retreated."

"Nay. You've ruined her and neither will you have her if I can't," said the earl.

"Drop your blade," ordered the king, riding forward. Rowen knew he had no choice but to do as ordered if he didn't want Cordelia hurt. He threw his blade to the ground.

"Nay, Rowen, don't," he heard Cordelia cry out, but he couldn't take the chance that she'd be hurt or killed, so he did as commanded.

"Now your dagger, and get off the horse," added the king. Rowen looked around him. Surrounded by the rest of the king's men all holding their weapons at the ready, he couldn't fight his way out of this one without his brothers. Neither would he try to make a run for it and leave Cordelia behind. He swore he would never walk away from her again and he wouldn't. He did what was needed to protect the woman he loved and his unborn child, but now he wished he had come up with a better plan. No matter what he did, he was doomed.

"Just don't harm Cordelia," he said, throwing his dagger to the ground and sliding off the horse.

"Leicester, drop your blade as well," said Edward.

"What for?" asked the earl.

"Because you are not marrying the girl. The plans we made no longer exist."

Angrily, the earl pushed Cordelia from his arms and headed down the stairs. Rowen reached out and caught her to keep her from falling and she threw her arms around him.

"We had a deal," complained the earl.

"You ruined that deal with your little charades," said the king. "I would have had them all if it wasn't for you. Now go! I don't want to see you again."

The earl stormed off in a very foul mood.

"Oh, Rowen, now we can get married," said Cordelia. Rowen almost believed it – for a moment.

"Take him to the dungeon," the king ordered. Before he knew what was happening, he was being ripped away from Cordelia and thrown into the back of the covered wagon. He heard Cordelia cry out.

Realizing there was nothing at all in the cart but a few empty crates and barrels, he felt his hackles rise. "You tricked us," spat Rowen. "This was naught but a trap."

"Your thieving has to stop. I will do whatever necessary to make certain that it never happens again," warned the king.

"Go ahead and hang me, or put my head on a spike if that's what you need to do," shouted Rowen. "My brothers will hunt you down and, this time, they will kill you."

"That's treason to your king," said Edward.

"Nay, it is not, because you are nothing to me. Not my king, not my ally, and certainly not my father!"

CHAPTER 25

It broke Cordelia's heart to see Rowen imprisoned in her dungeon at Whitehaven. He'd risked his life to try to keep her from marrying a man she didn't love and now he would die for it.

She wept bitterly into her pillow, not sure there was anything she could do to save him. If his brothers came to help him now, they might be captured and executed as well.

The door to her chamber opened and in rushed Annalyse and Summer. Autumn and Winter waited in the corridor.

"Oh, Lady Cordelia, this is terrible," said Summer, wrapping her arms around her. "Our brother is going to die."

"He's not your brother, he's your cousin," Cordelia pointed out.

"I'll always think of him as my brother and love him as one as well." Tears fell from Summer's eyes as she spoke.

"Us, too," said the other girls, hurrying into the room to join them.

"If only I could do something to help," said Annalyse. "I'll go to the king and talk to him. I'll tell him I'm the one he should be executing since I was the one to raise the boys in secret."

"Nay, Mother," cried Autumn. The girls clung to their mother, weeping.

"Nay, you'll do nothing of the kind. You have daughters to raise and I'll not let you get involved further. This is my problem and I'll go," said Cordelia, drying her eyes and sitting up on the bed. "I'll try to make a deal with the king to save Rowen's life, even if I can never marry the man I love."

"What will you say?" asked Annalyse. "You might anger the king even more."

"It doesn't matter," she told them, removing Summer's arms from around her and getting off the bed. "Because if Rowen dies, I won't want to live. I'll have to live to raise his baby, however, I would rather do it together."

She headed down to the great hall where King Edward and his wife were sitting near the fire speaking in hushed tones. Approaching cautiously, she curtseyed.

"Your Majesties, I would request an audience to speak with you."

"Hmmph, now you want to talk," said Edward. "Yet when I wanted you to do it, you wouldn't."

"What is it that troubles you, Lady Cordelia?" asked the queen.

"I request that you set Rowen free."

"I can't do that," snapped the king.

"He is your flesh and blood. Certainly, you won't execute him?"

"He has stolen from me, killed my men, and made me look like a fool in front of my country. Give me one reason why I shouldn't kill him?"

Cordelia knew there was only one reason she could give him that might change his mind. "Because I am carrying your grandchild and he needs someone like Rowen to protect him while he's growing up," she answered. The king seemed to think about it for a moment but just shook his head.

"I need to find out who saved these boys in the first place," he told her. "I have a feeling it was Gabrielle's sister."

"Nay, she's not to blame. It was me," said the queen sharply. Her husband's head turned with a snap.

"Philippa? Tell me it isn't so. Did you defy me and save the triplets? Why? Look what you've done with your foolishness. Now they are naught but monsters determined to make my life miserable."

"You are the monster, Edward, for ordering the death of infants, let alone ones you sired," retorted the queen. "How could you even consider such an outrageous thing?"

"Philippa, you know the superstitions of triplets. It is worse than twins."

"Nothing is worse than what you've done to your children."

They conversed as if they'd forgotten that Cordelia was still standing there.

"Nothing is worse than what they've done to me! That should prove to you that they were cursed from the beginning," said the king.

"I have put up with your mistresses and your bastards for years," argued Philippa. "How do you think our legitimate children feel by your carousing with other women? You brought this all on yourself. Only you are to blame that you've not been able to catch your thieves for the last three years."

"I don't have a choice," he said, shaking his head. "I may have made a mistake all those years ago, but what's done is done. I can't change things now."

"Aye, you can, my lord," said Cordelia, stepping forward to remind them she was still there. "You can change the way your sons feel about you by talking to them and making amends."

"They're my enemies," he ground out.

"Well, don't you make alliances with enemies?" she asked in exchange. "Make an alliance with Rowen."

"Why would you think he'd want to align with me?" asked the

king. "He and his brothers have hated me for years and vengeance isn't something easily forgotten."

"Forgotten no, but forgiven is another thing."

"Yes, Edward," said Philippa. "Talk to the boy. There must be some way to work things out between you."

"I'll think about it," he said. "Dismissed." He waved a hand through the air to rid himself of Cordelia. She hurried through the great hall and down the steps to the dungeon with hope in her heart. Mayhap, there was a way that she and Rowen could be together after all.

"Who goes there?" called out her guard when she got to the bottom of the stairs. It was dank and dark and only one torch lit the small outer room where the guards watched over the prisoners in the cells. There were two guards there, one being that of the king's. Rowen was the only prisoner.

"It's Lady Cordelia," she told her guard. "Let me into the dungeon. I need to talk to Rowen."

Her guard removed his keys from his belt, but the king's guard stopped him.

"Nay," he said. "It is by the king's order not to let anyone see the pirate."

"But I need to see him," she pleaded. "Please. Just for a moment."

"Let her go," said her guard and, finally, the other one agreed.

"You have two minutes only," said the king's guard opening the lock on the gate and letting her into the confined area. "And I'll be coming with you."

It was dark and dreary in the dungeon, and while it frightened her, she pushed forward since she knew her lover was inside. The guard followed with the lit torch in his hand. She'd never even been to the dungeon the entire time she'd been married to Walter. Now, she was glad that she hadn't because this was a place no one should have to be.

"Rowen?" she said, her voice echoing off the stone walls. "Rowen, where are you?"

"Cordy." She looked up to see Rowen's hands still scratched from climbing the rose vines, clamped to the bars of one of the cells. "Cordy, I am so sorry. I only wanted to come back to get you. I didn't know this would happen."

"You and your brothers came to raid the king," snapped the guard.

"Nay. I wasn't part of that. I came only for Cordelia," he tried to explain.

"Rowen, King Edward might make an alliance with you," she told him excitedly.

"What are you saying?" Hope showed for a second in Rowen's blue eyes.

"He's thinking about making you an ally instead of an enemy."

"Nay," he said, shaking his head. "I can't do that."

"What?" Her heart sank. She thought he'd be happy to hear the news, yet he wasn't. "Of course you can. Then mayhap we can be married and raise our child together."

"Sweetheart, it doesn't work that way." He took her hands in his through the grates and stared into her eyes. "Even if I made an alliance, King Edward would want one with Reed and Rook as well."

"Then do it."

"They would never agree to that. I can't betray my brothers."

"So you're saying . . . you won't do it to be with me?"

"Nay, that's not what I mean. Think about it. What will happen to my brothers if I align with the king? I'd have to fight them on the next raid. I'm sorry, but that is something I just can't do."

"Not even to be with your child and me?" Tears formed in her eyes and she felt that sickening feeling in the pit of her stomach again.

"I don't know what to tell you," he said, shaking his head. "Mayhap there is another way."

"This is the only way, Rowen. If you don't make an alliance with the king, we will never see each other again."

"Time is up," said the guard, dragging her away from the cell. She took one last look at Rowen, begging him to reconsider, because if he didn't, one of their lives would be over.

CHAPTER 26

Rowen jerked awake, hearing the sound of creaking from the outer gate to the guard's chamber. He sat huddled in a ball on the cold, wet floor, having dozed off from nothing more than pure exhaustion. He hadn't slept in days, so distraught over letting Cordelia walk out of his life. Now he had the chance to possibly be with her, but he just couldn't do what she was asking.

The sound of heavy footsteps came toward him and also the dim glow of a nearly extinguished torch. It was not Cordelia as he had hoped. She'd been ripped away from him by the guard so quickly that he hadn't even had the chance to tell her he loved her and was happy she would be birthing his baby. Now it was too late because his father would most likely have him killed as soon as he turned down the alliance.

"Rowen, where in the clootie's name are ye?" came his brother's voice. Rowen got up and hurried to the cell door.

"Reed?" he asked in a loud whisper. "Is that you?"

"And me," said Rook, stepping forward with the torch in his hand. "Here he is, Reed. Hurry and let him out."

Both his brothers were covered in long, dark robes like the

one he'd seen the monk wearing in Rook's crypts. Reed wore his tartan beneath his and it showed, but he could tell Rook wasn't wearing his chain mail.

"What? No chain mail to a rescue?" asked Rowen as Reed turned the key in the lock.

"Too heavy for scaling walls," Rook told him, glancing back over his shoulder to check for the guards.

"Scaling walls?" Rowen thought about his last ordeal with scaling walls and didn't care to experience it again. "How did you get in?"

"The same way we'll get out," said Reed. "Over the postern gate wall."

Rowen groaned. His hands hurt just thinking about it.

"Hurry, let's go before the guards wake up," said Reed, handing Rowen some weapons.

"Mayhap we can pilfer a few things while we're here," said Rook, always wanting more treasure.

"Nay. Don't anger the king more," said Rowen. "I don't want him to take it out on Cordy."

"Why would you even think dear old dad would do a thing like that?" asked Rook, leading the way out of the dungeon and past the guards they had knocked unconscious.

They sneaked outside and across the courtyard without being discovered. With only the light of the moon to guide them, they hurried to the back of the castle where the very tall wall awaited them.

"Yer ship is waitin' out of sight," said Reed. "My men are already on it and Brody is ready to set sail back to Scotland." He gripped on to the vines and started to climb.

"If we hurry, we can be down the cliff and out of here before sunup," said Rook, starting up the wall, too. Rowen knew how treacherous the climb was and that his brothers had risked their lives to come to his rescue. Still, it didn't feel right just leaving Cordelia, especially without even saying goodbye. He looked up the tower to her chamber and saw a soft glow and flickering of a bedtime candle through the open window. He needed to see her one more time and make sure she knew he loved her and that this wasn't the way he wanted things to end.

"Come on," whispered Reed, stopping at the top of the wall, ready to go over. Rook was right behind him.

"If I'm not there by sunup, leave without me and tell Brody the ship is his. He'll be the new captain of the Sea Mirage," said Rowen, looking up to Cordelia's window.

"What the hell are you saying?" Suspicion and irritation laced Rook's words. "Brother, don't do anything stupid."

Rowen stared at the tower window and his heart called out to go to Cordelia. "I have to tell her goodbye," he said, taking hold of the vines on the castle wall and starting to climb.

"God's teeth, ye're a fool," he heard Reed's oath.

"Let him get killed if he's that stupid," Rook said putting one foot atop the wall. "We'll not come back for you again, Brother."

With that, his brothers disappeared over the top of the wall. Rowen had the awful feeling he'd never see them again. Reaching out and grabbing on to the vines, he made his way upward in a climb that he wasn't looking forward to at all. Once at the top and still alive, he reached for the ledge of the window and hauled himself inside the tower for the second time. "Cordy," he whispered. When he dropped to the floor, a lantern lit up the room and he saw King Edward sitting at the table.

"I knew you'd show up here eventually," said the king, chuckling, and reaching forward to finish setting up a chessboard. "I've been waiting for you."

"Rowen," said Cordelia from the bed. Her eyes were red and swollen. He could tell she'd been crying. A half-dozen guards stood around the room with their swords drawn.

Rowen's eyes scoped the room. He tried to think of a way to get out of there and take Cordelia with him. But leaving through the door was not an option. His father probably had another dozen guards lining the hallway and he wouldn't risk taking Cordelia out the window because a fall could kill her and the baby.

"Drop your weapons and have a seat," said the king, pointing to a chair opposite of him.

Rowen did as ordered and sat down without a word. "Why didn't you have more guards posted at the dungeon and throughout the courtyard?" he asked.

"Because," said Edward. "I wanted to see how much you really loved Lady Cordelia."

"Are my brothers in any danger?"

"I didn't send my men after them this time if that's what you mean. I'm trying to make amends, Rowen, even if you don't believe it. I figure I'd start with you."

"You're right. I don't believe it," he said, a nerve twitching in his jaw.

"Philippa made me realize I might have acted a bit too hastily when you three were born. Honestly, I was just shocked and surprised to see you again after all this time. That's why I ordered my men to attack at the church."

"What is it you want?" Rowen growled, wanting the man to get to the point.

"I want to play a game of chess with you. I love the game and Lady Cordelia tells me that you are a chess player, too."

"She did, did she?" He glared at her, wondering what else she'd told King Edward.

"What is it you want in life, Rowen?" came his father's deep voice, almost sounding as if he cared.

"What I want can never be."

"Well, what if it could? Do you want a title and riches? How about being dubbed a knight?"

"How about being legitimized?" he threw back at him knowing the man would never do that.

"I'm afraid that is one thing I won't do. You see, I loved your mother and while she was noble, she was still only my mistress. You and your brothers are bastards and that is how it will stay."

"You've legitimized your bastards before. Why is this any different?" His blood began to boil with this conversation.

"The queen convinced me to make an alliance with you and if you come to my terms, I will. But I will never legitimize a bastard son who has stolen from me and made me look like a fool in front of my entire country."

"Then why don't you kill me?"

"Rowen, nay!" said Cordelia.

The king chuckled again. "It seems the legendary bastards of the crown are invincible and I'm not able to catch them or kill them," he said. "So we will set our terms and then have a game of chess. If you win, I will give you what you want. If you lose, you'll go back to the dungeon and we'll start over."

"Start over? What does that mean?"

"It means I'll have to rethink the entire situation. And I might not feel so generous the next time around."

"I won't play chess for something that is so important to me," he told him.

"Rowen, please. Do it for us," pleaded Cordelia, rubbing her hand over her belly. "The king has agreed to let us marry if you win the game."

"He did?" He glared at the man suspiciously, but part of him was beginning to be pulled in with his bait.

"I will let you marry Lady Cordelia if that is what you want," said the king.

"And receive the title of Lord of Whitehaven?" he asked.

"If you want the title of lord, it's yours, and the castle along with it." The man reached out and straightened the white pieces on the chessboard. "However, since you've stolen so much from me, I'll not give you land, coin, or anything more."

"I don't want land. I live on the sea."

"Speaking of that." King Edward fingered his long beard in

thought. "Your ship is one of the fastest I've ever seen and my ships have never been able to catch it. I want it for myself."

"Nay!" Rowen spat. "The Sea Mirage is mine and my crew will never do your bidding."

"I don't want your scalawag crew, just the ship."

The sound of Rowen's bird could be heard from outside the window. He wondered if his brothers had returned to the ship yet. Hopefully, they'd leave and not wait for him. Then, even if Rowen promised his ship to the king, the man would never get it.

"I want to be dubbed a knight as well," he said, being pulled into the temptation of getting everything he'd ever wanted.

"Fine, fine," said the king, running his finger along the edge of the chessboard. "I'll give you one of my best horses, too, so you can catch those brothers of yours next time they try to steal from me."

"I won't go against my brothers." He stood abruptly, only to be greeted by several tips of the guards' swords. Edward waved his heavily ringed hand toward his men, directing them to put down their weapons.

"Sit, Rowen. I think we both know an alliance will be the best thing for us."

"It won't matter. My brothers will keep attacking. You have no idea how much vengeance they hold for you."

"From one little incident when you were naught but babies?" asked the king. "Now I hardly think that is fair."

"Nay. Their vengeance also stems from the devastation of Scotland led by you on the night of Burnt Candlemas."

"Oh, yes. That," he said with a nod. "Rowen, as the son of a king – even if you are a bastard – you need to realize that war is a way of life. Don't take it personally."

"I want nothing to do with you, nor will I make an alliance. Forget it." He stood up, and, once again, was greeted by the tips of the guards' swords.

CORDELIA'S HEART went out to Rowen. She could see the position he was in and felt he had no choice. He would be thrown back in the dungeon if he refused an alliance with the king and, next time, he might be executed. Why hadn't he just escaped with his brothers and not come back for her? At least then, he wouldn't lose his life.

"Rowen," she said, stepping around the guards. The king motioned for his men to stand back as she did so. "Play the game and make the alliance," she pleaded. Reaching up to put her hands around his neck, she kissed him, hoping this wouldn't be the last time. "Do it for the baby and me. Your brothers will understand and, hopefully, come around in time. But this feud has to end."

"If I agree, my legend dies with it," he said.

"Nay. There will be a new legend and it will live on through our child. It'll be a better legend - one of honor and respect." She took his hand and laid it on her stomach.

"Oh, Cordy, I love you so much it hurts. I want nothing more than to see our child grow up and to be there for him. I know from experience how hard it is for a child to grow up without his father."

Over Rowen's shoulder, she saw an odd expression on Edward's face. She wondered if the king honestly did regret his action so many years ago after all or if he was just doing this to pacify his very persuasive queen. She'd heard that Queen Philippa had been the one two decades ago to convince Edward to spare the lives of the Burghers of Calais. She was known for her kind nature and compassion.

"Then align with the king and stop fighting," she said.

"If I do, I'll break any bonds with my brothers."

"It's your choice," she said, stepping away, knowing how hard this decision would be for Rowen. "I will respect any decision you make."

She saw the turmoil on his face. When his hawk cried from outside the window, once more, his eyes turned toward the sea.

Running his hand through his tangled hair, she could see him biting the insides of his cheeks in thought. The powerful captain of the Sea Mirage would be giving up so much, but gaining so much, too. But by aligning with the English king, he would be making himself an enemy of not only his brothers, but also the Scots. He was damned no matter what choice he made.

"All right," he finally said with a sad nod, biting his lip. "I will play chess. But if I win, I will also have your word that you will not harm my brothers."

"I can't agree to that," said the king. "However, I will agree that if you convince your brothers to stop stealing from me, I won't hunt them down to suffer the consequences of what they've done. But if they go back to their old tricks, I will come after them and you will be at my side to help me."

"Oh, Rowen," said Cordelia, not sure what was running through his mind right now. If only he had gone to the ship instead of coming back for her.

"Let's play," he said, sitting down on the stool. "I'm doing this for Cordy and the baby."

"Remember, your ship is mine as part of the deal," said the king.

"How could I forget?" Rowen asked, his eyes darting over to Cordelia. She felt sick to her stomach and, this time, it had nothing to do with being pregnant. This time, it was because she knew how bad Rowen was at playing chess and that he didn't have a chance in hell of winning.

CHAPTER 27

This was the most important game of Rowen's life, but hell if he could concentrate on what he was doing. He'd already made two vital mistakes and Edward had captured one of his knights and one of his bishops as well. He'd managed to collect a few of the king's pawns, but it wasn't looking good for him.

He heard his hawk calling to him from outside and wished to hell the ship would just leave already. Even if he won, he'd foolishly promised the Sea Mirage to King Edward. Plus, his brothers would never understand his decision. He had to try for Cordy and the baby, but either way, he was doomed. At least with making an alliance with his father, he'd be Cordy's husband and she wouldn't be alone or have to marry some old man. He would raise his child and the child would not be considered a bastard. The last thing Rowen wanted was for any of his children to be considered bastards and he would do anything to be with the woman he loved.

"Bad move," said the king, moving a piece and taking one of Rowen's rooks next. Rowen felt sick and longed for the rocking motion of his ship to soothe him. Instead, the only rocking was from the big man sitting on the chair across from him and the squeaking noise made it even harder to concentrate. He wouldn't be surprised if the chair broke under Edward's weight. He wanted more than anything to tell him to sit still, but he didn't.

Why had he agreed to play chess, of all things? And why had Cordy begged him to do it? She knew how terrible he was at the game. Did she want him to lose and end up back in the dungeon?"

"Your move," said the king and Rowen's mind clouded over. He reached for a pawn and was about to move it when he heard Cordelia clear her throat. He looked up to see her standing behind the king, shaking her head slowly. His eyes went back to the board and his hand quivered above the knight next. When he looked back up, she was frowning.

"Make up your mind," said the king. "Just move something, will you?"

Rowen's hand skimmed over the top of his bishop next and he glanced up to see Cordy crossing her arms as if she were getting angry. What the hell did she want him to move? He wasn't a mind reader!

"Rowen, when we marry, I will be so happy I will feel like your queen," she said, giving him the answer he needed. He touched the top of the queen and she smiled. Then he saw the move, plain as day. With Cordy's help, after a little while, he managed to capture the king's two bishops, one knight, one rook, a mess of pawns, and even his queen. He was feeling more confident by the moment that he was going to win.

"Lady Cordelia, I am thirsty," said the king. "I'd like you to go down to the kitchen and bring me more ale." Rowen's eyes interlocked with Cordelia's and his insides tightened.

"There are servants for that, don't make her leave," he said. "She needs to stay here." The king looked up in surprise and raised a brow.

"Son," he said, causing Rowen's stomach to convulse since he didn't like the man calling him that. "If I didn't know better, I'd think you wanted her to stay for some reason. You aren't by any chance cheating, are you?"

"Of course he's not cheating," Cordelia said before he could answer. "I'd be happy to go get you some ale, Your Majesty."

Rowen felt doomed. What was he to do now? Without Cordelia's help, he'd lose and end up back in the dungeon. She walked over and bent down to kiss him, putting her arms around him and whispered into his ear.

"Watch his bishop and use your queen and you'll win."

"What are you telling him?" snapped the king.

"I'm telling him that I have faith in him and that he will win." She smiled at Rowen and left the room. Although he'd felt powerful a moment ago, now he felt helpless.

"Leave us," the king said to the guards and they left the room as well. When the door closed, the king spoke.

"I wanted them all out of the room because I'm willing to make another deal with you, but I don't want anyone to hear it."

"What kind of deal?" Rowen studied his moves, trying to figure out how to put the king in checkmate and be done with this blasted game as quickly as possible. He hadn't felt this stressed since the night of Burnt Candlemas when he was a child.

"If you let me win, in a sennight, I'll release you from the dungeon and make another alliance with you, but we won't do it over a game of chess."

Suddenly, Rowen realized that this wasn't about deals and alliances, this was about the man's competitiveness to win a damned game of chess.

"You've never lost a game of chess to anyone, have you?" asked Rowen, still studying the board.

"Nay. And I don't intend to start losing tonight."

"Do you often bribe your competitors so you can win?"

"That is none of your business."

"I decline your offer, but thank you just the same."

"What?" the king sounded shocked and furious. It seemed he liked winning chess even more than Rowen's brothers did. "You can't turn me down."

"I just did," he said, moving another piece, being more focused on the game now that he knew the king wanted to bribe him to throw it. Losing at this point wasn't an option. He would win on his own and without Cordelia's help because, if nothing else, he wanted his father to feel the agony of defeat.

"I'll give you land as well as coin if you let me win."

"No, thank you."

The king moved a piece and now it was Rowen's turn. He felt as if he were getting closer and in a few moves, could possibly have the man in checkmate.

"All right, here is my final offer," said Edward. "I'll let you keep your ship if you take my new deal."

Rowen's eyes snapped upward and he contemplated the decision. If he didn't take the deal, it was going to kill him to have to hunt down his own ship to give it to a man who tried to kill him as a baby. The Sea Mirage was everything to him and this offer was very tempting.

The door opened, and Cordelia entered the room with a pitcher of ale in her hand and Queen Philippa at her side.

"I hope I didn't miss anything of importance," said Cordelia.

"More than you know," answered Rowen, focusing on the chessboard.

"Oh, really?" asked the queen. "Edward, what is going on?"

"Father," said Rowen, stressing the word, "just told me that if I win, I get to keep my ship as well, didn't you . . . Father?"

"Nay, that is not part of the deal," growled the king.

"It is unless you have any . . . secret moves you want revealed," said Rowen, knowing the king probably never had anyone turn down his offer of a bribe and wouldn't want anyone to know that he cheated. It would sully his reputation.

"What does that mean, Edward?" asked the queen.

Edward hesitated but finally answered. "It means he's keeping his ship if he wins," grumbled the king, making his move.

"Edward, are you losing?" asked the queen, glancing at the board. "I've never seen that happen before."

"Stop your incessant babbling, Wife. I'm trying to concentrate."

CORDELIA WAS ecstatic to see Rowen had done so well in her absence. Somehow, he seemed to have much more confidence than when she'd left the room. She tried to give him signals, but he no longer watched her for his next move. He studied the board with a look of determination on his face that told her he no longer needed guidance. She wasn't sure what happened while she was gone, but whatever was said had fueled his fire. Now, there was no stopping her restless sea lord.

Another three moves and she heard Rowen say the word she'd been longing to hear all night.

"Checkmate," he said, slamming down his queen and standing up and stretching his arms over his head.

"You won!" exclaimed Cordelia, rushing into his arms, hugging and kissing him in excitement. "We can be married now."

"Not yet," he said, getting down on one knee and taking her hands in his. "Cordelia, my love, will you do me the honor of marrying me and being not only my wife but the mother of our child as well?"

"I will," she said. He stood and gathered her into his arms. "Now we can be married and I suggest we do it as soon as possible."

"I love a wedding!" exclaimed Philippa, seeming as excited as they were. "It'll take place tomorrow morning at St. Mary's church. I'll send a page to contact the priest and let him know."

"Nay, the wedding banns need to be posed for a fortnight

first," grumbled Edward, getting up from the chair looking like he'd just lost a war.

"No, they don't," objected Philippa. "You were going to let Lady Cordelia marry the earl with no posting, so this should be no different. The wedding will be first thing in the morning and I'll be sure to tell everyone we have a lot of planning to do."

The king and queen left the room arguing. Once they were alone, Cordelia wrapped her arms around Rowen and kissed him again.

"I'm so happy," she said, but Rowen was staring out the window. The sun lit up the horizon in a glow of orange and it was the start of a new day. She heard the cry of two hawks and a raven. When she looked to the sea, she saw the Sea Mirage sailing away without him. "I'm sorry this will make waves between you and your brothers."

He bit his lip and nodded, looking like he'd just lost a good friend. "More than you know." Then he turned back to her, reached down and kissed her gently. "I love you, Cordy." Putting his hand on her belly, he bent over and kissed her there as well. "And I love our baby," he said, making her heart soar.

"Rowen, what was it that made you so confident and able to win the game?"

"He wanted me to lose and that's what made me determined to win even without you here to guide me," said Rowen. "I don't like to lose, but being bribed to lose is something that even I – a pirate – would never even consider."

"So you beat your father at his own game."

"Aye and nay," he said, once again watching his ship sailing away without him. "One game ends and another begins."

"At least you didn't have to give up your ship."

"It's not mine anymore. I instructed my brothers to tell Brody it's his if I didn't return before dawn."

"I'm sure he'd understand and give it back to you."

"I couldn't take it back even if he offered because everything is different now."

"You mean because you're going to be a knight and lord?"

"Nay. I mean because I've just betrayed my brothers, my crew, and all of Scotland by aligning with the enemy – my father."

CHAPTER 28

The wedding took place as planned the next morning, and Rowen felt happy inside to finally be marrying the woman he loved. He'd spent a good part of last night getting to know Autumn, Summer, and Winter, and decided to call them his sisters even if they were his cousins.

He'd also spoke with Annalyse and learned that his mother was a kind-hearted woman who had always hoped for sons. Lady Gabrielle was said to be smiling as she held the triplets when she died. His heart ached to know her, but by knowing her twin sister, he felt as if his mother were present at this wedding in spirit. Since Annalyse was the only mother he ever knew throughout his life, he would call her mother from now on. Annalyse loved the idea and, once again, that happy smile he remembered from childhood returned to her face.

Mya had returned to be with him this morning, abandoning the ship, and that made him happy as well. She sat up on a tree branch watching them. Rowen was thankful the castle was so close to the sea so the bird would still be able to fish and feel at home. So would he.

Cordelia joined him at the top of the church stairs while the king, queen, villagers, and occupants of the castle watched from the ground.

"You look beautiful," he told Cordelia, drinking in her beauty. She wore a rust-colored gown with a gold pattern upon it. The bodice laced up the front with ornate trim. It covered a long-sleeved forest green undertunic and her fiery red tresses were loose and long, the way he'd requested them. It was a breath of fresh air the way her vibrant hair contrasted with the dark green of her clothes. A metal circlet with colored gemstones was balanced precisely on her head, being a gift from the queen.

He felt as giddy as a child, having his dream come true of marrying a lady – that is, a lady he loved. To make things even more exciting, he would be a father soon. Both Annalyse and his sisters already told him they wanted to be included in raising his child. He and Cordelia decided to invite them all to live at the castle permanently. When they'd accepted the offer, he felt like he was truly home for the first time in his life.

He barely remembered saying his vows he felt so heady, but when everyone started clapping and Cordelia reached up to kiss him, he realized they were married. They hadn't had time to get rings but decided they would hire someone to create the rings they wanted when things settled down.

So much had happened in the last day that turned his life around, but he didn't have time to think about it because the king called him over.

"Lord Rowen, come here," said the king. Rowen found himself liking the sound of his new title. He took Cordelia's hand in his and they approached his father together. "Kneel before me," ordered Edward, removing his sword from his scabbard. Involuntary reaction had Rowen reaching for his own sword, but Cordelia tightened her grip and silently reminded him he was no longer an enemy of the king. Rowen released Cordelia's hand and his throat became dry. He knew this was the moment he'd become a knight.

"Go ahead," coaxed Cordelia. "You deserve it, Rowen."

"Aye," he said, releasing a deep breath, getting down on one knee and bowing before his father. He hadn't considered that being knighted would require him to vow to serve and protect his king. Although he had a hard time saying the words, he didn't want to disappoint his new wife and took the vows that made his father also his liege lord.

"I hereby dub you, Sir Rowen of Whitehaven," said the king, tapping him on each shoulder with his blade. It felt right for some reason as if this is what he was destined to be since the day he was born. But when he heard the cry of a red kite and the scolding guttural call of a raven overhead, he looked up to see both his brothers watching him from a distance. Now it felt wrong, really wrong, but there was nothing he could do about it.

His heart sank in his chest when he saw his brothers glaring at him. He wanted more than anything to run to them and explain why he'd made the choices he had.

"Rowen, get up," whispered Cordelia and he got to his feet. "What takes your interest?" she asked and then she saw them, too. "Don't worry about it. It'll be all right." She reached up and kissed him, and when he looked back to where he'd seen his brothers, they were gone and so were their birds. How could a man feel so alive and so empty all at once?

"Congratulations," said the queen. "To both of you on your wedding and to you, Sir Rowen, for being dubbed a knight."

"We have an alliance now," the king reminded him. "You are a knight and have vowed your allegiance to serve and protect me. I don't think I need to point out what that means."

"I know," Rowen said with a nod of his head. "You won't have to worry about me anymore."

"Now just convince your brothers to align with me, and things will be as they should," said the king. "My queen and I will leave you now, but I will be keeping a close eye on you, Sir Rowen of Whitehaven . . . Son."

Rowen felt choked up to hear the king call him *Son.* All the vengeance he'd held for the man seemed to wash away in that instant. He wondered if his bitterness had partially been because once he'd found out who sired him, he realized how much he'd missed out on in his life. Or could it have possibly been because he felt unloved?

"Rowen, what are you feeling?" asked Cordelia, snuggling up to his chest as they watched the royal entourage head back to London. "You don't still hold vengeance toward your father, do you?"

"I'm not sure what I'm feeling," he told her. "Neither does any of it matter. All that matters is that I'm married to the woman I love and have a new life now. I am happy that I will be able to give our child the life he deserves and that he won't have to grow up as a thief or a pirate. Our son will grow up with honor and someday be a noble knight as well."

"What if we have a daughter, instead?" she asked, looking up at him with love in her bright green eyes. "Will you love and admire her just as much as a son?"

"I will love any child you give me, Cordy, and I hope all our daughters will be just like you." He placed a gentle kiss upon her lips.

She giggled and ran a hand down his chest. "I love you, my knight."

"That doesn't sound real," he said, running a hand through her hair and looking out to the sea. The waves crashed against the shore calling to him and he felt a restlessness stirring inside his soul. He hoped to be able to make amends with his brothers and keep his alliance with his father at the same time. He'd felt all the weight of the world lifted from his shoulders and then dropped back down upon them within the course of one day.

"It is real, and you are a lord and a knight now," his wife reminded him.

"Aye, I am," he said, feeling pride swell in his chest. Mya called out and Rowen held out his arm. The bird landed on it, bringing comfort to Rowen that his hawk still accepted him, no matter how much he'd changed. With Cordy at his side, he'd have the strength he needed to face whatever trials life dealt him having to do with his new country and king, Scotland, his child, or his brothers. He'd do his best to keep his word through any challenge, because he was a lord now, a knight, a husband, and soon to be a father. He had almost everything he always wanted in life besides being legitimate, but now that didn't even seem to matter. With a good woman at his side, he could conquer anything. He no longer needed to be a ***Restless Sea Lord***.

FROM THE AUTHOR:

I hope you have enjoyed Rowen and Cordelia's story in ***Restless Sea Lord***. ***The Legendary Bastards of the Crown Series*** has been something I've wanted to write for quite some time. I often wondered what it would have felt like to be a twin or triplet back in medieval times.

During the Middle Ages, superstitions were not taken lightly. People didn't understand a lot of things. When two or three babies were born at a time, they thought any baby after the first one born was a curse and spawned by the devil. Left-handed people were feared back then, too, and thought to be evil. I'm left-handed, so I would have been on the wrong end of these superstitions if I had lived during that time.

Kings almost always had mistresses as well as bastard children and the queens just had to put up with it. Sometimes the bastards were legitimized, and sometimes not. I found it to be a much more interesting internal struggle for my bastard triplets if they were not legitimized, but remained bastards throughout their lives. Of course, who knows what might happen by the third story?

Rook the Ruthless and *Reed the Reckless* have their stories told i n***Ruthless Knight – Book 2,*** and ***Reckless Highlander – Book 3.***

The prequel of ***The Legendary Bastards of the Crown Series*** – Annalyse and Ross' story, can be found in ***Destiny's Kiss.***

This series is followed by my ***Seasons of Fortitude Series,*** which is about the boys' sisters. The first book is ***Highland Spring- Book 1, followed by Summer's Reign – Book 2, Autumn's Touch – Book 3, and Winter's Flame – Book 4.***

As in most of my series, I have crossover characters. Storm MacKeefe shows up in ***Restless Sea Lord*** and is the laird of Clan MacKeefe. He has always been one of my favorite characters. If you'd like to read his story, you'll find it in ***Lady Renegade – Book 2 of my Legacy of the Blade Series.*** It is one of the first books I've ever written and, to this day, remains one of my favorites.

All of my books are available in paperback as well as ebooks and some of them are now also in audiobook form.

Watch for the stories of the eldest daughters of Rowen, Rook and Reed in the **Secrets of the Heart Series** coming in summer of 2018.

You might also enjoy ***Forbidden: Claude-Book 2.***

Elizabeth Rose

ABOUT ELIZABETH

Elizabeth Rose is a multi-published, bestselling author, writing medieval, historical, contemporary, paranormal, and western romance. She is an amazon all-star and has been an award finalist numerous times. Her books are available as Ebooks, paperback, and audiobooks as well.

Her favorite characters in her works include dark, dangerous and tortured heroes, and feisty, independent heroines who know how to wield a sword. She loves writing 14th century medieval novels, and is well-known for her many series.

Her twelve-book small town contemporary series, Tarnished Saints, was inspired by incidents in her own life.

After being traditionally published, she started self-publishing, creating her own covers and book-trailers on a dare from her two sons.

Elizabeth loves the outdoors. In the summertime, you can find her in her secret garden with her laptop, swinging in her hammock working on her next book. Elizabeth is a born storyteller and passionate about sharing her works.

Please be sure to visit her website at **Elizabethrosenovels.com** to read excerpts from any of her novels and get sneak peeks at covers of upcoming books. You can follow her on **Twitter, Facebook, Goodreads** or **Bookbub.**

ALSO BY ELIZABETH ROSE

Medieval

Legendary Bastards of the Crown Series

Seasons of Fortitude Series

Secrets of the Heart Series

Legacy of the Blade Series

Daughters of the Dagger Series

MadMan MacKeefe Series

Barons of the Cinque Ports Series

Second in Command Series

Medieval/Paranormal

Elemental Series

Greek Myth Fantasy Series

Tangled Tales Series

Contemporary

Tarnished Saints Series

Western

Cowboys of the Old West Series

Please visit http://elizabethrosenovels.com

Made in the USA
Monee, IL
21 February 2021